Is It Me?

LK Wilde

For my boys x

Chapter 1

S arah rolled her eyes. In the chair beside her, her mother did the same.

'Cricket?' Sarah muttered to herself, wondering what had got into her father. He knew Sunday afternoons were a chance for the females of the house to catch up on their favourite soap operas. It was both unusual and irritating that he'd suggest commandeering the television to watch sport.

'Oh, ignore him. Likes to assert himself sometimes.' Cynthia tutted, her neck folding into multiple layers as she tipped her chin down and fixed her eyes on the television. 'Two G and Ts thanks, Colin,' she called to her husband.

Sarah and Cynthia reached the first advert break before they realised their drinks had not appeared. 'I'll go see what Dad's up to,' said Sarah, heaving herself up out of the recliner.

She wandered through the house, following the worn path in the carpet made from years of routine and traditions.

'Dad?'

There was no sign of her father in the kitchen. The gin bottle stood in its usual place, tucked in front of the brandy and whisky that were only opened on Christmas Day.

'Dad?'

Sarah spotted her father bent over a flower bed in the garden. The first bursts of spring colour peeked out of the beds guarding a bowling-green-perfect lawn. She opened the door, shivering at the nip in the air.

'Dad? What happened to our drinks?' Again, Sarah's father gave no answer, so she slipped on a pair of old Crocs and crossed the lawn. Perhaps he was going deaf? She'd suggest her mother take him for a hearing test. 'Dad?'

'What is it, love?' Colin's voice hinted at fatigue, and if Sarah heard right, impatience.

'It's Sunday afternoon. You always bring us a gin and tonic on Sunday afternoons. Is everything all right?'

'Everything's fine. I thought you could get your own drinks for a change.'

'Hilarious,' laughed Sarah, patting her father on the back and heading back into the house.

Back in the conservatory, Cynthia looked up at her daughter and raised an eyebrow.

'Dad's being weird. I'm sure he'll bring the drinks through soon. He's out in the garden.'

'He spends more and more time out there these days. Anyone would think he's trying to get away from me.'

Sarah reached over and patted her mother's hand. 'Don't be silly, Mum. You know what Dad's like.'

'Sometimes I think he loves those bloody plants more than he loves us.' Cynthia chuckled, her laugh turning to a choke as a lungful of cigarette smoke caught in her throat.

Sarah tried to concentrate on the television screen, focusing her eyes on an argument between a fictional husband and wife. But something niggled her. Yes, her dad loved his garden, but the only time she could remember him forgetting their drinks in twenty years was when he had the flu. Perhaps he was sickening for something? Perhaps he had dementia, or Alzheimer's? Sarah shuddered. As much as she loved her mother, the thought of being her sole companion didn't fill Sarah with joy.

By the time the second soap opera came on, Cynthia's plump feet tapped a drumbeat on the floor, her fingers doing the same on the chair's armrest.

'Shall I just get the drinks?' asked Sarah, knowing it was only a matter of time until Cynthia blew her top.

'No! Just because your father's playing silly buggers doesn't mean you should assist him. COLIN? COLIN!'

Her shouting gave Cynthia another coughing fit. She turned puce, banging her chest and sucking in big wheezy gulps of air.

'Dad? Mum could do with a drink.' Sarah heard a bang in the kitchen. Was that a door slamming? Or a foot kicking a cupboard?

By the time Colin appeared with a drink in each hand, Cynthia's breathing had calmed, the coughing fit leaving her with a sheen of sweat on her blotchy skin. Colin set the drinks down on the coffee table with enough force that gin lapped against the edge of the glass, spilling onto the polished wood.

'Coasters?'

Colin stared at his wife, a look in his eyes Sarah hadn't seen before. 'No.'

'What do you mean, no? Get the coasters, you lazy bugger. We don't want to ruin the table.'

'Get them yourself.'

Cynthia and Sarah sat in stunned silence as they heard the front door slam, followed by the revving of a car engine.

'Mum? What's going on?'

'How should I know? He says he's stressed at work as if that's any excuse.'

'Have you tried talking to him about it?'

'About work? Christ no. Why would I want to hear about his boring job? I told him to retire years ago, it's him who insists on still working. He'll be fine, don't worry. Give it an hour and he'll be back with his tail between his legs, begging for forgiveness.'

*

Sarah felt her heart rate increase, her palms grow sweaty. *Not now, please, not now.*

'I've got a migraine coming on, Mum. I need to lie down.'

Cynthia put up no resistance. Sarah wasn't sure she even heard, so glued was she to the television screen. Sarah put one foot in front of the other, keeping her steps regular, and her panic contained. As she climbed the stairs, she felt the pressure in her chest building, her breaths quick and light, never quite filling her lungs with air.

Sarah flung open her bedroom door, closed it behind her and slumped down against it. She put her head between her knees, trying to count away the panic. *In two, three, four, hold two, three, four, out two, three, four, hold two, three, four.* Her head was spinning, her legs like jelly, the tightness in her chest so painful she wondered if it was a heart attack this time.

It's all in your mind. Keep calm, keep calm.

As the feeling returned to her limbs, Sarah leaned her head back against the door and risked opening her eyes. There was something so comforting about the garish pink walls Colin had painted for her when she was eleven. There'd been no suggestion it could do with updating, and Sarah was glad. The pink-walled room and bed covered in cuddly toys was her haven. A place where nothing changed. A place where she could escape adulthood for a time.

Taking a gulp of water, Sarah congratulated herself on how well she kept her secret. Only her simpering, ineffectual boss Mel knew the truth, and she had promised secrecy. The first time had been the worst. She hadn't known what she was dealing with. The tight chest, lack of breath, all hit her on the most ordinary of days. She'd been on the phone behind the reception desk, dealing with an irate customer when the pain arrived. Mel was walking past at the moment Sarah clutched her chest and screamed. A more capable person would have called an ambulance, but Mel claimed she recognised the signs and bundled Sarah into her car.

At the hospital, they'd run every test under the sun before diagnosing a panic attack. Sarah could still picture Mel's smug face when proved right. It should have been a relief, but a heart attack or stroke could be treated with medication or an operation. A panic attack was a slippery beast, and one Sarah didn't have the first idea how to deal with.

The only saving grace that day had been that Cynthia and Colin were on holiday in Spain. Mel dropped Sarah back to an empty house, promising the story given at work would be an asthma attack. A week later, when Mel asked Sarah if she'd been to the doctor, Sarah lied and said yes. It wasn't a total lie, if you counted online medical sites as health-care.

Sarah had lost count of the number of panic attacks she'd had since that first one. But she had become adept at hiding them, controlling the symptoms until she could escape to her bedroom, or the disabled loo at work. Cynthia didn't believe in mental health. Every time the words 'mental' and 'health' came on the telly, she'd launch into an angry tirade that Sarah dared not contradict.

No, Cynthia could never find out about the panic attacks. They would remain Sarah's secret and she would deal with them alone. All she needed to do was keep life simple, avoid any stress. Everything would be fine. Sarah grabbed her oldest teddy bear from her bed and pulled it towards her. Arms wrapped around the squidgy bear, Sarah buried her face into its soft fur and cried.

Chapter 2

A patch of sunlight lit up the smiling faces on Sarah's wall. She closed her eyes and counted to sixty. When she opened them again, the sun had gone behind a cloud and the photo was in shadow once more. Sarah reached across and plucked the picture from the wall. She positioned her pillows behind her back and sat staring at the photo, daring her mind to go to places it shouldn't.

With the photo held tightly between her fingers, Sarah went through her daily routine: note all of Mark's worst features, run through the list of everything annoying he ever did, imagine how awful life would be if she was still with him.

Sarah pushed down the thought that if they'd stayed together, she'd be a married woman by now. She could be living in a three-bed semi of her own, thinking about starting a family. Mark would bring her a Sunday afternoon drink before getting started on the roast. They'd meet Mum and Dad at the local for a pub quiz...

No, the photo was her daily reminder not to settle for second best again. It would be better to go through life alone than with a weak man, and Mark was weak. Except for that last day. He wasn't weak then, just mean.

A memory flooded Sarah's mind of finding Mark's discarded bike on the cycle trail, his text message saying he was leaving her. After that point, the memories grew hazy thanks to all the beer she'd drunk. It hadn't been quite enough alcohol to remove the memory of crying on the shoulder of her Airbnb host, or throwing up on the train home.

Sarah stuck the photo back on the wall and heaved herself out of bed. She pulled on her old dressing gown and headed downstairs for her morning cup of tea and biscuit. In the kitchen, Cynthia was already up, curlers in her hair, nails slick with fresh varnish.

'You're up early, Mum.'

'Well, I couldn't wait for your dad to bring me up a cuppa. Too much to do today. You haven't forgotten you're picking up the flowers at nine?'

'No, I've set a reminder on my phone.'

'Don't you think you should get ready?'

'Mum, it's only just gone seven. We've got ages yet.'

'You won't be saying that when we get to the venue. The time will fly by then.'

'I didn't think we could get into the venue till after two?'

'Stop being so contrary and top me up. There's plenty left in the teapot.' Cynthia held out her mug and Sarah poured stewed tea inside it.

'Dad not up yet?'

'No, the lazy bugger was still snoring when I got up.'

'Did he say where he went last night?'

'Said he'd gone for a drive. He stunk like a brewery when he climbed into bed. I made him brush his teeth three times before I'd kiss him goodnight. What a night to go out drinking, just before our big day.' Cynthia huffed and inspected her fuchsia nails.

'Big evening, not big day. It's not like you're renewing your vows.'

'Pah, renewing vows is a stupid modern idea. A Silver Wedding anniversary is far more important. Couples these days are unlikely to make it to twenty-five days, never mind twenty-five years.'

Sarah felt the weight of her own failure sitting heavy on her shoulders. By the time they'd returned her unused wedding dress to the shop, it had picked up a stain from somewhere, a tiny mark that had cost her parents five hundred pounds. Two years later, Sarah was still paying them back. 'You're an inspiration,' muttered Sarah, putting the kettle back on to make a coffee.

'Isn't it about time you found a new man? I don't want to be an ancient mother-of-the-bride.'

'You said you didn't want me to settle for just anyone?'

'I don't. But time isn't on your side, girl. You'd better hurry or you'll find yourself an old, lonely, overweight spinster.'

Sarah sucked in her stomach and lifted her head to hide the double chin she'd gained over the past two years. Her mother loved pointing out how much weight her daughter had piled on. Cynthia was no waif, but in her book, once you'd snagged your man, it didn't matter if each passing year brought an increased dress size.

'I need to get ready for work.'

'Work? You haven't taken the day off?'

'I've taken the afternoon off, not the whole day. I'll collect the flowers on my way in and keep them in water in the staffroom.'

Cynthia tutted, folding her arms over her ample chest and pulling her face into a frown.

'I'd have thought my only daughter would have made more of an effort on my big day.'

'Big evening,' said Sarah under her breath as she filled her cup with coffee and carried it up to her room. Sitting on her bed, Sarah opened her banking app. At least the number was in the black, but not by much. Wasn't living with your parents supposed to be cheaper? With the rent Cynthia charged, Sarah could never save up for a place of her own.

Sarah yanked a shift dress over her mass of shiny dark hair and pulled her blazer on over the top. A sheet hung over the mirror and Sarah pulled a small corner aside to swipe tinted gloss across her lips. It was months since she'd viewed herself in the full-length mirror. She couldn't bear to see the image reflected. The kindest description of herself was *big-boned*, but she'd been called far worse by men on the street. Her cheeks burned with shame at the thought.

Mark used to call her beautiful. It had been nice, someone seeing something in her she failed to see herself. Of course, she hadn't believed him, but it was good to hear. Since Mark left her, the only person to compliment her was her dad and parents didn't count. She was Colin's only child. Of course, he was blind to her flaws. Sarah could have three green heads and Colin would still walk round the house singing 'The Most Beautiful Girl In The World' to her.

Grabbing her bag from the back of her door, Sarah raced through the house to avoid another conversation with Cynthia. Any interaction with her mother was bound to end in another job being added to her to-do list. Sarah reached the bus stop with moments to spare, only to find a notice detailing cancellations. Typical, the one day she needed to be early. At least the sensible pumps on her feet were comfortable to walk in.

With no time to lose, Sarah marched her way through the streets so familiar she could've walked them blindfolded. An unfamiliar sensation took hold as she sped past uniform grey buildings and concrete office blocks. No longer were the uniformed square boxes a comfort. That day, the monotony of her surroundings caused a tightness in Sarah's chest. She felt trapped. *It's just the stress of the day*, she told herself, pushing past early morning commuters to reach the florist as it opened.

*

Sarah kept her finger on the counter bell, ringing in a steady stream of tings until the wild-haired florist appeared at the counter.

'Are you going to be much longer? I need to get to work.'

'I'm going as quickly as I can. Why don't you come back at lunchtime like I suggested?'

'Because,' said Sarah, pushing back her shoulders in an attempt to emulate her mother's attitude, 'we agreed on collection at nine a.m. It is not my fault that you have a problem with time keeping.'

'And it's not my fault that your mother left a message on my answerphone at eleven o'clock last night, changing the order.'

'So, you're blaming the customer now, are you?'

'I'm pointing out that the last-minute changes meant I've been in here since seven this morning trying to make the alterations. I'm going as quickly as I can.'

'Please hurry. Goodness me, it's not as if we're not paying through the nose for these wretched flowers.'

'If you're unhappy with the service I provide, or the price, I'm happy to cancel the order. Good luck finding another florist at such short notice, though.'

Sarah tried to brush off the panic creeping into her chest. Cynthia would kill her if she turned up later empty-handed. Sarah took a deep breath and channeled the assertiveness Cynthia had drummed into her. 'You just get on with the job we're paying you to do. I'll be back at lunchtime to collect the flowers.'

Before the florist could respond, Sarah was out of the shop, the door slamming behind her. She found a quiet alley and leaned against a brick wall. *In two, three, four, hold two, three, four, out two, three, four, hold two, three, four.*

With the panic subsiding, Sarah walked the short distance to her office. There weren't any pretty corners of the town, but the small industrial estate Sarah worked on was grim, even by the rest of the town's standards. She reached the squat pebble dash office of the double-glazing company she worked with and checked her watch. Fifteen minutes late. Well, Sarah would not apologise for it. She worked at twice the rate of the other two receptionists, so deserved a late start once in a while.

Cathy and Miriam were already behind the reception desk when she walked in. They looked from the clock to Sarah, smirking at each other but saying nothing. Sarah put her bag away in the staff room, quickening her steps as she passed by her manager's office. Once installed behind the reception desk, she put on her headset and switched on her computer.

'I'm making a coffee, Cathy. Want one?'

'Thanks, babe.'

Sarah didn't bother looking up. Her once-held hope that work colleagues might become friends had long since vanished. She had tried at first, but with no knowledge of the latest fashion trends or celebrity gossip, Miriam and Cathy had long since given up on her and were open in their disdain for their prematurely middle-aged colleague. It was for the best. Sarah didn't have time to waste on making friends.

Miriam re-appeared with two steaming cups. It was only as the smell of cheap coffee reached her that Sarah realised how tired she was. Between the panic and preparations for her parents' party, it was weeks since she'd had a good night's sleep. She'd drink a bucket of the crap staffroom coffee if she could.

The morning dragged, time passing in slow motion. At eleven, Sarah took off the headset that was pinching her scalp and headed to the staffroom. A few of the fitters were on elevenses and their faces betrayed their disappointment when they saw Sarah walk in. They loved to flirt with pretty Miriam. Even Cathy could charm them into submission, despite being in her fifties and looking like a wrinkled Barbie doll. Sarah knew they called her *The Fridge* behind her back, after she rebuffed a creepy fitter at a staff party.

Sarah made her way to the coffee machine. A man stood beside it, looking fazed. With the high staff turnover, there was always a new face in the staffroom. Sarah huffed as he pressed all the wrong buttons, her frustration growing as she counted down the minutes until her break would be over.

'For goodness' sake, it's only a bloody coffee machine, not rocket science.' She leaned past the man, pressing the correct button and sending coffee spurting into the cup below.

'Thanks... I think. But I'm lactose intolerant. I was trying to get a black coffee.'

Sarah resisted the urge to punch the man and removed the cup. 'I'll have that one then,' she said through gritted teeth, setting the machine off to make a disgusting black coffee for the man.

'Cheers,' he said when she handed it to him. 'I'm Steve. Pleased to meet you.'

Suspicious of his outstretched hand, Sarah ignored it, marching past him and out of the room. As the door closed, she heard laughter and one fitter commenting that, 'That frigid cow isn't worth your breath.'

Desperate for air, Sarah carried her coffee outside. A fine layer of drizzle hung in the air, but she could feel herself dampening with sweat beneath her dress and knew she'd need to keep her jacket on to hide the marks. She found a low wall to sit on and spent the remaining five minutes of her break wondering why the universe was against her.

Chapter 3

B y the time Sarah finished work and collected the flowers, there was no time to go home, so she made her way to the ugly sports bar her mother had booked for the party. As she walked in, she found her father up a ladder hanging bunting and streamers from 1980s light fittings, and her mother arguing with a harassed-looking caterer.

Colin climbed down the ladder and father and daughter watched as Cynthia became irate.

'Should I help?'

'She looks like she can manage,' said Colin, winking at Sarah.

'The hall's looking good.'

'You think so?'

'Yes. Don't you?'

Colin looked at Sarah. 'Love, I know it's none of my business, but don't you want more than this?'

'More than what?'

Colin spread his arms out. 'This. What your mother and I have? Don't you want more for yourself?'

'How do you mean?'

'I mean adventures, excitement. Don't you want to go off and have adventures rather than finding yourself in a grotty hall at fifty wondering where your life's gone? You're a bright and beautiful young woman. You deserve more than this.'

Sarah let out an uneasy laugh. 'Been on the beer, Dad? You and Mum have a great life. I want to be just like you.' The thought of adventures made Sarah's pulse quicken, and not in a good way. What was wrong with her parents' life? Safe, secure, and comfortable. What was not to like? 'I'll check Mum's OK.'

'All right, love. You do that.'

'Can you believe they want to leave all the food here now?' shouted Cynthia, as Sarah crossed the room. 'The sandwiches will be dry as a rusk biscuit, and the ham will have gone bad before everyone gets here.'

'Madam, you told us to deliver the food at two.'

'Yes, but how was I to know the kitchen couldn't accommodate the buffet in their fridge? How is that my problem?'

'Well, it's not ours,' said the caterer, gathering up empty boxes in preparation to leave.

'How about I take all the perishable items back to the house and put them in our fridge?'

'No, you'll do nothing of the sort. You,' said Cynthia, jabbing a finger against the caterer's chest. 'You will sort this out for us.'

It was as though Sarah heard the snap resound in the room. The caterer grabbed tray after tray of food and tipped it out onto the floor. Cynthia stood in silence, so incandescent with rage, she couldn't find the words. The caterer turned on her heel and stormed out of the building. Cynthia found her voice and began hurling insults after her, Colin holding her back before she could commit an assault.

'You'll have to sort it,' said Cynthia, turning on Sarah.

'Me? Why me?'

'Because all this stress is going to give me a heart attack, and your father wouldn't know his way around the kitchen to save his life.'

'What do you need me to do?'

'I need you to prepare a buffet for a hundred people. What do you think I wanted you to do? Fly to the moon?'

Sarah went to speak, but Colin shook his head. She sighed and picked up her handbag. 'Could Dad come with me? I'll need a car to get everything back from the supermarket.'

'No, I need your dad here. You'll have to take a taxi.'

Sarah thought of the few pounds left in her bank account slipping away fast. She headed out of the bar, only stopping when she heard someone call her name. She turned to see her dad running towards her.

'Here,' he said, handing her a wedge of bank notes. 'Use these to buy the food and pay for a taxi. Just don't tell your mother.' He tapped his nose and headed back inside. Sarah steeled herself for the hours she had in front of her chained to the kitchen.

*

Sarah surveyed the groaning table of food and congratulated herself on doing a good job. Her fingers smelled of tuna. A piece of boiled egg lay tangled in her hair, but she'd surprised herself by how much she enjoyed preparing the buffet. The kitchen was Cynthia's domain, so it was a treat to be let loose without being watched like a hawk.

'You took your time,' said Cynthia, bustling across the room, her breasts spilling out of too-tight satin.

'Wow, love, you did all this in a few hours?' Colin's reaction caused Sarah to beam with pride.

'Yes. I even made a quiche.'

Colin stood beside Sarah and gave her arm a squeeze. 'Well done, love, well done.'

'Oh, stop fawning over her, Colin. You've still got balloons to blow up.'

'Yes, love,' said Colin, giving Sarah a weary smile as he walked away.

'Right, I'll just pop home and get changed, Mum.'

'What? But the guests will arrive in half an hour. You can't leave now!'

'But I'm still in my work clothes, which are covered in flour.'

Cynthia laughed. 'You think people will look at you, do you? Don't be daft, Sarah. You're not going anywhere. And no one will look at you, I guarantee.'

Too tired to argue, Sarah wandered off to find her dad and help with the balloons. There were too many balloons already. Garish primary-coloured balloon posies clashed with sickly pastel bunting, the tables glittering with plastic stars and confetti.

A band was setting up in one corner of the room. Sarah wondered where her mum had found them. They didn't seem like they'd be much in demand. The lead singer wore a tight shirt buttoned low to show off his chest hairs. Above his low-slung jeans, a beer belly spilled over his belt, straining the polyester fabric of his shirt. He'd done a valiant job of holding onto his hair, thin strands slicked over his bald patch and tied behind his head in a greasy ponytail.

'I hope they sound better than they look,' said Colin, noticing Sarah staring at the band. 'Has Mum told you their name?' The corners of his lips twitched as he spoke.

'What is it?'

'Melvis and the Cheeseburgers.'

'You're joking?' Sarah spluttered from behind her hand.

'I thought it was ironic, but after speaking to the band, they seem deadly serious.'

'Goodness me. I know this is your big night, Dad, but I wish I was at home with a cup of tea.'

'Me too,' said Colin, 'but don't tell your mother.'

Sarah smiled. 'How about we have a drink?'

'Good plan. Grab me a pint of bitter, would you? There are still a few balloons left to blow up.'

'I think there are plenty of balloons already.'

'Agreed, but if I don't get through the entire pack, your mother will have a fit.'

Sarah returned with their drinks just as the first guests were arriving. Some she recognised from her childhood, most she didn't know, and assumed they were friends from her mother's bingo nights. More than once she was mistaken for a waitress, and she decided it was easier to play up to the role, offering round plates of food to hungry middle-aged mouths.

The clink of a spoon on a glass signalled it was time for the speeches. People pushed their way to long trestle tables, vying for the best seats. Sarah sat herself down on a sticky plastic chair, wedged between two overweight men with large sweat patches forming on their shirts.

Never one to miss out on attention, Cynthia got to her feet first.

'Thank you soooo much for all coming out tonight to celebrate this very special anniversary. I'm honoured to count you all as friends.'

Applause sounded from across the hall, and Cynthia's chest puffed out a little.

'Well, what to say about my Colin? He's one in a million, that's for sure. I'd like to say I don't know how I'd cope without him, but I think we all know I'd manage just fine.' Cynthia gave a coquettish giggle, and her audience followed suit. 'On a serious note, apart from leaving the toilet seat up, spending too much time at the pub and still not knowing how to work the washing machine, Colin is the perfect husband.'

Sarah shifted in her seat as the rest of her table laughed. *Cynthia was only joking*, she told herself. But Sarah couldn't shake the feeling Colin was being laughed at, not with. Cynthia took a deep breath, and Sarah prayed her mother would end on a positive note.

'So here's to us, and another twenty-five years of wedded bliss.'

A chorus of 'To Cynthia and Colin' rang out across the hall.

As Cynthia sat down, Colin got to his feet. He seemed unsure of himself, his eyes darting from his wife, to the assembled crowd and back again.

'Get on with it!' shouted the sweaty man to Sarah's right.

'Yes, yes, of course,' said Colin, stumbling over his words, his face wearing a worried frown. 'Thank you all for coming...'

Colin's prompt cards dropped to the table, and he took a long swig of his beer. He placed the beer down and took a deep breath. 'I don't know who most of you are. I'm assuming you're Cynthia's friends and not just here for the free food, or even worse, rent-a-crowd.' The assembled masses laughed at what they thought was a joke. Sarah sat silently, knowing whatever was happening was not good.

'So, what to say about my wife? Well, we've been married twenty-five years and... and... I'm sorry, I can't do this.'

A stunned inhalation of breath resounded around the room.

'Don't be daft, Colin,' hissed Cynthia. 'It's only a speech. Grow a pair.'

Colin sighed. 'I wasn't talking about the speech,' he muttered, but Cynthia didn't hear. He turned back to face the room. 'In our first year of marriage, our beautiful daughter Sarah was born. My beautiful girl, I need you to know, whatever happens, I love you. You have so much going for you, if only you could see it. Be brave, love. Be braver than I've ever been.'

Colin looked straight at Sarah, who blushed at the scrutiny of many heads turning her way. Cynthia shifted in her chair, wondering what was happening. Colin's next words clarified any incomprehension.

'Cynthia, I'm sorry, but I think after twenty-five years it's about time we were honest. I've chosen the worst time and place for this, but it has to be said. We're no longer the people we were all those years ago. You married me with certain expectations and I've lived up to none. Your disappointment in me has turned you into the woman we all know...'

'And love,' interrupted Cynthia in an effort to break the tension. The crowd responded with muted laughter. Colin cleared his throat.

'I think it's best I leave it there. Apologies everyone, but I hope you have a good evening. Enjoy the buffet and free bar.'

As the crowd exchanged applause and confused glances, Cynthia tugged on Colin's sleeve. 'What is this? What are you saying?'

Colin bent down so only Cynthia could hear. 'It's time to stop pretending, Cynthia. It's over, you're free. I'll be in touch to discuss formalities, but for now I think it's best we each have some space.'

Colin prised Cynthia's hand from his sleeve, picked up his pint, downed it in one, and strode out of the room.

Chapter 4

S arah stumbled along the dim suburban streets in a daze. Her mind was a mass of cotton wool, a thin spear of pain piercing through with each step. Her arms gripped tight to Cynthia, who swerved and faltered along the pavement, stopping to lurch into the road and hurl insults at a husband who was too far away to hear them.

How had this happened? How had a celebration of stable family life turned into an imploding of all Sarah had ever known? At that moment, she hated her father. How could he walk away from them? What was he thinking? Was he having some sort of breakdown?

Sarah had no sympathy even if Colin was mid break-down. He'd abandoned them. He'd abandoned her.

The night had been a disaster from beginning to end. After the initial shock of Colin's departure, a shaken Cynthia had taken to her feet once again. With a glass of Prosecco held aloft, she announced a change of plan. No longer an anniversary party, she declared the night a divorce party, with the instructions that all present were to eat, drink and be merry.

After Cynthia's announcement, Sarah found herself in a room of drunk middle-aged strangers, dancing to an Elvis impersonator who would have the star himself turning in his grave. She tried her best to keep Cynthia away from the flowing booze, to no avail. By nine-thirty, Cynthia was grinding her hips against a spindly fifty-something on the dance-floor. By ten she was on a table, exposing her knickers to the crowd as she used an empty bottle of champagne as a microphone and sang along with the band. By eleven she had her head down a toilet bowl, Sarah stroking her back as the previous consumption of alcohol came back in violent bursts.

At midnight, the band packed up and, other than a few stragglers, the guests stumbled and slurred their goodbyes. By the time the last guest left, Sarah had to peel Cynthia from the floor, wiping her tear-stained face and heaving her towards the door. There had been no time to dwell on what had happened. Sarah was in survival mode.

As they left the building, the staff shouted about lost deposits and extra charges for the mess they'd left behind them, but Sarah didn't care. She needed to get her mother home. Everything else could wait.

The house lay in darkness when they arrived home. Sarah fitted her key in the lock and turned the door handle with trepidation. Would she find her father in tears at the kitchen table? Would he be sitting in the dark living room waiting for round two of recriminations and grievances?

The house was silent other than the usual white noise: the ancient grumbling boiler, a washing machine, dishwasher or tumble dryer, turned on at night to save on the electricity bill.

The first thing Sarah noticed was the empty banister. Colin always left his coat and hat on the end of the banister, much to the chagrin of his wife. Now his coat was gone. Sarah deposited Cynthia in an armchair and rushed through the house, checking room after room. All sat empty. Sarah paused in the doorway of her parents' bedroom. It looked the same as before, yet felt different. She walked across and opened the double wardrobe. On one side, Cynthia's outlandish dresses, kaftans and pashminas hung on padded hangers. The opposite side was bare. No shirts, no jackets, no trousers, no Dad.

Sarah slammed the wardrobe shut and moved to the chest of drawers, only to find the same story repeated. What Sarah hoped had been a spur-of-the-moment decision Colin would live to regret seemed more like a well-made plan. There was no trace of the man who had occupied the nineteen-thirties semi for the past twenty-five years. He'd even taken the hangers with him.

The sound of snoring floated up the stairs and, feeling that the best thing would be to leave Cynthia to sleep it off, Sarah retreated to her bedroom. On her bedside cabinet, a small envelope stood propped against a lamp. She tore open the envelope and pulled out a sheet of her father's blue writing paper.

My darling girl,

Please forgive me for the mess I've made of things. I never intended to hurt you or your mother, but I had reached breaking point and we couldn't go on as we were.

I take full responsibility for the mess I've created. When we met, your mother was young, feisty, beautiful, and I led her to believe I was all she wanted. In truth, I was a shy young man, content to develop my skills as a carpenter, but with no desire to run a business or climb a career ladder. She wanted an ambitious man who would provide the big house, big family, and big car she'd set her heart on. I did nothing to dissuade her notion that I was such a man. By the time she found out I was lacking in both the ambition and fertility departments, she was trapped, so it's no surprise she became bitter. Beneath her puff and bluster is the woman she once was. I hope by freeing her, she can find her way back to that girl. Perhaps I, too, will find the confidence to live a fuller life. We were never right for each other, and it's about time one of us admitted it.

I'll be in touch soon. Think about what I said to you today. I spent twenty-five years living half a life. Don't let life pass you by like I did. Much love, Dad.

Sarah scrunched up the paper and threw it at the bin. It missed and rolled across the carpet and under her bed. How could Colin be so selfish? In one fell swoop, he'd destroyed their family, destroyed their lives. Sarah buried her face in her pillow and cried hot, angry tears. She cried until the sun came up and she gave in to sleep.

*

Sarah walked into the kitchen to find Cynthia scraping butter on toast in quick, angry bursts. Crumbs flew out from beneath her knife, littering the table in tarnished confetti.

'How are you feeling this morning?'

'Like a new woman.'

'Oh?'

'Your father has done me a favour. I should write him a thank-you note.'

'You know where he is?'

'No, it was a figure of speech.' Cynthia took a bite of toast, a thin streak of melted butter trickling towards her chin.

'I can't believe he did that. I'm still in shock. It's so unlike him.'

'It's always the quiet ones you have to watch out for.'

Sarah stole a glance at her mother, the jovial attitude at odds with their situation. 'Mum, it's OK to feel sad. I'm here if you want to talk.'

Cynthia laughed, and a piece of toast flew out of the corner of her mouth. 'Sad? Why should I be sad? Like I said, your father has done me a favour. He's dragged me down long enough.'

'Aren't you angry about what he did?'

'Humiliating me in front of my friends? Of course! But I can use it to my advantage. *Unreasonable behaviour* I think it's called in lawyer speak. I intend to get my fair share from this divorce. He's got another thing coming if he thinks he can slip away into the sunset with his wallet intact.'

'Right.' Sarah's own toast popped up, but her stomach felt tied in knots and any appetite she'd had disappeared. 'I need to go to work. Will you be OK here by yourself?'

'Of course I will. I don't need babysitting. In fact, I've got plenty to occupy me. I need to see a man about a dog...'

'A dog?'

Cynthia sighed. 'Sometimes you're just like your father. It's an expression, Sarah. It means I've got a few irons in the fire.'

Sarah wondered if Cynthia was going mad.

'Don't tell me you've not heard that one either? I've got plans to make. That's what I'm trying to tell you.'

'Plans?'

Cynthia smirked and tapped the side of her nose. 'All in good time, Sarah, all in good time.'

'But...'

'We'll talk when you get home from work. I should have the details ironed out by then.'

'Right, OK. I'll see you later.'

Sarah grabbed her bag and left the house without touching her coffee or toast. She wanted to tell Cynthia not to make any big life decisions after a shock, but knew it would do no good. At least work would provide some normality.

Chapter 5

Sarah was in the office half an hour early. Fitters clocked in, some giving a halfhearted greeting, but Sarah kept her eyes down, scared that if she lifted them, they'd fill with tears. Cathy and Miriam walked in on the dot of nine, arms linked, laughing at some inane shared joke.

'Morning, Sara,' said Miriam, in her fake, singsong voice.

'It's Sarah,' muttered Sarah under her breath.

'Coffee?' Cathy asked Miriam.

'Hun, do you need to ask?'

'You realise it's already nine? Shouldn't you be waiting for your break?'

'Ignore her,' said Miriam, casting a glare Sarah's way. 'The boss knows we need caffeine to get us going.'

Cathy strutted off to the staff room, leaving Miriam and Sarah in tense silence behind the reception desk.

'Someone got out of the wrong side of bed today,' said Miriam, breaking the silence and Sarah's patience in one fell swoop.

'My mood has nothing to do with which side of bed I got out of,' said Sarah, pulling on her headset and praying a call would come through soon.

'What is it, then? Got dumped? Didn't get laid? Hate mornings?'

Sarah took a deep breath in, vowing to find another job where she wouldn't have to work alongside such imbecilic playground bullies. *Saved by the bell*, thought Sarah, as her phone rang.

'Good morning, this is Weatherwear Windows. How may I help you today?'

Sarah had to pull the headset away from her ears as the customer on the other end of the phone launched into a rant about his leaky conservatory.

'I'm sorry to hear you're unhappy with our product, sir. I'm sure...'

A stream of expletives reached Sarah's ears. Her face burned.

'Sir, I understand you're angry, but that's no excuse to speak to me this way. The best thing I can suggest for you is to piss off.'

Sarah slammed her finger against the 'end call' button. Cathy stood frozen mid-stride, two coffee cups held aloft in her hands. Miriam was staring at Sarah, her mouth open so wide Sarah could see her tongue piercing.

'What. The. Hell. Was. That?'

Sarah spun her chair round to face Miriam. 'He was being aggressive. What was I supposed to do?'

'Um, remember the customer is always right?' Miriam held her hands aloft and shrugged, flashing a confused glance to ally Cathy.

'Yeah, Sarah. That was well out of order. What if the boss finds out?'

Sarah ignored her colleagues, pulling on her headset and opening the list of emails that required her attention. Her heart hammered in her chest and for the next hour, she stole glances down the corridor, waiting for the moment her boss would appear. When Mel's door opened after an hour and a half of worry, it came as a relief.

'Sarah?' called Mel, her head poking out from behind the door frame. 'Can you come to my office for a quick chat, please?'

Miriam and Cathy didn't even try to hide their smirks as Sarah stood, patted her hair down and undertook the walk of shame to what she was certain would be a ticking off.

'Sit down, please,' said Mel, as Sarah appeared at her door. 'We need to have a talk.'

Sarah walked into the office. She hated it in there. Against the peach-coloured walls hung posters of smiling people staring out of cheap, plastic windows. As if getting a new window could bring world peace and happiness. On Mel's desk, photo frames cuddled into one another, a trophy cabinet of happy family life. Sarah thought Mel must be hiding a deep unhappiness. Why else would she need to overcompensate with that many photos? She even had a framed photo of her dog.

'If this is about earlier, I can only apologise. I had an awful weekend, my dad...'

'Sorry, Sarah. What are you talking about? What happened earlier?' Sarah flushed a deep red. 'Oh, nothing, nothing.'

'It doesn't sound like nothing.'

Sarah's brain whirred through a list of excuses, but in the end she decided it was best to stick as close to the truth as possible. 'I had an unhappy client swearing at me down the phone. I didn't deal with it as well as I should have.'

'Oh no, that's awful! You know how important staff well being is to us at Weatherwear. You should have come to me straight away. Are you OK? Do you need to meet with the on-site counsellor?'

Sarah suppressed the urge to scream that woke crap, as Cynthia called it, was the last thing she needed. Instead, she forced her lips into a thin smile. 'I'm fine, thank you. If it wasn't about this morning, why did you need to see me?' Somewhere deep down, Sarah wondered if she were about to be promoted, or get a pay rise. She might stay with the company then, if only to lord it over the two bimbos who shared her front desk.

'I'm afraid this is delicate. We've... um... well... how do I say this?' Mel took a deep breath and laid her palms flat against the table. 'We've had some complaints about you.'

'Complaints? From clients?'

'Yes, but not only clients. Sarah, this may be hard for you to hear, but your co-workers find you very difficult to work with.'

'What?' Sarah wracked her brain for what she could've done wrong. She avoided talking to colleagues at all costs. How was that ground for complaint?

'As you know, here at Weatherwear, we like to foster a positive working environment, taking care to protect not just the physical, but also mental wellbeing of our staff.'

God, thought Sarah, *this woman's so good at spouting nonsense she should pound the streets selling crappy windows herself.*

'Is any of this ringing true for you, Sarah? I'm hoping we're on the same page here?'

'Sorry, Mel, but I don't think we are. I don't know what you're talking about. Just because I don't like to socialise with colleagues doesn't mean I'm difficult to work with.'

Mel scrunched up her face, her fingers drumming against her desk as she sought the words she needed. 'This is about your attitude, Sarah. Your colleagues feel you view yourself as superior.'

Sarah laughed. 'Superior? Superior to window fitters with five GC-SEs between them? Hell yes, I feel superior.'

Mel sighed. 'This is just the attitude I was talking about. Those men you talk so disparagingly about are the backbone of this company. Your snide remarks and aloof attitude are causing disharmony within the company and I'm afraid I can't allow it to go on a moment longer.'

'What about the way they talk to me? I'm assuming you've heard the names they call me?'

Mel had the good grace to blush. 'That's a fair point, but there are also the clients.'

'What about the clients?'

Mel cleared her throat.

'You said there'd been complaints from clients?'

'Yes, several have commented on the abrasive nature of their interactions with you. Some have said you seem unwilling to problem-solve, that your communication style often verges on rude.'

Sarah laughed again, which was not the reaction Mel was hoping for. 'So what is this? A warning? A slap on the wrist? Am I going to be sent on some training course in the arse-end of nowhere?'

'I'm afraid it's not that simple. You may not be aware, but the double glazing market isn't what it once was. We're having to make cutbacks, streamline staffing, that sort of thing.'

'You're sacking me?' The room spun. This couldn't be happening. Not the day after her family life had imploded.

'I'm not sacking you. I'm offering you a very competitive redundancy package. You'll stay on at the company long enough to find a new job, and we'll offer you three months' salary at the time you leave.'

Sarah felt her chest tighten, her breaths coming too shallow, too fast. Desperate to leave the claustrophobic office, Sarah stood, pushing back her chair with such force it fell to the ground. 'How about this, Mel? Why don't you shove your crappy job where the sun doesn't shine?'

Mel's mouth dropped open and Sarah stormed from the room, grabbing her coat and bag from behind reception and ignoring the curious glances of Miriam and Cathy. It was only as she stormed out of the building and down the street that tears fell.

Chapter 6

S arah sat on a concrete bench in a concrete square surrounded by concrete buildings, eating a sausage roll. It was only midday and too early to go home. No way could she burden Cynthia with the news that she'd lost her job. An awful realisation flooded Sarah, and she swallowed down the overcooked pastry to avoid it coming back up. She had resigned. She had resigned and, in doing so, missed out on the chance of a redundancy payment.

At least you can hold your head high, she told herself. But pride would not pay the bills. She already struggled to pay the amount Cynthia demanded in rent. Now she would have no income for God knows how long. What would she do? Her business studies degree wasn't worth the paper it was printed on. She stood zero chance of getting a good reference from the company she'd been with since leaving university. She was screwed.

Sarah pulled the balled tissue from her pocket and wiped her eyes. She would need to compose herself before heading home to Cynthia. Her mother would spot the red-rimmed eyes a mile off and demand to know what was wrong. A sudden longing to call her father caused more tears to spring to Sarah's eyes.

'You all right, dear?'

Sarah looked up in surprise as an old lady creaked down beside her on the bench.

'Um, yes, fine. And you?' Sarah groaned at breaking one of her own rules. *Never engage strangers in conversation.*

'Can't complain. Just need to take the weight off these useless legs of mine.'

'Right.' Sarah observed the woman from the corner of her eye. Shrivelled and hunched, her skin hung from a gaunt face, creased like sand on a beach when the tide goes out.

'Guess how old I am.'

'Seventy?' Sarah thought the woman was far more likely to be in her eighties, but knew it would be rude to say so.

The woman laughed. 'Very kind of you, dear. I will turn ninety-seven next month. But don't ask me the secret to old age. There isn't one. I've taken none of my doctor's advice, but I can't die yet. Put a bet on myself reaching one hundred, didn't I?' The old lady cackled. 'Told my grandson he can have my winnings to buy a car. Got to keep my promises. Got to stay alive for a few more years yet. Anyway, what brings you to this miserable spot, crying your eyes out in the middle of the day?'

Wanting to avoid the old woman's questions, Sarah asked one of her own. 'Have you always lived in the town?'

'Yes, I was born here.'

'It must have changed a lot in that time.'

'Oh yes, and never for the better. Was more like a village when I was little. Green everywhere you went. Then some bright spark decided we were a commuter town, and in the sixties and seventies, turned our pretty village into a concrete jungle. A sacrilege if you ask me. And the master plan didn't work. Look at all these ugly, empty shops. There's no work round here, and nowhere to go shopping, even if you are lucky enough to be earning some cash. How about you? You always lived here?'

'Yes, I was born here too.'

'Then why haven't you left yet, like all the other youngsters?'

'My parents still live here.'

'That's not an answer. What is there here for you?'

Twenty-four hours ago, Sarah would have answered family and work, but now she had neither. 'I'm not sure.'

'Ah, you go off, girl. Go have some adventures. You're too young and pretty to be sitting in this dump bawling your eyes out. At least if you need a good cry, do it somewhere interesting. Find a place with trees, maybe a river. There's nothing so healing as nature.'

'Town life doesn't seem to have done you any harm.'

'Maybe not, but it doesn't seem to do you much good. Anyway, I'd better be on my way. No rest for the wicked. Nice to meet you, dear.'

'Likewise.'

The old woman hauled herself up on her walking stick and shuffled off down the dying high street. Sarah looked across at the empty building which once housed Woolworths. Next to it stood the empty building, which was once HMV. She'd spent so many afternoons after school searching through its shelves, trying to find the next up-and-coming band on CD.

What was left for her in the town? Her mother. And anyway, all this talk of adventures was utter crap. Only rich kids on gap years had adventures. Even the thought of setting off somewhere by herself made Sarah shudder. She was a home bird, a homing pigeon. She craved stability, not uncertainty. *There must be a way to fix this*, thought Sarah. Perhaps if she could get her parents to sit down and talk, things could go back to how they'd always been?

Sarah scrunched up the paper bag that had contained her sausage roll and threw it in a bin. She trudged her way along the high street, knowing she could no longer put off going home.

*

Sarah arrived home to banging and crashing upstairs. 'Mum? Is that you? Are you OK?'

Cynthia appeared at the top of the stairs, her face red and sweaty, her hair dishevelled. A layer of dust clung to her woollen skirt. 'What are you doing home?'

'I took a half day,' lied Sarah. 'I wanted to come home and check you were all right.'

Cynthia sighed. 'I told you, I don't need checking up on. Stick the kettle on, will you? I need to tell you my plans.'

Sarah set about making tea in the kitchen, all the while worrying about what her mother was going to announce. She wasn't the most rational woman at the best of times, so making any decisions after her husband had just left her could only spell disaster.

'Right. You and me need to have a chat,' said Cynthia, striding into the kitchen and standing with her hands on her hips. 'Sit down.'

Sarah carried two mugs to the table and passed one to her mother. 'Are you sure you're all right?'

'Never better. I've been on the phone to Auntie Marjorie and it's all settled.'

'What is?'

'I'm moving to Spain.'

'What? When?'

'Tonight. My flight leaves from Luton at eight o'clock.'

'Mum, don't you think you're rushing into this?'

'Not at all. I've been planning it for years. I always wanted to live in Spain, but your father couldn't cope with the climate. Me and Marjorie always said as soon as he died, I'd be on the first plane over there.'

'But Dad's not dead.'

'He is to me.'

'But where will you live?'

'With Marjorie to begin with, then I'll buy my own place. I've got an estate agent coming to value the house this afternoon.'

'This house?'

'Of course, this house.'

'But what about me?'

'Sarah, you're pushing thirty and still living at home. It's about time you stood on your own two feet.'

Sarah sat dumbfounded, nursing her cup of tea, staring at her mother. Cynthia had gone mad. That was the only explanation. Sarah was thinking of ways to head off the imminent arrival of an estate agent when the doorbell rang.

'That will be Greg.'

'Greg?'

'The estate agent. Keep up, love.'

Sarah looked on as Cynthia rushed to the front door, stopping at a mirror to slick a layer of pink across her lips.

'Greg, how wonderful of you to fit me in at such short notice.'

'It's no trouble at all, Mrs Lint. I'm pleased I can be of service. My, what a beautiful home you have here.'

'Thank you,' said Cynthia, giving a girlish giggle and leading the estate agent through to the kitchen.

When Greg walked in, Sarah spat her tea out across the kitchen table. 'Greg? When did you become an estate agent?'

'Around the same time Mark did. We've gone into business together.'

Mark? An estate agent? And here was his brother, standing in Sarah's kitchen like they were old friends.

'How is the lovely Mark?' asked Cynthia, batting her eyelashes at the scrawny man in an over-sized suit.

'He's good, thanks.' Greg turned to Sarah. 'Did you know he's met someone?'

Sarah blanched. She may still have Mark's photo on her bedroom wall, but she drew the line at internet stalking. 'No, I didn't know. Is she someone local?'

'He is, yes.'

'He?'

Greg laughed. 'Yes, that surprised us all. He's a dark horse is my brother. Anyway, Mrs Lint, would you like to do the honours and give me a tour?'

'Call me Cynthia, and yes, I'd be delighted.'

While Cynthia led Greg into the conservatory, Sarah took the stairs two at a time, racing to remove the photo of her and Mark before Greg reached her bedroom. She peeled it from the wall and ripped the photograph in two. Had she been such an awful partner that she had put Mark off women for life? Sarah leaned against the door frame, wondering if her life could get much worse.

Chapter 7

The house was as it had always been, but it no longer felt like a home. The furniture was the same, the kitchen smelled of twenty-five years of roast dinners, the bathroom door still squeaked on its hinge. And yet, everything was unfamiliar. There was no sound of her dad whistling, no nagging from Cynthia. The house was making unfamiliar noises that sent Sarah's imagination running wild.

Sarah checked the locks again. It felt different when her parents had gone on holiday and left her in the house alone. Knowing they were coming back made the house feel safe. Now all traces of them were gone. Cynthia had swept all the lotions and potions she used to hold back the advancing years from her nightstand and into her wash bag. Only winter clothes remained in the wardrobe, with the instruction that Sarah was to take them to the charity shop first thing the next morning.

There had been a brisk goodbye on the doorstep earlier that evening. The taxi driver had baulked at the amount of luggage Cynthia expected him to lift into his car. She'd been fidgety, excited, and the last thing she had wanted was an emotional goodbye with her daughter. There had been a vague suggestion Sarah should fly over and visit, but they had set no firm plans.

Sarah walked to the fridge and pulled off the list her mother had left for her. Greg had been certain that in a buoyant housing market, the nineteen-thirties semi with its high ceilings and well-proportioned rooms would sell in no time. Sarah's tasks included organising a removal van for the furniture, to be held in storage until Colin made contact, cleaning the house from top to bottom, and being Greg's contact should any problems arise with the sale.

Sarah wanted none of those jobs. Her home was being sold from under her and in a matter of weeks, she'd be homeless and unemployed. It wasn't as though she could stay with her father. He'd vanished off the face of the earth and even changed his phone number.

Colin would have to come out of the woodwork to deal with the legalities of his divorce and the splitting of profits from the house sale. But given Cynthia had inherited the house from her parents, she was free to sell it from under them without a second thought, or so she claimed.

The doorbell rang, and Sarah screamed. Her phone flashed with a text from a delivery company informing her food was at the door. She peered through the spyhole. Reassured the caller was indeed a delivery boy, Sarah opened the door a crack and exchanged cash for two boxes of pizza.

Not wanting to be reminded of her parent's absence, Sarah took the pizza to her bed and climbed under the duvet. She flicked on the TV and poured herself a glass of wine from the bottle beside her bed. With no one around to question her dietary choices, Sarah ate until she felt sick, took a ten-minute break, then started again until she had consumed both pepperoni pizzas.

The self-recriminations started as soon as she'd swallowed the last bite. Sarah turned up the TV, trying to drown out the voices in her head that were screaming with words such as *fat, loser, useless, spinster.*

The TV wasn't doing its job, so she opened her phone and began scrolling through social media. All the people she'd known at school seemed successful, with shiny lives, shiny partners, and shiny cars. *Just got my first promotion! She said yes! New house, new baby.* Sarah swallowed down bile as she read the chirpy captions accompanying photos of slender women and muscular men.

Against her better judgement, Sarah searched for Mark's name. She'd un-friended him the second he left her, but with his profile public, he was easy to spy on. At first, she didn't recognise him. He'd grown a beard, filled out. He may not be conventionally handsome, but Sarah felt a glimmer of attraction. *It's just the new clothes his partner's got him wearing*, she told herself.

Sarah scrolled down to another post. Mark and his partner Gary were in the centre of a large family group. A fluffy cockapoo snuggled into Gary's neck, Mark's arm draped across his shoulder, tickling the dog's fur. The smiling faces around the couple suggested they'd met Mark's sexuality bombshell with acceptance and love. Sarah wondered how Cynthia would react should she make a similar announcement. She couldn't imagine many smiles being involved.

It was gone midnight when Sarah fell asleep, phone in her hand, a piece of pepperoni stuck to her cheek. Playground bullies filled her dreams, and handsome Spanish men dancing Cynthia off into the sunset. She woke before the sun rose, feeling like she'd not slept at all.

*

Sarah sighed as the bus crept past the high street for the third time that day. The ache of her feet was nothing compared to the deep aching in her heart. Going cap in hand to local businesses with her CV and no reference had been a humiliating experience.

Sorry, we're not looking to take on any new staff.

Thanks for dropping by, but you don't have the skills we're looking for.

No, we're not hiring.

We don't employ anyone without references.

Have you tried the job centre?

Sarah thought back to conversations with Cynthia about the people they saw loitering outside the job centre. *Scroungers, wasters, spending all their money on fags.* No way was she letting herself become one of those people. Sarah reached across and rang the bus bell. The bus squeaked to a stop, and she climbed down the steps.

The high street was bleak. Only a handful of people shuffled along its depressing pavements, heads down, thick coats wrapped around themselves, avoiding each other's eye.

'Watch it,' said a scruffy man as he staggered to avoid Sarah. He wove along the pavement in unsteady lurches, a can of cider clamped between his fingers.

Sarah squared her shoulders and walked towards the last place on her list. 'What are you doing?' She muttered to herself. 'You're worth more than this.'

The faded sign of the burger restaurant was missing a few screws, and several letters drooped, as though about to fall into a deep sleep. Through the windows Sarah saw tables of youths, as greasy as the burgers in their mouths. She took a deep breath and opened the door.

'Hello, what can I get for you today?' The boy behind the counter looked like he was twelve years old. A failed attempt at a moustache clung to his top lip, his puckered acne-prone skin shimmered with oil and his hair hung in a replica of a 1980s mullet.

'Good afternoon. I was wondering if you are looking for staff?'

'Have to ask the manager.' The boy turned to serve another customer. Sarah pushed in front of him.

'Could you fetch the manager for me?'

'Not in.'

'Sorry, do you mean the manager's not at work?' Sarah swallowed her frustration. Why couldn't the boy speak in full sentences?

'Yeah.'

'Well, could you tell me what time he'll be here?'

'It's a woman. She'll be here to close up at five.'

'Fine. I'll wait.'

'Suit yourself.'

Sarah squashed herself behind a dirty plastic table and pulled out her phone. She checked the council website again, but as expected, all the jobs advertised required experience and references. Sarah opened a new tab and began scouring the job listings of a local recruitment firm. She stopped scrolling and stared in horror at an advert for her old job. *So much for budget cuts and slimming down the team.*

By ten past five, Sarah was giving up hope of ever meeting the elusive burger joint manager. She stood and gathered her coat and bag just as a teenage girl with slicked back hair walked in.

'Alright, Nuts? Everything good?'

Nuts? Sarah looked over at the counter. The greasy boy nodded in her direction.

'That lady wants to talk to you about getting a job.'

The girl stopped by Sarah's table and gazed at her through narrowed eyes. 'What's a person like you doing looking for a job in a place like this?'

The girl chewed gum as she spoke, and Sarah tried to ignore the way it made her stomach churn. 'I need to be earning money.'

'You worked in a restaurant before?'

Sarah thought calling the burger joint a restaurant was a stretch, but bit her tongue. 'I did a bit of waitressing while I was at uni,' she lied.

'Uni, hey? La-di-da. Got references?'

Sarah shook her head.

'Lucky for you we're short staffed. Can you come in for training tomorrow? I'll put you on a two-week trial, see how you get on. Wait there.' The girl disappeared behind the counter and came back, holding out several sheets of paper. 'Have this application filled out by the time you come in?'

'Will do,' said Sarah, taking the outstretched paperwork 'What time tomorrow?'

'Ten sharp.'

'See you then.' Sarah pulled on her coat and forced her feet to walk rather than run out of the door. At least it was a job. A job was a job. *It's only a stop-gap*, she told herself.

On her way to the bus stop, Sarah's phone rang, and she rifled through her bag to find it.

'Hello?'

'Hi, Sarah. Greg here. I've got a viewing booked in for tomorrow morning.'

'A viewing?'

'Yes, a viewing of your parents' house.'

My house. 'OK. What time?'

'Nine. That's all right? If you can't be there to let us in, just leave the keys somewhere safe.'

'I'll be there,' said Sarah, hating the thought of strangers waltzing through her home without her there. It would be tight, getting to her new job in time, but it was a risk she'd have to take.

Sarah got off the bus a stop early and called in to the corner shop. An evening of form filling and cleaning stretched ahead of her. The least she could do was to ease the pain with a few bags of crisps. With her cleaning snacks paid for, Sarah walked the street she'd been walking for twenty-five years, wondering how long it would be before someone else walked this path, put their key in her front door, slept in her bedroom. With a job under her belt, she'd need to get onto the next urgent matter on her list. Finding somewhere to live.

Chapter 8

S arah leaned against the oven door, wiping a rubber gloved hand across her forehead. She'd been cleaning since six, despite working until eleven the night before. Cynthia's claims to always keep her home ship-shape rang hollow given the dust and grime Sarah had found during her toil. Perhaps she'd gone a little over the top. Would prospective buyers be looking inside the oven, or behind the wardrobe?

Given how little she wanted the house to sell, Sarah wondered why she'd spent so long making it sparkle. Deep down, she knew the answer. Pride. Not only pride in her home, but she was too proud to admit her life prospects were fast slipping down the drain. At least when the prospective buyers stepped into her home, they'd smell lemon freshness tinged with fresh coffee and decide the current owner must have her shit together.

The scrubbing and polishing in the kitchen left no time for a shower. Sarah ran a brush through her hair, threw on an old pair of jeans, a passable T-shirt, and was waiting by the front door when the knock came.

Sarah opened the door, then slammed it shut again. She leaned against it, fighting to regulate her breathing. What was he doing here? The doorbell rang.

'Sarah? Sarah, please open up.'

With a deep breath, Sarah opened the door. 'What are you doing here?'

'I'm so sorry. Greg was supposed to do this, but he came down with food poisoning last night. He said he'd let you know, but I guess he had other things on his mind.'

Sarah stared, open-mouthed. Mark not only looked different, he sounded different. There was none of his usual stuttering. He no longer spoke in snatched, whispered sentences. Just as his shoulders had broadened, so had his voice. He sounded confident. He was a changed man.

'You'd better come in.'

'Sorry. I can postpone the viewing till Greg's better if you'd prefer?'

Postpone the viewing? Sarah weighed up her options. Postponing would mean less chance of selling and give her more breathing space to find a new place. On the other hand, postponing would signal to Mark that she still wasn't over their break-up and she wouldn't give him the satisfaction.

'No, it's fine, come in.'

Sarah and Mark walked through to the kitchen. Fresh coffee stood cooling in the pot, but rather than offer him any, they stood in the kitchen, throwing awkward glances at one another.

'So, your parents are selling up?'

'Good news travels fast.'

'I'm sorry to hear that, Sarah. I thought Cynthia and Colin would live here forever.'

'Me too.'

'Well, I'm sure wherever they're moving to will be just as lovely. This place will sell in no time. I'd be tempted to buy the place myself. Gary would love it.'

'Gary?'

'My partner.'

'Oh, so you work together?'

'No, he's not my colleague. He's my life partner. My boyfriend.' Mark turned to her. 'But you knew that, didn't you?'

Sarah had the good grace to blush. 'I'd heard a rumour.'

'It wasn't easy for me, you know.'

'What wasn't? Leaving me, or coming out?'

'Both.'

Sarah laughed. 'Do you think it was easy for me? I thought we were going to get married! Have you any idea how humiliating it was being abandoned like that?'

'Sorry.'

'Yeah, too right, you should be sorry.'

'I'm sorry for the way I handled things. Not for the decision I made. It was the right one for both of us.'

'It may have been right for you, but you don't get to tell me what's right for me.'

'Sarah, be honest with yourself. You never loved me.'

'I did! I...' Sarah thought back to their time together. She loved being part of a couple, she loved showing off her shiny ring. But Mark... had she loved him?

'You need to take some responsibility for what happened. How you treated me.'

'How I treated *you*? Oh, that's brilliant, that is. I wasn't the one who ran away from a holiday and changed my number.'

'And I've apologised for that. I'm talking about how you treated me while we were together. Of course, it was also my fault. I let you get away with it.'

'Get away with what?'

'The bullying.'

'Bullying? I never bullied you! I would never bully anyone. Don't you remember me telling you how badly I was bullied at school?'

'It's not unheard of for the bullied to become the bully.'

Sarah stared at Mark, too stunned to speak.

'Sorry, Sarah. I didn't come here to fight, just to do my job. I'm pleased you're here, I've been wondering how you were.'

'Yeah, well, you're about two years late for that. If you cared so much, you wouldn't be standing here accusing me of bullying you.'

'I'm not saying you meant to do it. It's not as though your parents gave you a great model for a healthy relationship.'

'What have my parents got to do with anything?'

'Oh, come on, Sarah. You must see how badly your mum treats your dad, and how he lets her get away with it. I hated being around it, because it was like looking into our future.'

Sarah stared down at her feet. Colin had yet to make contact, and she hated him for it. But was she right to lay all the blame at his door? 'Mum and Dad are getting a divorce. That's why they're selling the house.'

'What? Cynthia left him?'

'No, it was the other way round.'

Mark chuckled. 'Good for Colin. I didn't know the sly old dog had it in him.'

'It's not something to laugh about. They're selling the house from under me. They've abandoned me, left me homeless. I don't see how that's funny.'

'Homeless? You know if you're looking for another place I could help with that?'

Sarah gave a joyless laugh. 'Thanks, but no thanks.'

'I wasn't trying to...' Mark sighed. 'I'm sure something will turn up. There's plenty of housing stock around. What are you after? Flat?

House?' The doorbell rang and Mark looked at his watch. 'That will be the couple coming to view this place.'

Mark turned to leave the kitchen, but Sarah stepped into his path, blocking the door.

'Did you know you were gay while we were together? Is that the real reason you left me?'

'I know that would make it easier for you, but no, that's not why I left you. I'm not sure I'd even label myself as gay. It's too black and white. There was no sudden revelation about my sexuality. I just fell in love. I fell in love with a man.'

Sarah picked at a piece of loose lino with the toe of her boot. She'd spent two years hating the man in front of her, but as much as she tried to pull those feelings to the surface, she couldn't. Standing in front of her was an old friend, his calm, genuine way of speaking reminding her of all she'd liked about him when they first met.

'You'd better let them in,' said Sarah, as the doorbell rang again. She stepped aside. As Mark passed her, he placed a hand on her shoulder and squeezed. 'I'm pleased we got the chance to talk, even if the circumstances aren't ideal. And I mean it, if you need help to find a new place, just ask.'

Sarah walked to the sink and stared out into the garden. She heard Mark greeting the young couple coming to snoop around her home. Why was everyone's life moving forward but hers? No doubt the young couple would pop out babies before they'd even wiped their feet on the mat. Mark was happy with his new love. Even Cynthia was having a wild old time of it reliving her youth.

'This is the kitchen. As you can see, there'd be an opportunity to knock through and create one large open-plan living-dining space.'

The young couple nodded at Sarah, and she gave them a curt smile. For the next ten minutes, she did her best to stay out of their way. The last thing she wanted to see was them knocking on walls, talking about interior decor, or assigning bedrooms to their future children.

Sarah checked her watch. If she didn't leave soon, she'd be late for her first shift. She ran up the stairs and found Mark and his clients squished into the small family bathroom.

'Hi, um, I'm sorry, Mark, but I have to get to work.'

'Oh, right, OK.' Mark looked at his watch. 'We've still got a few rooms to view...'

'No worries. Look, why don't you take your time? Put the keys through the letter box when you're done. I'll take my spare set.'

'If you're sure, that would be very helpful.'

Sarah forced a smile onto her face and said her goodbyes to Mark and the couple. As she left the house and closed the door behind her, sadness flooded through her, followed by anger. How dare her parents sell the house from under her? How dare the couple talk about knocking down walls and changing the colour of her bedroom? How dare Mark rub his lovey-dovey new life in her face?

Sarah strode towards her new job, her legs powered by anger and resentment and a creeping feeling that she was standing still while the world kept turning. She was being left behind and could do nothing about it.

Chapter 9

T he drinks machine spurted into life and Sarah filled a cup with sickly sweet brown liquid. She moved to the kitchen, grabbed an ageing burger from the stand and scooped fries into a cone.

'Here you go,' she said, dumping the tray of poor-quality food in front of the customer.

'Got any mayo?'

'That will be an extra fifty pence.'

The man in front of her scowled, shook his head, and carried his tray to a table.

'Getting the hang of it, aren't you?' The greasy boy known to all the staff as Nuts appeared by her side.

'It's hardly rocket science.'

Nuts sniffed and wiped his nose on his sleeve. 'How you finding it?'

'What?'

'Working here. Almost two weeks, isn't it?'

Two long weeks of serving oily customers oily food, going home stinking of oil. What a waste of a life. 'It's wonderful, just the opportunity I'd been looking for.'

Nuts missed the sarcasm in Sarah's voice and held out his hand for a fist bump. Sarah stared at him in confusion until he sighed and stuffed his hands in his pockets.

'Well, just shout if you need a hand with anything.'

'I have a question. Why are you called Nuts?'

The boy in front of her howled with laughter. 'You don't wanna know, babe. You don't wanna know.' He walked away laughing and shaking his head. Sarah looked around her and sighed. She must have done something awful in a past life to end up here.

By lunchtime the restaurant was filling up and Sarah faced a snaking queue as she tried to keep up with orders. It amazed her that so many people would come to the restaurant by choice. She ate the food, but only because she got it for free. No way would she pay good money for it, especially after seeing how they made it. Nuts was still outside on a cigarette break, but despite needing help, Sarah refused to humiliate herself by calling his name out loud.

'How can I help you?' Despite hating the bright orange cap that made up the worst part of her uniform, it had its uses. It meant she could keep her head tipped low and remain incognito.

'Sarah?'

Sarah whipped her head up. No. Please no. 'What are you doing here?'

'Lunch, hun. What else?'

Sarah's heart hammered in her chest. She wondered if she'd die of embarrassment right there and then. 'What can I get you?'

Miriam pretended to study the menu. *In two, three, four. Hold two, three, four. Out two, three, four. Hold two, three, four.* The breathing exercises weren't working. Heat flooded Sarah's face, her legs turned to jelly. She needed to regain control. It was bad enough Miriam finding out she worked in a burger bar, without also reporting back that Sarah had collapsed under the weight of her embarrassment.

Just in the nick of time, Miriam placed her order. 'Two burgers, two fries and two cokes.'

'Coming right up.'

'Hey,' Miriam called, as Sarah turned to make up the order.

'Yes?'

'I bet Weatherwear doesn't seem so bad now, does it?'

In two, three, four, hold two, three, four, out two, three, four, hold two, three, four.

'Here you go,' said Sarah, placing two bags of food in front of her ex colleague.

'Oh, sorry, didn't I say? I wanted those to eat in, not take away. Cathy's joining me in a minute. I'm sure she'll be delighted to see you.'

Miriam's smirk proved too much. 'Excuse me,' said Sarah, rushing through the fire door to find Nuts.

'You all right?' he asked, dropping his cigarette to the floor and crushing it beneath his shoe.

'No... no... don't feel well...'

Panic scoured Nuts's face as he looked at Sarah. 'I got a first aid certificate, but I slept through most of the training. I'll call an ambulance.'

'No! Please, I just need a minute out here. Can you take over inside?'

'Course,' said Nuts, looking grateful to get away. 'Take as long as you need.'

As the door closed behind Nuts's retreating body, Sarah crumpled to the floor. She curled up among the bins, tears streaming down her face, her breaths coming in quick, ragged bursts. Pins and needles crept along her limbs. *You're over-breathing,* she told herself. *It's happened before. Calm down, calm down.*

Sarah wasn't sure how long she'd been lying by the bins. By the time Nuts reappeared with a glass of water, her breathing had slowed and feeling was returning to her limbs.

'Lunch rush has died down,' he said. 'How are you feeling?'

'Bit better.'

'I called the boss. She said she'll come in and cover so you can take the afternoon off.'

'There was no need to do that.'

'Come on, babe. I saw the state of you. You should be home in bed, not flipping burgers.'

At that moment, Sarah could've hugged the spotty teenager in front of her. 'Thank you,' she said, pulling herself off the floor and dusting herself off. 'I'll stay till the boss gets here.'

'No, you get on home. I can manage by myself. Afternoons are always quiet.'

'Thanks,' said Sarah. She walked back into the restaurant and straight to her locker. It was only as she headed to the door she realised there were still two customers left in the restaurant.

'Sarah, how the hell are you?'

Cathy and Miriam stared up at her, empty food wrappers strewn on the table in front of them.

'Hi, Cathy. I'm surprised you guys are still here. Isn't your lunch break over?'

'Still a stickler for the rules, hey?' said Miriam, a sly grin creeping across her face. 'You know, the place isn't the same without you?'

'Oh?' A flutter of hope stirred in Sarah's stomach. Could she could get her old job back?

'No, it's not,' simpered Cathy. 'Everyone's happy for a start.'

'Oh.'

'Yeah, it's just so much more relaxed. Longer breaks, less stress. You did us all a favour by quitting. We should get back, but I couldn't leave without thanking you.'

Panic prickled the edges of Sarah's body. She pictured Cathy and Miriam reporting back on Sarah's fall from grace. How they'd laugh.

With horror, she realised it wouldn't be long before the fitters turned up at the restaurant to see Sarah's downfall for themselves.

'I have to go,' said Sarah, heading for the door.

'Love the uniform,' called Miriam, the sound of her and Cathy's laughter following Sarah out of the door.

Sarah ran down the high street, only stopping when she reached a park. Paint peeled from children's play equipment, empty cans of lager spilled out of a bin, but at least it was quiet. Sarah sat on a bench and looked down at herself. Her black trousers bulged at the thighs. The orange T-shirt they had given her was too small. Around her middle, it looked like someone had shoved several rubber rings up her top, her breasts straining at the seams above.

A thought nagged her that perhaps it was time to move on. But if she did, there was no guarantee things would be any better in a new place. The scenery would change, not her life. Sarah kicked an empty beer can in frustration. It wasn't like she was asking for a lot. All she wanted was a decent job, a decent place to live, a safe, comfortable life. She didn't want to be rich; she didn't want to be famous. God, it wasn't like she was asking for the earth.

Sarah pulled a crumpled piece of paper and pen from her bag. It was no use wallowing. She began making a list of how to crawl out of the pit she'd fallen into:

Look for a place to live
Search online for a different job.
Try to get hold of Dad.

Her pen hovered over the paper. If she wrote the next action point down, she'd have to stick to it. Damn her own efficiency. Was it worth the risk? Sarah took a deep breath and put pen to paper.

Register with a dating site.

Sarah folded her to-do list into her pocket and left the park. At least the latest panic attack had resulted in an unexpected afternoon off. Sarah wondered if she'd get sick pay, but decided it was unlikely. The working practices at the burger bar were less than standard.

Leaving the park bench behind, Sarah walked home with a new sense of purpose.

Chapter 10

O ver her morning coffee, Sarah perused the latest goings on in the local paper. Her home town wasn't so bad; there was a new bar opening, a local school fund-raiser and an interview from a B list reality TV star who had grown up in the town.

Things were looking up. Sarah had four flats to view, had circled six jobs in the paper, and within minutes of signing up to a dating site, had her first date booked in for that evening.

She'd had to tell a white lie to get the day off, phoning her boss to say she still felt under the weather. It wasn't a complete lie. The panic attacks left her exhausted, and a good night's sleep still proved elusive. With a positive day stretching before her, Sarah downed the dregs of her coffee and pulled on her coat, ready for her first appointment.

The first flat Sarah viewed was in the town centre, above a boarded-up shop. The outside wasn't up to much, but Sarah told herself not to judge a book by its cover as she waited for the estate agent to arrive.

'Hi, you must be Sarah?'

'That's me.'

'Great. Let's head up to the flat, shall we? Like I said on the phone, it needs a bit of updating, but a lick of paint should do the trick.'

'Isn't that the landlord's job?'

'You'd think so, wouldn't you?' said the estate agent, giving Sarah a shrug and opening the door.

They climbed a shabby staircase that ran up the side of the building. Sarah tried to hide her shock at seeing the front door. There was a splintered dent at the bottom, a boot mark in the middle, and the tangled remains of police tape hanging down the side.

'My God, what happened here?'

'Ah, yes, sorry, I should've mentioned that. The previous tenant got into a bit of bother with the police. Drugs.'

'Why the police tape?'

'An unhappy customer assaulted the man, put him in hospital. Hence the crime scene. Right, let's get you inside.'

If anything, the inside of the flat was worse than the outside. Devoid of furniture, the rooms were a decent size, but that was the only positive Sarah could find. A lingering smell of cigarette smoke hung in the air, the walls a telltale yellow colour. The frayed, dirty carpet housed a suspicious stain covering the middle of the living room floor.

'Is that where...?' asked Sarah, pointing to the stain.

The estate agent shuffled his feet, whilst wringing his hands. 'Yes, well, it's possible, although it could be a red wine stain.'

Sarah looked at him in horror. 'The landlord didn't think it would be a good idea to change the carpets?'

The estate agent coughed. 'Shall we look at the kitchen?'

'I think I've seen enough,' said Sarah, leading the estate agent out of the flat. 'How much did you say they're charging in rent?'

'Seven hundred a month.'

'Including bills?'

'Um, no.'

Sarah felt her positive mood slipping through her fingers. 'Shall we go to the next one?'

'Yes, of course. It's only a couple of streets away. Are you all right to walk?'

'Yes, that's fine.'

The estate agent made awkward small talk as they walked the short distance to the next flat. 'Right, here we are,' he said, pulling out a set of keys.

Sarah looked up at the building in front of her. It was a definite improvement on the last place. The house was part of a nineteen seventies terrace. Some houses in the row even had pots of flowers outside. 'At least there's no police tape here,' said Sarah.

The estate agent gave a nervous chuckle. 'Now, it's the ground-floor flat, so no stairs this time.'

'And the listing said it has a garden?'

'A yard, yes.'

'Great, let's have a look.'

The estate agent unlocked the front door, then paused before letting Sarah in. 'I think I told you, but this flat has lain empty for quite some months. An elderly gentleman occupied it, so it may require a bit of imagination to see its full potential.'

A ball of dread settled in Sarah's stomach. 'Let's just get in there, shall we?' Sarah followed the estate agent inside. Their hands flew to their noses. 'My God, what is that smell?' The previous flat smelled like roses compared to this one.

'I think the previous tenant had cats...'

'How many cats?'

'A few...'

'And no litter tray if this smell is anything to go by. I'm sorry, but I don't want to see any more. I need to get out of here.'

The estate agent and Sarah fled the house, taking deep lungfuls of air and slamming the door behind them.

'The next flat's a little way out of town. Do you have a car, or would you like a lift?'

'A lift would be helpful.'

*

As soon as she arrived home, Sarah headed straight for the shower, keen to wash away the dirt and grime she'd been exposed to. The third flat proved just as disgusting as the first two. Mould grew throughout the kitchen and bathroom, large black patches of damp covered the walls like wallpaper. Sarah had pinned all her hopes on the final flat, only to have them dashed before they'd stepped foot over the threshold. The estate agent had received a call to say the flat had already gone, taking all Sarah's positivity with it.

Oh well, at least there's tonight to look forward to, Sarah told herself, scrubbing her skin with twice the amount of soap as usual.

Adam sounded nice on his dating profile. *Professional man in my thirties, looking for friendship with the hope it leads to something more.* His profile picture showed a friendly face with good proportions. Just what Sarah was looking for.

Sarah arrived at the pub a fashionable ten minutes late. Scanning the room, she found no trace of the man she had met online. Sarah perched on a bar stool, ordering a gin and tonic and feeling a momentary pang of loss for comfortable Sunday afternoons in her parents' home. She was halfway through her G and T when a man coughed beside her.

'Hi, are you Sarah?'

Sarah turned to face the man. There was no way this was the same man she'd been speaking to online. 'Yes, I'm Sarah. Who are you?'

'Adam, of course. Don't you recognise me?'

Sarah didn't. White stubble covered his chin. The thick head of blond hair in his profile picture was thin and white in real life. There was no way the man in front of her was in his thirties. Even fifties would be a stretch.

'Right, hello, nice to meet you,' said Sarah, recovering from her first impressions.

'I've grabbed us a table in the corner. More privacy,' said Adam, winking and making Sarah's flesh crawl. This man was older than her father.

Sarah followed Adam to the table. She could see why he'd picked it. The low lighting knocked ten years off him.

'Shall we call the waiter over?' said Sarah.

'No need. I've already ordered.'

'Yes, but I haven't.'

Adam laughed. 'No, silly, I've ordered for both of us.'

'You ordered for me?' asked Sarah, astounded at the cheek of the man.

'Sure did.'

'But how did you know what I like?'

'Everyone likes seafood.'

'I'm allergic to seafood.' This was not true, although there had been one occasion when Sarah had suffered at the hands of a dodgy mussel.

'Oh. I ordered bread as a side. You could eat that?'

'Or I could just order for myself?'

'Too late,' said Adam, pointing to a waiter who walked through the bar carrying an enormous tray of seafood, its crowning glory a lobster on top.

'Excuse me, do you think we could order a bowl of chips to go with this?'

'Of course,' said the waiter.

'Chips?' Adam laughed. 'You look like a girl who enjoys her food.'

Sarah shivered as he looked her up and down with hungry eyes. She'd chosen a loose- fitting black dress to wear, which she hoped hid her lumps and bumps. It seemed she'd been wrong.

'Yes, I like a girl with meat on her bones. Can't stand these awful stick insects you see on TV. Give me a woman with plenty to grab hold of any time.' Adam took a large bite of lobster, his eyes glued to Sarah's chest.

'I need to visit the ladies,' said Sarah, pushing her chair back.

'Sure thing,' said Adam, putting the lobster down and sucking a mussel from its shell, a thin trickle of sauce dribbling down his chin.

Sarah grabbed her coat and bag and ran. She didn't stop running till she reached the corner shop and was certain Awful Adam hadn't followed her.

'You look lovely this evening,' said the shopkeeper as Sarah lay a frozen pizza and a bottle of wine on the counter. 'Off out somewhere nice?'

'What do you think?' said Sarah, grabbing her meal for one and heading home.

Chapter 11

S arah looked down at her crumpled dress, thrown into a pile on the floor the night before. She groaned and sat on top of it, leaning against her bed frame and planting her face in her hands. She couldn't get anything right; dating, house-hunting, employment. Perhaps Colin was right and she should set the bar higher, seek adventure? Perhaps her hometown had given up all it offered? It seemed to have left her the dregs.

Her alarm clock showed six a.m. How Sarah longed for a good night's sleep. She couldn't remember the last time she'd fallen asleep before midnight, or woken after six. Sarah's bedroom floor felt like shifting sand, everything around her unstable, threatening to collapse and drag her further down at the first opportunity.

Sarah flicked on her phone, desperate to fill the few hours before the rest of the world was awake. She'd blocked Awful Adam and deleted the dating app after a stream of curse-filled insults disrupted her movie-watching-pizza-eating marathon the evening before. Flicking on to social media, Sarah's thumb swiped away inane posts about pets, boasting parents showing off their children, beautiful people flaunting fun nights out.

Just as Sarah was ready to throw her phone against the wall, a post came up that made her heart jolt. She went on social media so rarely, it surprised Sarah to find she followed the B&B she had stayed in on her final fateful holiday with Mark.

This looks like a great opportunity for anyone wanting a summer job!

Below the caption was a photograph of an old stone cottage in the woods. A sign above the front door informed her it was now a café. Outside it were picnic tables, a children's play area and a tree-lined stream. A friendly-looking waitress stood in the doorway holding a tray of tea and cakes.

Waitress wanted. Basic accommodation provided. Immediate start.

Sarah scrolled past the post, then back up to it. Waitressing wasn't so different from what she did at the burger bar, and the café looked an improvement on her current working environment. Could she quit the burger bar so soon into her new job? It wouldn't look good on her CV, holding down one job for four years but leaving without a reference, then leaving another job after two weeks. But she didn't owe them anything, and they'd find someone new. A monkey could flip burgers. God, if Nuts could do it, anyone could.

Sarah frowned at her phone screen. She was supposed to be moving up in the world, not sideways. A summer job in a café wasn't a step up. And yet... And yet... Was she desperate enough to be a skivvy for rich holiday makers and chirpy hikers? Sarah looked at the empty food containers and wine bottles scattered around her bedroom floor. They didn't scream success, or happiness, or a lifestyle worth clinging on to. She pictured the posts she could share on social media if she got the job. *Forest bathing after work. Quick hike before breakfast.*

Her disastrous CV was a concern, but the *immediate start* suggested the café manager was desperate for staff, and it wasn't like she was incapable of making a pot of tea. God knows she'd had plenty of practice making thousands of cups of tea for Cynthia over the years.

Before she could change her mind, Sarah clicked the *like* button on the café's page and fired off a message. *I saw your advert and wondered if you're still looking for staff? I've just left my previous job and I'm looking for a fresh start as my parents have moved to Spain.*

It wasn't all lies. One parent had moved to Spain, and she was looking for a fresh start, regardless of whether she wanted to. There was the small matter of handing in her notice at the burger bar, but it wasn't as though it would come as a surprise given their high staff turnover.

The ping of her phone made Sarah jump. Had they replied already? It was only twenty past six in the morning.

Hi, good to hear from you. Yes, we are still looking for staff. Would you be able to pop in on Saturday for an interview? X

P.S. Us early risers need to stick together! ;-)

Saturday. That was only a few days away. Sarah thought of the long to-do list Cynthia had left on the fridge. She couldn't abandon her duties, could she? A wave of anger caught Sarah by surprise. Why should she clear up her parents' mess? It wasn't like Cynthia was trekking through the jungle. They had internet and phone signal in Spain. For the second time that day, Sarah typed a rushed, rash message on her phone.

Hi Mum. Hope all's going well over there. Something's come up and I need to go away for a few days. I'll give Greg your number and tell him to call you if there are any issues with the sale. Likewise, I'll pass your number onto the removal company. I'll leave a key with Mr Merryman next door so they can get in. I leave on Friday, so I'll pack any valuables up before I go. Sarah x

Sarah turned her phone off even though she knew Cynthia wouldn't be up for hours yet. The last thing she needed was her mother tearing down her newfound sense of purpose. Her shift at the burger bar started at ten, and she'd hand in her notice straight away. It shouldn't cause too many ripples, given she was still just within her trial period. There was a call Sarah needed to make, but it was too early, so she made herself a coffee and began packing up belongings in her room.

Sarah waded through her wardrobe, throwing all her ill-fitting clothes into a pile destined for the charity shop. When she had finished, there were only enough clothes left to fill one small suitcase. Sarah pinched at her expanding waistline, hating herself for binging the night before. If she got the job, perhaps she could do a bit more exercise, get a bit more healthy? Anything was worth a try.

Next, Sarah tackled her bookshelf. It had been years since she'd read anything and the piles of Nancy Drew and Jacqueline Wilson books felt too immature to keep. By the time Sarah had sifted through her soft toys and knickknacks, items headed for the charity shop covered the bed.

Sarah glanced at the clock. Almost nine. She turned her phone on, her pulse quickening as she waited for messages to come through. Her phone remained silent. Perhaps Cynthia had been on the sangria the night before and hadn't yet woken to Sarah's message? Sarah scrolled through her list of contacts until she found the number she was looking for.

The dial tone went on for so long Sarah was ready to give up. Just as she was about to hang up, a woman's voice came on the line.

'Hello? Kate Tremain speaking.'

'Oh, hi, um, I'm not sure you'd remember me, but I stayed at your house a few years ago.'

'OK. What's your name?'

'Sarah. Sarah Lint.'

There was an awkward, almost imperceptible pause on the other end of the line before the woman gathered herself. 'Sarah, of course I remember you. How are you?'

'I'm good, thanks. The reason I'm calling is I saw your post on Facebook about the job.'

'Job?'

'Yes. You shared a post about a waitressing job in the woods.'

'Oh, that. I'd forgotten. Yes, lovely place to work.'

'Well, I've got an interview there on Saturday, and I was wondering if you had any room at your place for a night or two?'

'Hmm,' said Kate. 'I don't think we have any bookings. Have you checked on our online calendar?'

'No, um, I was kind of hoping I could go direct through you. You know, avoid the extra fees.' In the silence that followed, Sarah wished she'd just sucked up the extra cost and booked through the conventional route. 'I'm sorry, I shouldn't have asked. It's just I lost my job, my dad left my mum, then Mum moved to Spain and... and...' To Sarah's horror, she found herself choking back tears. The last time she'd seen the Airbnb host she'd been a snotty mess. Now here she was, confirming the impression that she was emotionally unstable.

'Oh no, that all sounds awful. I'm not supposed to take private bookings, but I guess there's no harm just this once. Do you know what time you'll be arriving?'

'Not yet,' said Sarah, wiping her eyes on the sleeve of her jumper. 'I need to book my train tickets. Can I message you when I know?'

'Yes, no problem. It will be lovely to see you again.'

Liar, thought Sarah as she put down the phone. She knew Kate hadn't liked her the first time they met, and there was no reason to assume she'd reconsidered in the intervening years. Sarah didn't dwell on it, though. For the first time in days, something had gone her way.

By Friday she'd be on a train to Cornwall, and if she was lucky, a whole new life.

Chapter 12

S arah wriggled in her seat, trying to find a comfortable spot. She should have been travelling by train, but after checking the cost of fares, had settled for a bus. And this wasn't just any bus, at a whole ten pounds cheaper, the night bus was the obvious choice.

Beside her, a plump middle-aged woman let out a snore, a trickle of saliva creeping down her chin. Sarah shuddered. She'd tried to claim the seat beside her with her large holdall, but with the bus full, she'd had five minutes to herself before being forced to give the spare seat up.

At least if she was sleeping, the woman couldn't talk. She'd been bending Sarah's ear from London to Exeter, only submitting to sleep when her watch hands passed one a.m. Sarah had tried every trick in the book to avoid conversation: headphones in, book in hand, eyes closed. None of it had worked. In the end, Sarah's patience had snapped, and she'd told the woman to shut up. Thankfully, the frosty silence that ensued ended with the woman's drooping eyelids.

Sarah ground her teeth. The snoring was worse than any amount of inane chatter. Two rows back, an elderly gentleman was singing to himself, whisky bottle in hand. Four rows back, a woman threw up at regular intervals. Sarah bristled. Why would you travel by coach if you suffered from motion sickness?

It wasn't only the bus making Sarah uncomfortable. Memories of her last encounter at the burger bar made her insides squirm. Nuts had been upset at her leaving, the boss angry. They spoke of her letting them down, leaving them in the lurch. Anyone would think she'd been a doctor, abandoning patients. Sarah tried to bring perspective to the situation, telling them a crappy minimum wage job would be easily filled, but that hadn't gone down well. The only comfort was picturing Miriam and Cathy turning up to gloat, only to find Sarah gone. With the thought of their disappointed faces in her mind, Sarah drifted towards sleep.

When the bus pulled into Bodmin at six a.m. Sarah had endured two hours of fitful sleep and felt like death warmed up. As she stood to disembark, every bone in her body clicked, her limbs stiff after ten hours in a cramped seat.

What a relief it was to be out in the fresh air. Sarah stood for a moment, enjoying the light sheen of drizzle settling on her face. The bus creaked away and Sarah prayed she'd never have to experience it again.

With her bag hauled on her back, Sarah walked through the quiet Bodmin streets, desperate for a bed and a cup of coffee. The town was sleeping, not a car on the road. Despite the mizzle hanging in the air, Sarah compared the town to that which she'd grown up in and found Bodmin won hands down. It might be grotty in places, with several empty shops, but each building on the high street differed from the last, freshly painted shop fronts and houses popping with colour on the grey day.

On reaching the Airbnb, Sarah dumped her bag down on the floor and pulled out her phone to find the code Kate had sent. She removed the key from the key box, opened the front door, and crept into the house.

The house was smaller than Sarah remembered, a floral scent coming from a vase of flowers in the fireplace. Any nerves at returning to a place from her past dissipated as the warm colours and cosy furniture enveloped Sarah's tired brain. Last time she'd been here, Mark had carried her heavy bags for her. On this occasion, she carried the holdall upstairs herself, struggling for breath and deciding to begin a fitness regime as a priority.

The bedroom was as pretty as Sarah remembered, the large, old bed calling to her from the middle of the room. Sarah kicked off her shoes and climbed between the covers. Hadn't she complained about the mattress the last time she was here? Either she'd been in a bad mood back then, or the bus had lowered her standards, for on this occasion she snuggled down, more comfortable than any time she could remember.

Sarah's alarm blared out from the pillow beside her. Ten a.m. Good. Three and a half hours' sleep was better than no sleep. She pulled off her crumpled clothes and headed to the shower. Downstairs, the sound of a radio playing and a man's deep baritone singing along reached her. There was no man on the scene the last time she was here. Sarah was curious to see what Kate's type was and meet the tuneful man downstairs.

She showered, towel drying her hair and climbing into the black skirt and white shirt, which she hoped looked the part for a waitressing role. In the guest sitting room, Sarah made herself a coffee and took advantage of the croissants her host had left for her. The diet could wait until tomorrow.

Sarah was gathering up croissant crumbs with her thumb when a knock came on the sitting-room door.

'Come in.'

'Morning, Sarah. It's good to see you again.'

The host, Kate, stood in the doorway, looking even prettier than Sarah remembered. Sarah swallowed down her envy. If she tried to pull off scraped-back hair and a pair of dungarees, she'd look like a builder on his way to work.

'Thank you for letting me book direct.'

'No problem at all.' Kate walked into the room and sat opposite Sarah at the small dining table. Sarah bristled at the proximity and over friendliness on display. 'So, how have you been?'

'Good, yeah, all good.'

'Oh?' Kate arched an eyebrow. 'It didn't sound like things were that great when we spoke on the phone.'

Sarah flushed as she remembered over-sharing her disastrous situation. 'Oh, yeah, all that. It's not as bad as I made out. I'm an adult, after all. It's not like I'm ten and my parents are getting divorced. I'll get over it.' Sarah squeezed out a small, unconvincing smile. To Sarah's horror, Kate placed her small hand on hers and squeezed.

'Parents getting divorced is hard whatever age you are. I don't want to be presumptuous, but I know a great counsellor if you ever need to talk?'

Sarah choked on her coffee, rushing to the sink for a glass of water to ease the coughing fit which ensued.

'Sorry,' said Kate. 'That was a stupid thing to say.'

'It's OK,' said Sarah, feeling like it wasn't and her host had more than overstepped the mark. 'I'm OK, honestly.' There was nothing Sarah hated more than a power imbalance. If she was a regular guest, she could've told Kate where to go. By trying to save a few pounds, she was now indebted to the woman and therefore required to bite her tongue.

'What time's your interview? Do you know how you're getting there?'

'It's at twelve. I thought I'd get a bus.'

Kate laughed. 'You'll be lucky round here. It's hard enough finding a bus that goes to Wadebridge, never mind the woods.'

'Oh.'

'How about we give you a lift? When I say we, I mean my partner. I'm up to my ears in paperwork for my uni course. He's free all day, though.'

'I wouldn't want you to go to any trouble.'

'It's no trouble at all. He'll enjoy the excuse to get out of the house and have a walk. I'm not much fun when I'm working on an assignment.'

Sarah knew the polite thing to do would be to ask what Kate was studying, but she didn't have the energy to care. 'If you're sure, that would be great. How long does it take to get there?'

'Twenty minutes at the most, but I'd leave longer in case you get stuck in traffic.'

Traffic? A traffic jam in Cornwall would be an empty road to anyone living elsewhere in the country.

'OK, shall we say half eleven? If that's OK with your partner?'

'I'm sure it will be fine. You get yourself ready and I'll let him know the plan. See you later.'

'Thanks,' said Sarah, breathing a sigh of relief when Kate left the room and she was on her own again.

Chapter 13

S arah gave one last glance in the mirror. There was no need for makeup, her unblemished skin, wide eyes and rosebud lips her saving grace. Sarah wondered if she should've been a nun, for with her body hidden by swathes of black fabric, she might pass as pretty. She ignored the pinch of her waistband and the pain shooting through her big toe as it squished against the end of her heeled shoes.

'I'm ready when you are,' she called as she reached the bottom of the stairs.

'Coming,' called a gruff voice.

A large man appeared in the doorway. His hair was wild, his face had a five o'clock shadow and his clothes had seen better days.

'I'm Bob,' said the man, holding out a paw-like hand for Sarah to shake. 'I don't think we met the last time you were here. Before you panic about getting in the car with a strange man, I should let you know I'm a respectable solicitor. I'm usually much smarter than this, but I've been trying to tame the garden all morning and didn't see the need to change for a trip to the woods.'

Sarah, feeling very overdressed, gave him a smile. 'I appreciate you giving me a lift. It's very kind of you.'

Bob guffawed so loud it made Sarah jump. 'It gets me out of the gardening. Kate's a hard taskmaster when she wants to be. Don't let her appearance fool you. She wears the trousers in this operation.'

Bob led Sarah out of the house and to an old Volvo parked outside. 'Bloody hell, not another parking fine. There's a lot to recommend this town, but the ferocious parking attendants aren't one of them.' He peeled a bright yellow parking ticket from the windscreen and squashed it into his pocket.

Sarah climbed into the ancient car, hoping the journey wouldn't be too long. 'Have you lived in the house long?' she asked, wanting to sit in silence but knowing it would be uncomfortable.

'No, only a few months. Me and Kate have been friends since the day she arrived in town, but we dragged our heels with anything more. How about you? Do you live alone? I think Kate misses the solitude sometimes.'

'No, I live with my parents. Lived with my parents, I should say. They're selling up.'

'Hence the move?'

'Yes.'

The car putted its way through the town's streets, spewing out smoke from the exhaust and contributing more than its fair share to global warming.

'Kate wants me to get rid of this old beast,' said Bob. 'But I love this car for all her faults.' He stroked a hand across the dashboard and Sarah wondered if he were mad.

'I've never learned to drive,' said Sarah.

'Really?' said Bob, so shocked he stared at her too long for someone who should watch the road. 'How do you manage?'

'There's good public transport where I live.'

'Crikey, you'll have your work cut out getting around if you move down here. Our public transport system leaves a lot to be desired.'

'So I've heard.'

'Might be time to get your licence, hey?'

'If I could afford it, I would.'

'Have you thought about getting an electric bike? I know they're expensive, but it would save you a fortune in the long run.'

'Maybe,' said Sarah. The last time she'd been on a bike was the day Mark left her, and she had no intention of taking up cycling now.

Bob turned into a lane only narrow enough for one car at a time. Sarah felt frustration building as they waited, drove, reversed, reversed some more, before pulling into a large car park.

'If you go down to the woods today...' sang Bob.

Sarah winced in embarrassment. She hoped he wasn't planning to come inside with her. It would be like turning up to an interview with her dad.

'Thanks for the lift. I can make my own way back if you have things to do?'

'All I have planned is a stroll through these beautiful trees. I'm happy to give you a lift home after your interview. There's no rush, I've got my book with me,' he said, patting the back pocket of his trousers.

'Thank you, that's very kind. I'll call you when I'm done.'

Sarah and Bob swapped numbers, and she left him by the car, pulling on a pair of wellington boots. As she walked through the car park, Sarah realised the error of her ways. Her heels caught on stones, flicking mud up the back of her tights. She straightened her smart jacket and ran a hand through her hair.

The café appeared through the trees like something from a fairy tale. Strings of glittering lights brightened the stone exterior on the dull day, bunting hung from the door-frame and pots of ferns and flowers garnished every window.

Sarah pushed the door open, a tinkling bell announcing her arrival. The first thing to hit her was the heat. An open fire blazed in the far wall, sofas and armchairs pulled around it as families and walkers warmed up after their time outside.

'How can I help you?' asked an attractive woman as she rushed around from behind the counter.

'Hi, I'm Sarah, I'm here for the interview.'

'Oh,' said the woman, looking Sarah up and down.

Sarah flushed as she realised the error of her ways. This was not a smart shirt and skirt establishment. The woman behind the counter had her auburn hair flung on top of her head in a messy bun. An apron covered a lime green tunic and strings of coloured beads clinked each time she moved.

'I'm Hattie. Pleased to meet you. Sorry, this was a stupid time to invite you for an interview. As you can see, we're run off our feet. Would you mind mucking in for a bit? Think of it as a trial. We'll sit down for a chat once things have calmed down.'

'Um, OK,' said Sarah, feeling like she had little choice in the matter. Hattie flung an apron over the counter and Sarah put it over her smart outfit.

'Take these to table five, please,' said Hattie, passing a tray laden with cakes and coffee across the countertop.

'Which is table five?' asked Sarah, but Hattie had her back to her and could hear nothing over the noise of the coffee machine.

Sarah moved around the room checking for table numbers, but found none. She carried the tray through to a back room, where large bi-folds led out to a damp garden. 'Table five?' she called. No one turned to look, all the customers distracted by either conversation or children. 'Table five?' she called, louder than before. A couple of people looked her way before shaking their heads. 'TABLE FIVE?' Sarah shouted, getting the attention of the entire room.

'Coffee and cakes?' asked a man in waterproof trousers and a fleece. 'That looks like us.'

Sarah laid the tray down, handing out coffees and cakes. She smiled, despite the sweat dripping down her back and the quickening of her breath as she fought the panicked voice in her head telling her she was out of her depth.

'No one told you the table number system?' asked a tall young man as she walked back towards the counter.

'No, they didn't,' said Sarah, thinking it must be very obvious she was new.

'One, two, three, six, seven, ten in here,' said the man, pointing to tables too fast for Sarah to follow. 'Four, five, eight and nine are in the back room.'

'Wouldn't it have been easier to number them in order?'

The man's deep brown eyes narrowed, the corner of his lips curling in amusement. A flush crept across Sarah's face, which she told herself was from the fire and nothing more.

'Wanting to change things on your first day, are you? Don't worry, you'll get used to how we do things here.'

'Yes, but if the system made more sense...'

'Take a chill pill. Don't stress about it. Like I said, you'll get the hang of things soon.'

Take a chill pill? Had this guy stepped out of the nineties? Sarah saw his lips curl again as he watched her walk away. *Idiot*, she thought, hoping she wouldn't be rostered on with him again.

'I see you've met Felix,' said Hattie, as Sarah walked behind the counter. 'He's a bit of a joker, but you'll get used to him soon enough.'

I'd rather not, thought Sarah, as to her horror her cheeks flushed once more. 'What would you like me to do next?'

'Plate up the cakes on that order, please. Knives are next to the cakes, plates are on that shelf down there.'

It was several hours before the café was quiet enough to sit down. Sarah could feel the blisters forming because of her inappropriate shoes and had a stomach ache from her pinching waistband.

'Here you go,' said Hattie, placing a cup of coffee down beside Sarah. 'You've earned it. I'm sorry about that. It's impossible to tell when we'll be dead and when we'll be run off our feet. We're busier on wet days if you can believe it. I should have scheduled our chat for later in the day, but I suppose it doesn't hurt to get stuck in. How did you find it?'

'Fun,' lied Sarah.

'Good. Now, do you have questions?'

'Um, shouldn't you be asking me questions rather than the other way round?'

Hattie laughed. 'Yes, you're right. OK, so I just have the one. How soon can you start?'

Chapter 14

S arah found Bob at a picnic bench outside, head in his book, oblivious to the drizzle.

'Hi,' she said, tapping him on the shoulder.

'Ah, hello. How did it go?'

Before Sarah could answer, Felix came jogging towards them. 'Hattie wants to know if you'll be needing the on-site accommodation?'

'Yes, please, if it's still available.'

'Sure is. Hey, we'll be neighbours.' Felix stuck his thumbs up, then jogged back to the café, leaving Sarah with more questions and a sense of foreboding.

'So I take it you got the job?' asked Bob.

'Looks like it.'

'If you don't mind me saying, you don't sound all that excited at the prospect.'

'The job seems fine. I could do it standing on my head. It's the company I'm worried about.' Sarah marched off, hoping to hide another spontaneous blush, leaving Bob trailing in her wake.

On the journey back to the house, Bob was quiet, and Sarah was glad. She needed to think. A million and one questions popped into her head she should have asked when given the chance. *What was the salary? What were the hours? What was the on-site accommodation like?*

Sarah picked at the skin around a nail. It wasn't like her to be so careless, so casual about life decisions. Was it a mistake in coming here? What had she let herself in for?

'A penny for them,' said Bob as they drove up Bodmin's high street.

'I was thinking of all the things I should've asked. The only thing I know about this job is that I start tomorrow. I was beating myself up about not asking questions, but now I come to think of it, what kind of organisation doesn't provide a detailed welcome pack to new employees?'

Bob suppressed a chuckle, but not well enough to hide it from Sarah. 'Sorry,' he said, noticing her glare. 'I've just never heard of hospitality jobs providing that level of information. Waitressing is pretty casual, isn't it?'

'How should I know? I've never done it before.' She wasn't about to admit to working at the burger bar despite her desire to inform Bob of the induction videos they had forced her to watch as part of her training, or the policies and procedures she'd had to read.

'I see. So what's this accommodation like?'

'I don't know.'

'Right. Well, if it's not up to scratch and you need a few days to sort something else, you're welcome to stay at our place.'

'Thank you, but I'll be fine.'

'Well, the offer's there,' said Bob.

Bob parked the car and let them both into the house.

'Hello you two. How did it go?' Kate was sitting at her computer, notebooks and text books piled up beside her.

'Sarah's got good news,' said Bob, leaning over to kiss Kate on the head.

'You got the job?'

'Yes, I got the job.'

'Wow, that's fantastic. Well done, you.' Kate jumped off the sofa and stunned Sarah with a hug. Conscious of how hot, bothered, and smelly she was, Sarah extricated herself from Kate's arms.

'Thanks. I'm going up to my room now, think I'll have an early night.'

'Are you sure? I was going to order a takeaway. You'd be welcome to join us.'

'That's kind of you, but no thanks. I'm exhausted.'

'But you have to eat.'

'They gave me something to eat at the café,' lied Sarah.

'Ah, OK. Well, we'll see you in the morning.'

'I'm happy to drive you again,' said Bob.

Sarah would have liked to refuse, but knowing she didn't have enough in her account for a taxi, she accepted his offer, made her excuses and headed to her room. With the door shut, Sarah kicked off her shoes and undid the zip on her skirt, letting it fall to the floor. She moved across to the mirror to inspect her wounds.

A crimson band sat against her stomach. In some places, the too-tight skirt had drawn blood. She reached into her wash bag and found a tub of skin cream. Each dab at her skin caused her to wince. With a comfortable pair of jogging bottoms on, Sarah sat on the bed to inspect her feet. Huge blisters had formed on her heels, the nail on one big toe had turned black, and red marks lined her toes where her shoes had chafed.

Whilst the thought of a bath was tempting, the sting of water on her wounds was not, so Sarah climbed into bed, turning on the TV and snuggling down. She reached inside her bag and pulled out her phone. There had been nothing from Cynthia since Sarah's announcement she was leaving, and the silence troubled her more than any typed recriminations.

Sarah's phone pinged with ten notifications. Steeling herself for what was to come, she opened the messages.

Having a great time in sunny Spain.

I was a little cross you've abandoned ship, but Dad has come out of hiding and I've passed the list onto him.

Dad said he'll call you soon.

Where are you?

Are you with a man?

Are you ignoring me?

Fine. Have it your way.

The remaining messages were photos of Cynthia lying on a lounger by a pool, wearing nothing other than a bikini and a sarong. Sarah deleted the photos from her phone and put it on the bedside table to charge.

Halfway through a boring murder mystery show, a door downstairs slammed and not long after the smell of Indian food wafted its way up the stairs. Sarah's stomach growled, and she wished she hadn't lied about eating at the café. Now she'd done that, she couldn't even go out and buy a sandwich.

Half an hour later, a knock came on her bedroom door.

'Come in,' she said, resenting the intrusion when she'd made it clear she wanted to be alone.

'Hi,' said Kate, carrying a plate in one hand and a glass of wine in the other. 'I know you said you'd already eaten, but we ordered way too much food for the two of us. You'd be doing us a favour if you helped us out. Also, I thought some prosecco was in order to celebrate your good news. And don't worry, I know you're exhausted. I'll just leave this here for you.'

Kate placed the plate and glass on the bedside table.

'Thank you.'

'No problem.' Kate made to leave, but hovered in the doorway. 'Look, this is delicate, but I wanted to say sorry.'

'Sorry?'

'Yes, I should have checked you were OK sleeping in this room after what happened last time you were here. I could make the bed up in the sitting room if you'd prefer?'

For a moment Sarah was confused, then she realised what Kate was referring to. 'Oh, you mean being dumped by Mark?'

Kate grimaced. 'Yes, that.'

Sarah laughed. 'Water under the bridge. Don't worry.'

'If you're sure.'

'Quite sure. Me and Mark are on friendly terms.'

'Oh, I'm so pleased to hear it. How is he?'

'Gay. Thanks for the food.'

'Right. OK. Um, have a good evening, and, um, good for him.'

Kate scuttled from the room and Sarah lay back against her pillows. She knew it was envy making her irritable. There was no evidence to suggest Kate was anything other than a decent human being, but Sarah found her too decent, too perfect, too pretty. The kindness she showed had to be an act, didn't it? Sarah considered leaving the food, but hunger won out, and she ate so fast she gave herself indigestion.

After several hours of rubbish TV, Sarah turned off the light and tried to sleep. Her mind buzzed with thoughts of starting a new job. She ran through all the possibilities of what the on-site accommodation would be like. At best, it would be a little cottage tucked away somewhere, at worse, a log cabin with no running water. Then there was the job itself.

Frustration swept through her as she thought of all the events that had led her here. Less than a month ago, she'd been part of a happy family, living in a comfortable home, with a secure job. Now she was waitressing in the back of beyond. She was better than that. She deserved more. As her eyelids grew heavy, Sarah resolved to move onwards and upwards as quickly as she could.

Chapter 15

S arah sat on the bathroom floor trying to take deep, steady breaths. This was the first time the panic had woken her, and she didn't know what had caused it. Could it have been the messages from Cynthia? Or fear of the unknown?

Panic at night was nothing like panic during the day. During daylight hours, she could feel it creeping up and head it off at the pass. Being woken by panic was greeting it in its full-blown anger, too late to contain or control the painful squeezing in her chest, too late to breathe.

When she was sure the panic had receded, Sarah turned on the taps of the bath. It was too early to be running a bath above where Kate and Bob were sleeping, but Sarah needed to submerge herself to stay calm.

Sarah had been up for an hour before she heard any signs of life downstairs. Bob was singing along to the radio again. Did he not realise how loud his voice was? Perhaps she should leave a note to let him know before other guests complained?

By half past nine, Sarah was packed and ready to go. Her shift didn't start till midday, but Hattie had messaged, suggesting she arrive early to settle in to her new accommodation. Sarah had replied, asking if Hattie would pay her for the extra hours but received no response.

'There you are,' said Bob. He walked through to the living room looking a very different man to the one she'd met the previous day. Instead of old, torn gardening clothes, he wore a shirt and tie, braces holding up his pressed trousers.

'You look smart.'

Bob laughed, looking down at his clothes. 'I'm taking Mum to church this morning. She's old-fashioned and likes me to look the part.'

'Right. Do you go every Sunday?'

'Yes. Church, lunch, then off we go to visit Dad.' Bob's face creased in pain and his voice cracked with the mention of his dad. His expression piqued Sarah's curiosity, but she needed to get a move on so, without further chatter, let herself out of the house and headed to Bob's car.

Lost in his thoughts, Bob was quiet on the journey to the woods. For once, Sarah could have done with some inane chatter, the silence leaving her brain to fret over the day ahead. Sarah pushed down her annoyance as they reached the car park and Bob stayed in the car. Did he expect her to get her bag out by herself? She hovered by the car boot for a minute, then, realising he had no intention of moving, opened it and heaved her heavy bag out onto the ground.

'See you,' said Sarah.

'Good luck. Remember, we're only round the corner if you need anything.'

I needed a hand with my luggage, but that wasn't forthcoming, thought Sarah, giving her best impression of a cheery wave goodbye.

Sarah reached the café only to find it closed. She banged on the door, to no response. She tried again, and again, and again, until a dishevelled Hattie appeared at the door.

'Sorry,' she said, brushing a strand of hair from her eye. 'I overslept. I rarely sleep here but we had a bit of a *sesh* last night, so I slept on the sofa.' Hattie laughed, while Sarah wondered what on earth a *sesh* was.

'No problem. If you could show me to my accommodation, I'll get settled in and be ready to start at twelve.'

'Yes, of course. Come through. It's easier if we go out the back.'

Sarah followed Hattie through the café and out to the garden beyond. At the far end, Hattie opened a gate and turned to Sarah. 'You don't have wellies, do you?'

'No.'

'Sorry, I should have told you to bring some. It can get pretty muddy out here. What size shoe are you?'

'Six.'

'We've got some spares kicking about somewhere. I'll dig them out while you get settled in. Come on, it's this way.' Hattie walked Sarah out to a large grass area covered by a giant tipi. 'This is where we hold our events. There's often an extra shift to pick up at events.'

'What events?'

'Weddings, but we've had all sorts. It gets rowdy sometimes, but often the staff are invited to join in.'

'Great,' said Sarah, thinking it wasn't. She hadn't come here to make friends. This job was a means to an end, a chance to get back on her feet, then get the hell out again.

Grass gave way to the forest floor, squelching mud and rotting debris spilling up the sides of her shoes. A branch caught Sarah in the eye and brambles tore at her jeans.

'See what I mean about wellies?' chuckled Hattie. 'Don't worry, we're almost there.' Hattie and Sarah emerged into a clearing, grand old trees creating a canopy above them, encircling the space like giants holding hands. 'Ta da,' said Hattie, spreading her arms out wide.

'Oh,' said Sarah, 'I didn't realise you offered camping here.'

Hattie laughed. 'You're a funny one, you are. I'll show you to your tipi.'

Hattie walked towards a flimsy-looking tipi, while Sarah stayed pinned to the spot. A tent? She was supposed to sleep in a tent? She hadn't spent a single night under canvas in her life. Now she was supposed to *live* in one?

'Come on,' said Hattie, pulling back canvas and clipping it out of the way to reveal Sarah's new canvas home.

'This is my staff accommodation?' asked Sarah, her heart hammering in her chest.

'Yes. Cool, isn't it?' Hattie noticed the expression on Sarah's face and gave her arm a squeeze. 'Not a camper? Don't worry, they're kitted out well. Come and see.'

Sarah followed Hattie as she bent beneath the canvas walls. At least the tipi was bigger than it looked from the outside. In its centre lay a full size double bed, covered in a bright pink woollen throw. Beside the bed was a chest of drawers, colourful rugs leading to a tatty armchair. Sarah looked around, stunned.

'Right, so what do you need to know?' Hattie tapped a finger against the corner of her mouth, looking at her surroundings. 'Oh yes. In here,' she said, pulling an old chest out from beneath the bed, 'are blankets. You'll need them at night, but the weather should warm up soon. It's cosy in here as long as you're wrapped up. Clothes go in there. There's room for your luggage under the bed. Oh yes, I almost forgot. This is an essential.' Hattie pulled a china bowl from under the bed.

'Is that? Is that... Please tell me that's not what I think it is?'

Hattie laughed. 'Yep, this is your toilet. At night, anyway. Trust me, if you wake up needing a pee, you won't want to be fumbling around outside in the dark.'

'You mean there aren't even proper toilets?' Hot tears pricked at Sarah's eyes, anger suppressing the despair she knew would follow.

Hattie laughed again, and Sarah wanted to scream. 'Don't worry, we provide you with a shovel for more serious business.' Seeing the look on Sarah's face, Hattie laughed. 'I'm kidding, I'm kidding. Come on, I'll show you the facilities.'

Hattie led Sarah back outside, past an identical tipi to Sarah's. 'That's where Felix stays. You'll be relieved to know you're not alone out here.'

Relieved wasn't the word Sarah would have used.

'Here we are,' said Hattie, after they'd scrambled through more undergrowth. A wooden structure stood amongst the trees. It was like no toilet Sarah had seen before. 'Have you used a compost toilet before?' asked Hattie.

'A what?'

'I'll take that as a no. It's much nicer than using a flushing loo.'

'Hang on. The toilet in there doesn't flush?'

'No. If I had my way, we'd all have these in our homes. It would save a crap ton of water, excuse the pun. You do your business, then shovel sawdust over the top. It's hygienic and doesn't smell. God, you look so worried. Don't be. You'll find normal toilets weird after a few days using this. Trust me.'

Trust her? The woman who had led Sarah out into the woods and shown her a tent and a compost toilet in the same way someone would show off a luxury hotel room, was asking Sarah to trust her? Sarah wanted to run through the woods and never come back.

'The shower is round the other side. It runs off a solar panel so the water temperature is temperamental, but you'll get used to it. Right, I'd better get back to the café and start setting up. Are you all right to find your way back and get settled in?'

Sarah nodded, too shocked to speak. She picked her way through nettles and brambles to find her tipi. Crawling inside, she climbed up onto the bed, put her head in her hands, and screamed.

Chapter 16

Sarah dabbed her eyes with a tissue and picked up her phone. She'd need to remember to charge it at work as there was no electricity in the tipi. Taking a deep breath, she fired off a message to Cynthia.

Hi Mum, how are things in Spain? I was wondering how the house sale is going and if I'd be able to go back there for a few weeks? Have you heard from Dad again? Has he called you? Could I have his new number, please? X

The last thing Sarah wanted was to speak to her father, but sitting beneath the canvas walls, she was prepared to lose all her pride if it meant getting out of there. She stared at the phone for a good ten minutes. Cynthia hadn't even seen the message yet. Sarah resigned herself to the fact that her escape would not happen that day and rifled through her bag to find something suitable to wear for her shift. From what she'd seen, there was no set uniform. If anything it seemed they favoured scruffiness over smartness. Perhaps it was a deliberate ploy to blend in with the rustic woods beyond the café's walls?

In the end, Sarah settled on jeans and a smart shirt. A compromise. She pulled her long hair back into a ponytail and slipped on her old pair of trainers. No way was she going to add more blisters to her problems.

'Knock knock.'

Sarah jumped at the voice outside her tent. 'Hello?'

'Only me,' said Felix, walking into the tipi like he owned the place.

'Oh, it's you.'

'Hello to you too, neighbour. How do you like the tipi? Cool, isn't it?'

'That's not the word I'd use to describe it.'

Felix threw himself down on the bed. 'Don't tell me you don't enjoy camping?' he asked in mock surprise. 'You look just the type to enjoy a night under the stars.'

'Sarcasm is the lowest form of wit.'

'Ha! You sound just like my old maths teacher.'

'Don't you have someone else to annoy?'

'No. In case you haven't noticed, we're the only two here.'

'There must be more staff than that. Why don't the others live here too?'

'They all come from the local town. Have you been to Bodmin yet? Gem of a place, isn't it? They have some great live music events lined up. I'll take you to one, if you like?'

'No thanks.'

'So you don't enjoy camping and you don't like music? What do you like?'

'I never said I don't like music.'

'Ah, so it's me you don't like. Shame you're living with me for the summer then.'

'Not if I can help it.'

'What? You're going to up and leave before you've even started?'

'This wasn't what I signed up for,' said Sarah, waving her arms to show she was talking about the tipi.

'That's out of order, you know. They're a good bunch here; hard working, decent, look out for their staff. They deserve to be treated with more respect than someone who's hunting for a better option.'

'I never said that.'

'Whatever. See you at work.'

Felix left the tent, and Sarah groaned. Now she could add an enemy to her list of problems. She kicked her bag under the bed, not bothering to unpack. There was no point when she intended to get out of there as soon as possible.

The café was already busy when Sarah arrived. Hattie was in the same position as the previous day, rushing round behind the counter like a blue-arsed fly.

'Sarah, hi. Have you ever used a coffee machine?'

'No.'

'OK. Well, could you help in the kitchen today? Our KP's called in sick and we could do with a hand with the dishes.'

'I thought I'd be waitressing.'

'We all do a bit of everything here. Waitressing, making coffee, cooking, cleaning. We work as a team rather than having specific job roles. I'll teach you how to use the coffee machine later when it's not so busy. The kitchen's just through there. Fran's in there, she'll show you what to do.'

'OK,' said Sarah, tying her apron over her jeans.

'Don't worry, the cavalry's here.' Felix burst into the building, all wide smiles and big brown eyes. He hadn't bothered to shave or brush his hair from the looks of things. His faded blue T-shirt had a stain down the front that looked as though he'd dribbled red wine at some point.

'Thank God,' said Hattie, throwing him an apron. 'I need six Americanos, two cappuccinos, one flat white and a mocha.'

'Yes, ma'am,' said Felix, saluting Hattie before heading to the coffee machine.

Sarah walked through to find the kitchen. Behind a swing door, she found a hive of activity.

'Ah, you must be Sarah. I'm Fran,' said a short, plump woman, wiping a flour-covered hand on her apron before holding it out to Sarah. 'Welcome to the team. I'm so glad you're here. My KP has called in sick and I can't manage this lot on my own.' Fran pointed to the pans bubbling on the stove, and various mixing bowls lining the worktops.

'You make everything from scratch?'

'Of course I do. It's what keeps people coming back again and again. I used to be a school cook if you can believe it. But then they started making us cook things from packets and I chucked the job in. Have you heard of Turkey Twizzlers?'

Sarah shook her head.

'Then you're lucky. Let's just say you'll find no junk food here.'

'What would you like me to do?'

'Start on those dishes, would you, love? The dishwasher's self-explanatory, but those pans will need scrubbing by hand.'

'Sure,' said Sarah, pulling on a pair of rubber gloves. 'I don't want to sound stupid, but what's a KP?'

'Kitchen Porter, otherwise known as a general dogsbody, otherwise known as my slave.' Fran chuckled. 'The chap who works with me is a lovely lad, but very unreliable. He's always off sick with some complaint or other. If you ask me, he's a bit too fond of the wacky baccy.'

'Wacky baccy?'

'Goodness me, love. You are an innocent, aren't you? You watch those folks out there don't corrupt you too much.'

'How would they do that?'

'Best you find that out for yourself. I'm not one to tell tales. Now, enough chatting, these pies and cakes won't make themselves.'

Sarah spent the next four hours elbow-deep in dirty plates, cups, and pans. Water trickled inside her rubber gloves and she could feel the skin wrinkling beneath them. This was not what she had signed up to. The job advert had specified waitress, not skivvy. It was all very well Hattie saying they all mucked in where needed, but she and Felix looked quite at home behind the counter, and she couldn't imagine either of them washed up much.

In her pocket, Sarah felt her phone vibrate. *Please let the house still be on the market, please let me be able to go home.* Sarah resisted the urge to check her messages, knowing if it was bad news, she wouldn't be able to hide her disappointment.

Fran announced it was time for a break. She plated up two slices of cake fresh from the oven and made two cups of tea from her personal kettle. 'If I asked that lot through there for a cuppa, I'd been waiting all day,' she explained.

'Thanks,' said Sarah, carrying her plate and cup to a step outside. 'How long have you worked here?'

'Ooh, getting on for ten years I should think.'

'And you enjoy it?'

'Love it. I complain a lot, but they're a good bunch here. We rarely get fresh faces joining the team, as most folk who come here don't want to leave.'

Unlike me, thought Sarah, taking a bite of lemon drizzle cake. 'Wow, this is delicious. I'm supposed to be on a diet, but I worry working with you will have the opposite effect.'

'Diet? What nonsense. You're lovely as you are, love.'

No, thought Sarah, *I'm not. Kate and Hattie, they're lovely as they are. They don't get cut in the flesh by too-tight waistbands, or have muffin tops spilling out every time they put on a pair of jeans.* 'That's kind of you, and I wish it were true. I'm so unfit I find climbing a flight of stairs tricky.'

'Ah, now if you're talking about fitness, that's a different matter. Health is important. At least you're in the right place. There's no shortage of walks around here. And if it makes you feel better, take a walk for every piece of cake you eat. That's how I like to balance it.'

Sarah looked at Fran, at ease with her voluminous bosom and tiered middle. What she'd give for a fraction of Fran's contentment. But as Cynthia said, Sarah couldn't afford to be so complacent, not if she wanted to start a family before her eggs dried up.

Sarah's phone buzzed again, and comforted by the cake, she risked a glance.

Forgot to tell you, house has sold. Full asking price! New owners moving in in a couple of weeks, so you'll need to find somewhere else to stay. Mum.

Sarah sighed. It looked like she had no choice but to stay put.

Chapter 17

Sarah folded her apron and laid it on the counter. 'What time do you need me tomorrow?'

'Oh, sorry, I forgot to say. I don't need you tomorrow. We're closed on Mondays.'

'OK. Well, a rota might be helpful. I know I'm living on site, but it would be nice to have a life outside of work.'

'Of course,' said Hattie, her tone cooler than before. 'I'll get a rota dropped round to you tomorrow. Sorry, we're pretty casual here, but I'm not usually this disorganised. Truth be told, we've been so short-staffed I've let some things... like rotas... slide. I'll try to up my game.'

'Thanks.'

'How was your first full day?'

'Good.'

'Right, well, I'll see you Tuesday at ten. Are you OK to work ten till six?'

'Yep.'

Sarah walked out of the café and back to her tipi. She longed for a hot shower, but it had rained all day so she wouldn't risk the dodgy solar panel. The evening stretched before her like an abyss. What did people do before electricity, TV, light bulbs? Sarah considered taking up a hobby. Maybe she could learn the guitar?

As though reading her mind, strumming started up in the tent next door. Of course Felix played the guitar. He was such a cliché. Scruffy, hippy clothes, laissez-faire attitude, he probably had a trust fund tucked away, enabling him to be a free spirit. Sarah would put money on him spending the cold winter months on a beach in Thailand or at a commune in India. Or perhaps he returned to Mummy and Daddy and their big house in the country?

The evenings were drawing out, but inside the tipi any daylight that made its way in glowed dull orange. Sarah lit the paraffin lamp beside her bed and picked up her book. She read the same paragraph again and again before throwing her book to the ground in frustration.

The guitar playing stopped, and Sarah heard rustling footsteps heading her way.

'Sarah?'

'Yes.'

'OK if I come in?'

Before Sarah could say no, the tipi's door opened, and Felix ducked inside the tent. He filled the space, stealing any comfort Sarah might have felt by his presence.

'What do you want?'

'I just wanted to check in and see how you're doing.'

'I'm fine.'

'Good. How was your first day?'

'I was stuck with a pile of dirty dishes all day, so how do you think it went?'

'Not a fan of washing up?' Felix laughed and Sarah bristled. 'I love washing up duty.'

'Why don't you do it then?'

'I'm too good at making coffees. Taken loads of barista courses since I rocked up here so my skills are better served front of house. I'd love the occasional day up to my elbows in soap suds, but it's never gonna happen. Did Hattie show you how to use the coffee machine?'

'No. She was supposed to but claimed she was too busy all day.'

'Well, that's true,' said Felix. 'It was mad busy. Ever since we were in the local paper, people have been flocking here for our cakes and coffees. Did Fran tell you we're up for an award?'

'No.'

'Yeah, some big awards ceremony up country. All thanks to Fran's wizardry in the kitchen. You'll learn a lot from her.'

'You mean I'm going to be stuck in the kitchen all the time?'

Felix frowned and scrubbed his hands through his messy hair. 'You hate it that much?'

'Yes.'

'Then how about I give you a lesson in coffee making now?'

'Now?'

'Yes, no time like the present.'

'But the café's closed.'

Felix dug around in his pocket and pulled out a bunch of keys. 'Ta da. Problem solved.'

'Won't Hattie mind?'

'No, I'll be doing her a favour. Training newbies is a bit much on top of everything else she has to do.'

'So I've noticed.'

'That's harsh. She's doing such a great job running the place with so little back-up.'

'If you say so.'

Felix let out a loud sigh. 'Do you want me to train you up or not?'

'Fine. It's not like there's anything else to do around here.'

They left the tipi and squelched their way back to the café. It was eerie with no one there, like a school with no pupils, or an empty train station. Felix switched on the lights and set the coffee machine spurting into life.

'We'll start with the basics and work up to the more complex orders. I'll be your taste tester.'

'Isn't it a bit late to be drinking coffee?'

'Not for me. I can sleep anywhere, anytime.'

'All right for some.'

'You don't sleep well?'

'Not lately.'

'Oh dear. If you have any trouble sleeping in the tipi, you know where to find me.'

'What? In the middle of the night? Thanks, but no thanks.'

Felix laughed. 'I didn't mean it like that. Right,' he said, turning to the coffee machine, 'you start off by putting fresh ground coffee in here.'

Two hours later, Sarah found herself on the brink of tears. Despite Felix's best efforts, she had wasted about a hundred pounds' worth of coffee and milk on botched attempts at fancy-named coffees she could not master.

'Stupid machine,' said Sarah, smacking her hand against it.

'Hey, watch it. That thing is worth thousands of pounds, you know.'

'Yeah, well, it's not working.'

'Watch.' Felix moved behind the machine, pressing buttons, twisting knobs, disappearing in a plume of steam, then turning round and handing Sarah a perfect cup of coffee topped off with a fancy leaf design. 'It's not the machine, Sarah. You'll get there, don't worry. I had to take a ton of courses to get to this point.'

Sarah sighed. She was due a break, not another thing to add to the list of things she couldn't get right. 'Can we try again tomorrow? If you don't mind, I need to get myself to bed.'

'Sure. You OK finding your way back? I'll stay and clear up here.'

'Thanks.'

'Night.'

Back at her tipi and unwilling to navigate the undergrowth in order to get to the toilet, Sarah pulled a water bottle from her bag and brushed her teeth outside the tent. Back inside, she pulled out the chamber pot and eyed it as though preparing for battle.

Sarah weighed up the options. She could fight through brambles to the disgusting compost loo, she could pee behind the tipi and risk Felix stumbling across her, or she could swallow her pride and pee in a pot. Pushing away thoughts of the comfortable bathroom in her parents' house, she unbuttoned her jeans. With a deep breath, Sarah emptied her bladder into the chamber pot, her cheeks burning despite no one to witness how far she'd fallen.

Pyjamas on, she climbed into bed. Sarah hated to admit it, but it was more comfortable than she had expected. Pulling the duvet up around her chin, Sarah snuggled down with her book. Before long, her eyelids grew heavy, and she put down the book and blew out the lamp.

In the dark, the tipi felt different. Something tickled Sarah's cheek, and she leapt out of bed, screaming.

'Sarah? Sarah?' Felix appeared at the door. 'Are you OK?'

'There's something in my bed. I felt it on my face.'

'OK, OK, don't panic. Let me see.' Felix walked in, torch in hand and threw bright yellow light onto the bedsheets. Sarah looked down in horror at the chamber pot beside the bed. She threw a towel over the pot, praying Felix hadn't seen it.

'Ah ha,' he said, cupping his hands against the sheet. 'I've found the culprit. Nothing worse than a harmless house spider. Want to see?'

Sarah shook her head, clutching a pillow to her chest. Felix carried the small creature out of the tipi and appeared a moment later, reassuring Sarah it was over the other side of the field and wouldn't be troubling her anymore that night.

'Is there anything more I can do for you?'

'No, thanks.' Sarah climbed into bed.

'Right,' he said. 'I'll see you in the morning. Goodnight.'

'Goodnight.'

Sarah tried her best to sleep, but hadn't anticipated the forest coming alive at night. Growing up in suburbia, Sarah assumed when she tucked herself up in a comfy bed, all the animals of the forest snuggled down into a bed of leaves, sleeping away the hours until the sun came up again. How wrong she was.

If anything, the forest was noisier at night than in the day. Each time Sarah started drifting towards sleep, a shriek, howl or cackling call would jolt her awake, sending her pulse rate through the roof and sweat beading her forehead.

I've landed in hell, was Sarah's final thought before she succumbed to sleep.

Chapter 18

S arah rolled over and switched on her phone. At first she thought her sleep-blurred eyes were mistaken. It couldn't be ten already? She'd never slept that late in her life. A series of messages popped up. One from Cynthia.

Where do you want us to send your stuff from the house? Need an answer ASAP!

A beach photo followed, Cynthia wearing a hat so broad it flopped down to her shoulders, and a bikini so small Sarah saw far more of her mother's body than she'd like. She ignored the message, her heart beating faster as she clicked on a series of messages from an unknown number.

Hi, love. Dad here. This is my new number. It would be good to talk to you soon.

Sorry, me again. There are things I need to sort out with the house. Could you call me?

I don't just want to talk about the house. I miss you.

Me again, I'm so sorry for what happened. Please call me and let me explain.

Sarah sighed. She may as well get this over with.

'Hello?' Colin picked up on the second ring.

'Hi, Dad, it's me.'

'Sarah! So lovely to speak to you. Thank you for calling me back.'

'You said you had things you needed to speak to me about.'

'I do, I do, but that can wait. How are you? Where are you?'

'In a forest in Cornwall. How about you?'

'On a boat in the middle of the Norfolk Broads.' Colin laughed and Sarah's hackles rose.

'On a boat? What's going on, Dad?'

'I've always wanted a holiday on the Norfolk Broads, but your mother wouldn't let me.'

'Oh yes, 'cause this is all Mum's fault, isn't it?'

Colin sighed down the phone. 'No, of course not. I take full responsibility for my actions, and the last thing I want is for you to have to take sides.'

Sarah let an awkward silence develop. It would do Colin no harm to be left squirming. In the end, he broke the silence with a chuckle.

'We're a fine pair, us two. One of us is in the woods, one in the middle of a river. Who'd have thunk it?' He chuckled again. 'Mum said you're working down in Cornwall?'

'Yes, in a café. It wasn't like I had much choice, what with my house being sold from under me.'

Colin cleared his throat. 'Yes, I'm sorry about that.'

'So you should be. I don't have time for small talk about your mid-life crisis. What did you need to speak to me about?'

'I know this will be hard to hear, but we've already had an offer on the house.'

'I know. Mum told me.'

'Right, well, it's a lovely young couple about to have their first child.'

'Good for them.'

'Yes, right, well, with the baby imminent, they'd like to move in as soon as possible.'

'What's that got to do with me? It's not like I have any rights over the house.'

'No, yes, I mean, I'm sorry. I know this is hard.'

'You've got no idea.'

Colin sighed again. 'There are a lot of your belongings still in the house. Do you have an address where I could get your things delivered?'

Sarah looked around her one metre square tipi. 'My new accommodation is on the small side.' No way was she telling him she was living in a tent. 'I can't have the stuff here. You'd better dump it.'

'I'll figure something out.'

'Dump it.'

'Sarah, I know you're hurt by what I did, but...'

Sarah hung up the phone. She couldn't bear to listen to his flimsy excuses for upending their lives. There were more practical matters to deal with. Sarah poked her head out of the tipi to check no one was around, then carried the chamber pot behind the tipi and emptied it in the undergrowth.

'What you got there?'

Sarah groaned as Felix jogged across the field, full of the joys of spring. His timing was impeccable. 'Nothing,' she said, holding the chamber pot behind her back.

'An essential part of camping,' he said, peering behind her.

'If you don't mind, I'd like a little privacy.'

'Sure. You must have slept well. I popped my head in around nine and you were dead to the world.'

'You came into my tipi?'

'Not inside. I just had a little squint through the door.'

'I'd rather you don't do that again.'

'Sure, no problem. Are you heading to the shower? I can show you how it works if you like? It's temperamental.'

Sarah swallowed down impatience. She was plenty old enough to shower by herself. 'I think I can manage.'

'All right, well the offer's there if you have any problems.'

Sarah walked back to her tipi and gathered up her wash bag and clothes. She braved the nettles and brambles to get to the shower and took a deep breath before walking into the primitive facilities. Sarah's heart sank as she closed the door and looked around the small room. There wasn't even a proper sink, just an old metal bucket with a hole drilled into the bottom. What kind of place was this?

After checking the door was locked, Sarah undressed and stepped into the shower cubicle. Moss poked its way through the wooden walls and she shivered as a chill breeze met her through holes in the tin roof. She turned on the shower and screamed as a blast of icy water hit her skin. Despite a good five minutes fiddling with the shower controls, she couldn't get the water above tepid. With a deep breath, she jumped back under the water, washing as fast as she could.

Sarah had read about people who took cold showers by choice. *Weirdos*, she thought, scrubbing herself dry and flinging on clothes to warm up. Felix was hanging up pants and socks on a line outside his tipi when she arrived back.

'How was the shower?'

'Lovely,' Sarah said, giving an involuntary shiver that caused Felix's lips to curl into a smirk. 'Don't tell me you've been washing your clothes in the river?' she asked, trying to avoid looking at his boxer shorts.

'No, we're not that primitive. There's a washer and dryer in the café, but I prefer to air dry my clothes. Saves on electricity.'

'Bloody eco warriors', muttered Sarah under her breath.

'What are your plans today?'

'Nothing much. I thought I'd explore the woods a bit.'

'Want some company?'

'No.'

Felix laughed and disappeared into his tipi. Sarah wished she hadn't said she was exploring. Now he'd ask her about it so she'd have to do some walking. Sarah wasn't a fan of nature. It was all right in a well-kept park, but the wildness of the forest scared her. There could be anything out there amongst the dank, moss-covered trees and muddy footpaths. Give her a shopping mall or tarmacked roads any day.

With boots on and a raincoat stashed in her bag, Sarah set off into the woods. She came across a noticeboard, the different routes colour-coded for difficulty level. Opting for the easiest wheelchair and pushchair friendly path, Sarah began walking. Her face warmed as she strode along the gentle incline, the forest opening up, the curling river at its base falling away as her feet carried her up. 'Wheelchair friendly? How unfit must I be?' Sarah muttered to herself, wiping her brow and taking deep lungfuls of air.

Footsteps sounded on the path behind her, and Sarah turned to see Felix jogging up to her.

'Are you following me?'

'What?' Felix slowed his pace, pulling headphones from his ears and jogging on the spot.

'I said, are you following me?'

Felix chuckled. 'No, I have better things to do with my time than follow grumpy women around the woods. This is my warm-up.'

'Warm up for what?'

'My warm-up lap. I run this kiddie route before tackling the harder trails.'

God, could this man be any more annoying? 'And how often do you do this run?'

'Every day. Helps with this,' said Felix, tapping a finger against his head. 'You should try it sometime. The endorphins help lift your mood.'

Before Sarah could answer, Felix replaced his headphones and sprinted off. *What an irritating man*, she thought, picking up speed to burn off some of her frustration. It was going to be a long summer with Felix for a neighbour.

Chapter 19

'Felix? Is that you?' Sarah reached for the paraffin lamp as a shadow passed beside her tipi. 'Felix? This isn't funny. Stop messing around.'

No reply came from outside. Sarah pulled her blankets up higher to stop the shivering. What was he doing creeping around outside her tipi? The shadow passed by again.

'Please, you're scaring me.' Shaking beneath her bedding, Sarah reached to the ground, scrabbling around for anything weapon-like. If the shadow belonged to Felix, wouldn't he have said something by now?

An unearthly scream tore through the air. Blood drained from Sarah's face, her lips quivering in a whimper. She buried deep beneath her blankets, covering her ears to block out the sound, wondering what she'd done wrong in a past life. She didn't want to die in a tent. This wasn't what was supposed to happen.

The screaming outside the tipi continued. 'Please go away. Please leave me alone,' whispered Sarah through chattering teeth. Certain no human could have made the sound, Sarah ran through all the wild beasts that might lurk beyond the canvas walls. How was Felix sleeping through the racket?

As quickly as it started, the screaming stopped. Sarah took her hands from her ears and pulled her blankets down. All was quiet.

Too quiet. She lay still as a statue, listening for any sound, the pad of footsteps, the crunch of leaves, the snapping of a twig. Nothing.

Sarah told herself that if the intruder was coming for her, it would have acted by now. Instead, the tipi remained intact, she still had all her limbs, and the moment seemed to have passed. *But they might come back*. The thought caused Sarah's legs to renew their shake. There was only one thing for it.

Sarah slipped on her borrowed boots and opened the tipi's door an inch. She poked her head out into the night air. In the distance she heard an owl call, but around the tipi, all was still. *One, two, three, GO!*

Sarah sprinted across the field to where Felix's tipi lay in darkness. Her fingers fumbled with the door clasps, her head snapping back and forth in case whatever had been lurking reappeared.

Sarah pulled back the door to Felix's tipi and stepped inside.

'Felix? Felix? Wake up.' She walked to the bed and patted her hand against it. The bed was empty. Sarah felt around on the bedside table until her fingers settled on a box of matches. She struck one, holding it to the paraffin lamp and flooding the tipi with a warm, orange glow.

Despite the fear flowing through her, Sarah was impressed by what she saw. The inside of Felix's tipi wasn't just spotless, but welcoming and homely. A little bigger than her own, a wood burner sat at the end of the bed, logs and kindling stored in a basket beside it. Colourful rugs covered the floor, a dreamcatcher danced at the door. Beside the bed, a guitar sat on a stand, but most surprising to Sarah was the stack of books on the bedside table.

Sarah picked up the dog-eared book sitting on top of the pile. *The poems of John Betjeman*. Did Felix read these poems or was the book there for show? And who was John Betjeman, anyway? Curiosity got the better of Sarah and she sat down on Felix's bed, opening the book and flicking through. A bookmark fell to the ground and Sarah picked it up. She held it by the lamp to get a better look. The neat letters had faded but she could make out *I love you*, in feminine curls and loops. Around the lettering, someone had stuck flowers and leaves, all now brown from age.

So Felix had a mystery woman. Perhaps she was the reason he read poetry, so he could impress her with his cultured mind? Was it this mystery woman who had given him the book in the first place?

A noise outside reminded Sarah why she'd come to Felix's tipi. Her muscles tensed, the hairs on her arms standing on end. She sat statue-like on the bed, listening as footsteps crept around the tipi, muffled by the grass, but drawing near.

Sarah let out a scream as the doors flung back. The screams turned to relieved laughter as she saw Felix standing in the doorway carrying a thick tree branch.

'Thank God it's you,' he said, flinging the branch to the ground and stepping inside. 'I knew I'd blown out the lamp before I left, so though there was an intruder. What are you doing here?'

'There was someone outside my tent. Was it you? Was that your idea of a joke?'

'Me? No, I've been... I've been... out.'

'Out?'

'Yes, out.'

Sarah observed Felix through narrowed eyes. A woollen hat covered his hair, he was bundled up in a thick winter coat, and a backpack was slung across one shoulder.

'Out where?'

'Toilet.'

'And do you always take a backpack with you to go to the loo?'

'Fine. I was out walking.'

'Walking? You realise it's one in the morning?'

'I'm aware of the time.'

'Then why?...'

'I just fancied a walk, OK?'

Felix's eyes wouldn't meet Sarah's, and she wondered what he was trying to hide. Was it was the mystery woman? 'Whatever.'

'You said there was someone outside your tipi?'

'Yes, I saw a shadow moving around, then there was this awful screaming.' Sarah shivered at the memory.

Felix scratched his chin and stood looking thoughtful. Then he burst out laughing.

'Grab that lamp and follow me.'

'No way am I going out there again.'

'I'll be with you. I've got a torch.'

'It may still be out there.'

'It may. Here, take this if it makes you feel safer.' Felix handed the tree branch to Sarah. 'Come on.'

Sarah followed Felix out into the night. The paraffin lamp threw pools of light onto the damp grass, the moon bathing the forest in a ghostly half-light. Beside Sarah's tipi, Felix bent down to inspect the ground.

'Aha. I think I've discovered the culprit. Look.' Felix pointed at the grass beside his foot and Sarah leaned over to see for herself.

'What am I looking at?'

'Droppings.'

'Droppings?'

'Poo.'

'Poo? This night just gets worse and worse.'

Felix laughed. 'It's not human, don't worry.'

'Well, I guess that's something.'

'Look, can you see it's in a sort-of pit?'

'Um, yes.'

'That's how I know Madge is responsible.'

'Madge? I thought you said this wasn't human?' Sarah took a step back.

Felix looked back at Sarah and laughed. 'Madge isn't human, don't worry. She's not a ghost either. She's a badger. Madge the badge.'

'A badger? Aren't they dangerous?'

Felix laughed again. 'They're not after you, if that's what you're worried about. Did you know they can eat hundreds of worms every night?'

'Gross.'

'Yeah, but they'll also eat hedgehogs, so I'd rather they stick to worms. Madge is often round here. You'll get used to her.'

'I'm not sure I want to.'

'Don't worry,' said Felix, standing up and taking the stick from Sarah's hand. He used it to flick the badger poo into the undergrowth. 'How about a quick nightcap to help you sleep?'

Sarah wanted to refuse, but despite knowing the intruder's identity, she didn't relish the thought of being alone in her tipi. 'Fine.'

'Don't sound so enthusiastic.'

Sarah followed Felix back to his tipi. He rummaged around under his bed and pulled out a bottle of whisky. Sarah hated whisky, but hated the thought of being alone in the dark more, so accepted the glass he held out to her.

'So where do you walk?'

'Huh?'

'At night. You said you went walking?'

'Yeah, just around the woods,' said Felix, but not before Sarah noticed him pause and look at the floor. Why was he lying? What had he been doing, out in the woods in the middle of the night?

'Sounds a strange hobby to me.'

'Don't knock it till you've tried it,' said Felix, sounding a little too jolly to Sarah's ears. He picked up the poetry book from his bed. 'Did a bit of reading, did you? I love his poems. Do you know them?'

Sarah didn't want to admit she didn't know the poet, let alone his poems. 'No, poetry's not my thing.'

'What do you read then?'

The women's magazines my mum buys. 'Novels. I like the classics.'

'Oh yeah? Like what?'

Sarah wracked her brain, but couldn't remember the last time she picked up a serious book.

'I'm not sure.'

'Hmm. Well, how about you give this a go?' asked Felix, holding up the book of poems. 'You won't be disappointed.'

'OK,' said Sarah, thinking it was easier not to argue.

Before Felix handed her the book, Sarah watched him slip out the bookmark and tuck it under his pillow.

'Sorry,' said Sarah, yawning. 'I think I'm ready to sleep now.'

'Looks like it,' said Felix. 'You know where I am if any more wild beasts come pooping beside your tent.'

Sarah frowned at him, then said her goodbyes and headed to bed.

Chapter 20

'Morning, how did you sleep in the end last night?'

Sarah didn't know where to look. She'd risen early to avoid bumping into Felix on her way to the compost loo, but there he was, blocking her path, a brazen smile on his face, only a towel covering his modesty.

'Fine, thank you.' *Don't look at his chest, don't look at his chest.*

'Did you have time to read any of the poems?'

Please put some clothes on. 'Not yet.'

'Something to look forward to later. I've got more books you can borrow once you've finished that one.'

Does he think we're friends? 'I'm a slow reader.'

'Not to worry. No rush, keep the book as long as you like. See you at work.' Felix squeezed past her and made his way back to the tipi.

Thank God. 'See you at work.'

*

'Good news,' said Hattie, as Sarah walked in to the café. 'The KP's turned up for once, so no dirty dishes for you today.'

'Great,' said Sarah, surprised at the slight tug of disappointment. She'd try to time her break to fit in with Fran's.

'Felix gave you some coffee training, didn't he?'

'Um, yes.'

'Great. I need two flat whites.'

'Sure,' said Sarah, moving to the coffee machine. She eyed the machine, her nemesis, an unruly monster. *How the heck do you make a flat white?*

Sarah was on her fourth attempt when Felix appeared at her side. 'Watch and learn,' he said. He made two coffees with such ease, Sarah wanted to scream. 'Like I said, it takes time to get the hang of this.'

'Take these to table three, please,' said Hattie, carrying a tray from the kitchen and handing it to Sarah.

Table three, table three... Sarah looked around her, trying to remember the illogical table number system.

'Over there,' said Felix, pointing to the back room. 'Elderly couple in matching cagoules.'

'Thanks,' said Sarah through gritted teeth.

When Sarah dropped a slice of cake into the old man's lap, Felix appeared with a stack of napkins. When Sarah smashed a coffee cup against the slate-flagged floor, Felix was there with a brush and dustpan. When the milk overflowed all over the coffee machine and worktop, Felix was poised with a damp cloth ready to mop it up.

By lunchtime, Sarah was fighting back the urge to yell at him to give her some space. By closing time, she was red-faced with humiliation at all the mistakes he'd witnessed and how small he'd made her feel with his *helpful hero* act.

'You were a legend today,' said Hattie, walking up to Felix and squeezing his arm. 'First round's on me.'

'Coming?' Felix asked, turning to Sarah.

'Where?'

'The pub.'

'No, I don't think so.'

'Oh, come on,' said Hattie. 'You're part of the team now.'

'She's coming,' said Fran, bustling through from the kitchen and taking Sarah's hand. 'I've missed chatting to this one today. Our chap in there isn't a patch on Sarah. All I get from him are grunts.'

Right on cue a skinny young man wearing a T-shirt covered in skulls appeared from the kitchen.

'You coming to the pub, Dave?' asked Felix.

'Nah, got band practice tonight.'

'OK, see you tomorrow.'

The young man grunted as he left the café.

'I bet you five pounds he doesn't show up for work tomorrow,' Hattie said to Felix.

'Deal,' he replied, shaking her hand.

'Come on, I'm parched,' said Fran. 'I'll drive.'

'No!' shouted Felix and Hattie in unison.

Fran turned to them, hands on her hips. 'So rude. Sarah, love, would you like a ride in my classic car?'

'Yes, that sounds great.'

Hattie rolled her eyes. Felix sighed, earning himself a whack on the arm from Fran.

'You don't know what you've let us in for,' he muttered to Sarah as they followed Fran out of the café.

The four of them squeezed into Fran's ancient Mini Cooper, clutching onto door handles or each other as she tore along narrow country lanes.

'Take it easy, Fran,' said Hattie, her knuckles white as she gripped the seat below.

'Fran's a bit of a speed demon,' whispered Felix.

'Oi, I can hear you. Don't worry, love,' said Fran, taking her eyes off the road to catch Sarah's in the rear-view mirror. 'There's a reason I have such a compact car. It can get past anything.'

'Woah!' yelled Hattie. Sarah screamed. Colour drained from Felix's face.

Fran skidded the car to a stop, narrowly escaping a nasty encounter with a very large tractor. Laughing, she pulled the Mini as far as she could into the hedge.

'That will teach me for being so cocky.'

'Christ, Fran. You're more suited to *Top Gear* than working in a kitchen.'

'I'll take that as a compliment,' said Fran, turning to wink at Felix.

By the time the car pulled up outside a quaint country pub, all its passengers were grey, their legs shaking, relief etched on their faces as they climbed out of the car.

'Now I need a drink,' said Hattie.

'Me too,' said Sarah, following her colleagues into a pretty beer garden.

Hattie headed to the bar, appearing minutes later with four pints of beer. Sarah hadn't had Fran down as a beer drinker. Then again she hadn't had her down as a racing driver. It seemed her new colleague was full of surprises.

'Right, Sarah. We want all the gossip,' said Hattie, wiping a foamy moustache from her face.

'What do you mean?'

'Come on. You message me out of the blue about a job miles from home, turn up to the interview dressed for the office with no references. There's more to it than wanting a change of scene. Oh, and by the way, you caught me at a weak moment. I've never employed someone with no references before.'

'Right. Well, I'm afraid there's not much to tell.'

'Start with the lack of references.'

Sarah sighed. There was nothing to be gained from lying. 'I had the same job ever since I left uni. I quit after pointing out a few flaws in their working practices, so as you'll understand, I couldn't ask for a reference.'

Hattie and Felix exchanged a glance. Had they been talking about her behind her back?

'Where did you work?'

'At a double glazing company.'

'You were a window fitter?'

'No. Office manager.' Sarah flushed at the white lie of her inflated job title.

'That explains your coffee making skills, or lack thereof,' said Felix, chuckling to himself. Sarah flushed a deeper red.

'Yeah, sorry about that. I did work in a restaurant after leaving my office job, but the coffee came straight from an instant machine.'

'What restaurant was it?'

'Oh, just an independent one. You wouldn't have heard of it.'

'OK.' Hattie threw another look Felix's way. 'I get why you needed a job, but why so far from home?'

'My parents are getting divorced and selling up. I live in the commuter belt near London. Rental prices are out of reach for someone earning minimum wage.' Sarah stared into her pint. These people didn't want to be her friend, they just wanted to interrogate her and find out some gossip they could discuss behind her back. If she wasn't reliant on Fran for a lift, Sarah would have walked out there and then. *Don't you ever learn*, she told herself, *you're not friend material.*

'My turn,' said Fran, taking a swig of beer then setting her pint down. She leaned forward on folded arms. 'Where did you learn to love cooking?'

'Cooking? I don't love cooking.'

Fran laughed. 'We may not have known each other long, Sarah, but you've shown more interest in my recipes in five minutes than Dave has in the three years we've worked together.'

'Oh, right? Well, um, I never got the chance to cook at home. Mum always did it. But I love those cookery shows on TV. It's like magic what they produce from a few simple ingredients.' No way was she mentioning the successful buffet she'd produced for the very unsuccessful anniversary party.

'Hmm,' said Fran, leaning back in her chair and looking pensive.

'Well, cheers to having Sarah on the team,' said Hattie, raising her glass to clink against the others. 'We'll make a barista out of you yet.'

Chapter 21

The scream tore through the forest, sending birds scattering from nearby trees and bouncing off the surrounding ancient trunks.

'Get out, get out, GET OUT!' Sarah yanked her towel off the door and buried her face in it. *No, no, no, no, no. This could not be happening.* She wrapped the second towel in a turban around her hair. With eyes fixed on the ground, she slammed open the shower door and set off through the forest.

'Sarah, wait. I didn't mean to do that. I'm so, so, sorry.'

Sarah spun round, sending mud and fallen leaves up in a trail against her bare legs. 'You didn't mean to? Do you think I was born yesterday? The shower was on. You would have known I was in there.'

'I had my headphones on,' said Felix, holding out his fancy-looking headset. 'They're noise-cancelling. I promise you, I didn't know you were in there.'

'Bollocks. I don't care if they were noise whatevering, it's impossible you didn't know I was there. I've heard about men like you.'

'Sarah, I was half asleep. Please, it was a genuine mistake.'

'The only genuine thing around here is my dislike for you.'

Sarah turned and half-walked, half-ran towards her tent.

'Sarah...'

'LEAVE ME ALONE! Did you hear me? LEAVE ME ALONE!' Sarah turned her head enough to see Felix standing with his palms raised, admitting defeat. 'Idiot, bastard, cockweasel, arsewipe, A-hole, crappycrapster.'

Sarah muttered her way to her tent, only realising as she stepped inside she had left all her clean clothes in the shower, including her bra and knickers. Her greying, fraying, over-sized, grandma-style bra and knickers. She flung herself down on the bed, buried her head in a pillow and screamed. When her throat was too raw to make a sound, the screams gave way to hot, angry tears.

There was no way Felix could not have known she was there. He was a dirty perv who enjoyed teasing and tormenting. The past week working with him had been insufferable. All his attempts to help her were thinly veiled ways of showing she wasn't up to the job. So what if she'd broken a few cups, annoyed a few customers and still not got the hang of the coffee machine? Everyone had to start somewhere, and she'd never promised she was a quick learner. God, she hadn't even filled out an application form or had a proper interview.

If anyone was at fault, it wasn't her. She was trying her best. What more could anyone ask? It wasn't her fault customers were so finickity, with their gluten-free this, lactose-free that, double-expresso-chai-berry-caramel-soy-chicken-milk lattes. OK, so no one had ordered one of those, but they'd come close.

Sarah wiped her face dry and sat up on the bed. What had Felix seen? He couldn't have been in the shower room for longer than a few seconds. Sarah unfolded her towel and looked down at her naked body. Her face burned with shame. Her stomach lay in rolls against her wide thighs, her breasts drooping down as though in conversation with her feet. Felix would be texting his mates now, laughing at the disgusting creature he'd walked in on. At least it might stop him trying the same trick again. There was no way he could have liked what he saw.

'Sarah?'

Sarah could see the silhouette of Felix outside the front of her tipi. She grabbed the towel from her bed and wrapped it round herself. 'Go away.'

'I will, I promise. I just wanted to say that it was an honest mistake. I was half asleep, my music was blaring in my ears, and I guess I'm still getting used to sharing the facilities. I honestly didn't realise you were in there.'

'Whatever. Can we just leave it, please?'

'Yes sure. I just didn't want you to think badly of me.'

'I thought we were going to forget it happened.'

'Fine. See you at work.'

Sarah dressed with speed. It was important she was at work early to do what needed to be done. By half-past nine, she was ready and waiting outside the front door of the café for Hattie to arrive.

Considering Hattie was managing the place, her time keeping left a lot to be desired. Sarah had been waiting ten minutes before Hattie scuttled up to the café, waving a set of keys and jabbering on about flat car batteries.

'God, it's been one hell of a morning and I haven't even started work yet. How come you're here so early?'

'I need to talk to you. Do you have a minute before setting up?'

'Yes, sure. I wanted to talk to you, too.'

'OK.' Sarah wracked her brain for what Hattie could want to talk to her about, but came up with nothing.

'How about we have a coffee with our chat?' asked Hattie, firing up the coffee machine.

'If there's time,' said Sarah, glancing at the clock and praying Felix wouldn't be in early for once.

Five minutes later, Hattie directed Sarah to one of the comfy sofas and placed two steaming cups of coffee down on the table.

'How about you go first? What did you want to talk to me about?'

'I'm having problems with Felix.'

'Felix? We've never had complaints about him before.'

Sarah frowned

'Go on,' said Hattie, blowing on her coffee before taking a sip.

'This morning was the final straw. He walked in on me in the shower.'

'He what?' asked Hattie, nearly spitting out her coffee. 'That sounds out of character.'

'Well, maybe you don't know the real him. He came up with all sorts of excuses, but I didn't believe a word of it. It's verging on sexual harassment, if you ask me.'

'God, that's a serious allegation to be throwing out there. Could you tell me his side of what happened?'

'You don't believe me?'

'No, it's not that. It's just there are always two sides to every story, and I'd like to know the full picture if possible.'

'He claimed he didn't know I was in there.'

'How's that possible?'

'Exactly.' Sarah folded her arms and humphed with victory.

'No, I mean, how is that possible? What reasons did he give?'

'He claimed he had his headphones on and was half asleep.'

'And you don't think that's plausible?'

'And you do?' Sarah looked at Hattie, ignoring the niggling feeling that she might have gone too far. There was no option but to stick to her guns.

'I suggest we leave this conversation here for the moment. When Felix comes in, I'll listen to his account of what happened and take it from there. I'm not saying I don't believe you,' said Hattie, leaning over and patting Sarah's arm. 'But it's only fair I talk to Felix, too.'

'OK. Why did you want to talk to me?'

'Yes, um...' Hattie took a swig of coffee and avoided catching Sarah's eye. 'Now, I don't want you to take this the wrong way, but I'm not sure you're cut out for waitressing.'

The room began to spin, and Sarah felt the telltale signs of panic seeking her out. What would she do? She had no money, nowhere to go. She'd be homeless on the streets. 'You're... you're... you're... firing me?'

'God no!' Hattie leaned forward and met Sarah's eyes with her own. 'Sarah, take deep breaths, in, out, in, out.'

Sarah closed her eyes. *In two, three, four, hold two, three, four, out two, three, four, hold two, three, four.* 'I don't understand what you're saying,' she managed when her heart rate reduced to a scamper rather than a full-blown samba band.

'What I'm saying is I think you're better suited to working in the kitchen with Fran. You get on well with Fran, don't you?'

'Yes.'

'And she's keen to work with you. She told me you have potential. Between you and me, I think she's eyeing you up as her protégé.'

Sarah decided Hattie must be lying. There was no way after a few days working together, Fran would have said all that.

'I've just been finding my feet, that's all. Please don't demote me so early into my time here.'

Hattie laughed. 'Sarah, this isn't a demotion. Fran's a modest lady, but she has a stellar reputation. If anything, being her sidekick is a promotion, not a demotion.'

'But why won't you give me another chance at waitressing?'

'Urgh, I didn't want to go here, but you may as well know. I've had some complaints about you.'

'Complaints? From who?'

'Customers, but also two Saturday girls.'

Sarah thought back over the past week. Nothing stood out as being cause for complaint.

'I don't get it. What am I supposed to have done?'

'It's not what you've done. It's more your attitude. The complaints have all centred on the way you speak to people. You've been called rude and a little aggressive.'

Sarah let out a mirthless laugh. 'Aggressive? Me? That's nonsense and you know it. I'll work in the kitchen because I like and respect Fran. You don't need to make up silly reasons to convince me.'

Sarah stormed through to the kitchen, leaving Hattie shaking her head and wondering what the hell she'd done bringing Sarah into the team.

Chapter 22

'Fran, could you give us a moment?'

Sarah looked up from her pile of dirty dishes. The muscles in Felix's face were taut, his words spat from between pursed lips. Sarah pushed her shoulders back. Hattie must have spoken to him about her allegation. If he couldn't admit what he'd done, it wasn't her fault.

'Felix, I'm in the middle of making a Bakewell tart. I can't up and leave it now.'

'Just one minute, I promise.'

'OK. But if that burns, you're making another one for me.'

'Deal.'

Fran removed her apron and wandered out of the kitchen. Once the door closed, Felix turned on Sarah. 'How dare you!'

'How dare I do what? Speak the truth?'

'I explained what happened. I told you it was an accident. Do you know what happens to guys falsely accused of sexual harassment?'

'Do you have any idea what happens to women who are victims of it?'

Felix scrubbed a hand through his hair. His eyes fell to the floor, but not before Sarah noticed them filling with tears. 'I do. Far more than you. Crying wolf does nothing to help actual victims.'

'Crying wolf, was I?'

'Oh, for God's sake. Here, put these on.' Felix pulled his headphones from his bag and handed them to Sarah.

'This isn't the time to impose your music on me.'

'I'm not asking you to listen to music. Just put them on.'

'No.'

'Fine. Have it your way. I'm going to leave these here,' said Felix, laying his headphones on the counter. 'If you change your mind, put them on and you'll understand what I meant.'

'Yeah, well, even if you couldn't hear me, you would've seen the steam.'

Colour flooded to Felix's face, but the way his fists bunched told Sarah it wasn't through embarrassment. 'Steam? STEAM? My God, what planet are you on? Have you had a single hot shower since you got here? Where would the steam be coming from? Oh yeah, from your ARSE! And just for your information, the shower lock doesn't work. Never has, never will.'

Felix stormed out of the kitchen, leaving Sarah staring at the space where he'd stood. Though she hated to admit it, part of her was now questioning her version of events. Wiping her hands on a tea towel, she reached across and grabbed the headphones. As soon as she placed them over her ears, the world around her fell silent. Sarah turned back to the dishes, staring into the water, a creeping sensation that she'd made a huge mistake causing her own cheeks to burn. Sarah jumped as someone touched her back. She pulled off the headphones and turned around.

'I've been nattering away to you since I came in and you haven't heard a word of it, have you?'

'Sorry, Fran. I didn't realise you were back.'

'I heard what happened. Let me get this Bakewell out of the oven, then you and me need to have a little chat.'

With Fran's latest creation cooling on a rack, she opened the door and ushered Sarah outside. They sat on a step, each nursing a cup of tea from Fran's pot.

'Right, love. I know what happened this morning must have been very embarrassing, and I understand why you might have got the wrong end of the stick, but you're way off the mark accusing Felix like that.'

'But isn't it important women speak up when things like this happen?'

'Things like what? An honest mistake?'

'I didn't know that. I barely know Felix from Adam.'

'Fair point. I understand where you were coming from, but I think embarrassment has clouded your judgement?'

Sarah gave a small nod.

'There's something I think you should know about Felix.'

'Go on.'

'A couple of years back, he lost his little sister to suicide after she suffered a sexual assault.'

'Oh my God. I'm the worst person in the world.'

'You weren't to know.'

'No, but his explanation for what happened made sense, I was just too embarrassed to admit it.'

'That's understandable.'

'I'm not sure he'd see it that way.'

'Give him time. That boy's come a long way in the past two years. When he first joined us, he was a different person, quiet, withdrawn, wouldn't say boo to a goose.'

Sarah struggled to imagine the cocky Felix ever being shy. 'What changed?'

'Time. But also family, our little family we've got going here. Hattie and her partner Millie were wonderful. Millie used to work here too, till she got a job in a posh restaurant on the coast. They mothered that boy, licked his wounds, held him when he cried, fed him, gave him somewhere to stay when he couldn't go home.'

'Couldn't go home?'

'Felix didn't have the easiest home life to begin with. I don't think it was a happy household before Mia died, and it certainly wasn't after. His parents blamed him for what happened, but it wasn't his fault. Mia snuck out to a party while Felix was sleeping. No one knew what happened at the party till months after when she couldn't go on anymore and wrote it all down in her suicide note.'

'Where were his parents?'

'The night of the assault? At the pub. Same thing the night she died. Felix was more of a parent to Mia than they ever were.'

'God, that's so awful.'

'Yes, it was. He's been with us for two years now. Hasn't spoken to his parents since Mia's funeral.'

'He's lived in the tipi all that time?'

'Yes. He stays with Hattie and Millie when it's freezing, but he says he likes his own space. He even fitted a wood-burner into his tipi this year so he can stay in it all year round. Hattie still insists he come to theirs for a hot meal each night during the winter, but he's happiest out in the woods. I've never seen a transformation like I've seen in Felix. Finding his purpose was the last piece of the puzzle.'

'Purpose?'

'Coffee.' Fran laughed. 'It might not sound like much, but that boy's a genius at making coffee. He's won too many awards to count. He's often head-hunted by other restaurants to train their staff.'

'Wow, I must be a terrible pupil.'

'What do you mean?'

'He tried to teach me, and I was awful at it, even after two hours of trying.'

Fran laughed. 'Don't you worry, love, you only had two hours. He's had two years to perfect his talent. Besides, I think your skills lie elsewhere.'

'You do?'

'Yes. Stick with me and you'll find your calling soon enough.' Fran winked at Sarah. 'Come on, best get back to it. I've got thirty scones to make and could do with a hand.'

As they entered the kitchen, Felix stood beside the sink, unloading a tray of dirty dishes. Fran gave Sarah an encouraging nod.

'Felix, I need to apologise. I was out of order, embarrassed. I...'

'Are you done? I need to get back to work.'

'Yes, sure.'

Felix left the kitchen, and Sarah held her forehead in her hands. 'He's never going to forgive me.'

'Give him time, love. Give him time. Now, have you ever made cheese scones before?'

*

Sarah saw nothing of Felix for the rest of her shift. In fact, she was sure he was avoiding her. She waited in her tipi until she heard his guitar start up, then bit the bullet and went to find him.

'Knock knock,' she said, hovering outside Felix's tipi. The guitar continued its strumming. 'Felix? It's Sarah. Can we have a chat?'

From inside the tipi, Sarah heard a loud sigh, and the guitar being laid on the ground. Felix came out of his tipi, his brow furrowed, his lips turned down at the corners.

'If you're here to apologise again, please don't. You've said it enough and I accept your apology. I'd like to leave it at that.'

'OK. I just wanted to clear the air, seeing as we're neighbours and colleagues.'

'Consider it cleared. But Sarah?'

'Yes?'

'We may be neighbours and we may be colleagues, but we're not friends. I'll be civil to you at work, and if I see you around, but what you did today was toxic. I've come too far in my life to get dragged down again. I hope you understand.'

'Yes,' said Sarah in a small voice as Felix disappeared back inside.

Back between her own canvas walls, Sarah climbed up onto her bed and pulled her knees up around her chin. A hollow sadness filled her, colouring the world around her grey despite the orange glow of the paraffin lamp.

Sarah thought back over her life and the few friends she had made. School had been a lonely experience. After years of being bullied, she'd collected a couple of odd-bods to hang around with when she started high school, but no genuine friends. There had once been a girl at work she got on OK with. What was her name? Susan, that was it. Sarah and Susan. It had a nice ring to it, but their friendship only lasted a few months. When Susan got a better paid job in a different town, the friendship fizzled out as quickly as it had started. Mark had been her friend. But he was living a different life now.

You're on your own, Sarah, she told herself. *It's about time you got used to it.* Kicking off her shoes, Sarah climbed into bed, pulling the covers up over her head. It was stupid feeling so sad about a friendship she'd never had. She didn't even like Felix. His retreat from her was no great loss. And yet, she wished he'd appear at her tipi door to annoy her. She couldn't even hear the guitar anymore. Was this the way her life would be from now on? All alone, with only trees for company?

Chapter 23

S arah was elbow-deep in pastry dough when Hattie appeared in the kitchen. After telling Fran about the buffet she'd prepared for her parent's ill-fated anniversary party, making quiche had become a daily task.

'Sorry, I know you're busy, but someone is here to see you. It's about time you took a break, anyway.'

'Someone's here to see me? But I don't know anyone.'

'Well, this lady says she knows you.'

A flutter of fear tickled Sarah's insides. 'How old is the lady?'

'Dunno, late twenties, early thirties, something like that.'

Thank God, not Cynthia then. 'OK, give me a minute to clean myself up and I'll come through.'

'Great. I'll give your friend the sofa by the fire. It's so quiet out there you'll have plenty of time to chat. Don't feel you need to rush your break today.'

'Thanks.' Friend? Hattie said friend, but Sarah didn't have any of those. She washed her hands and arms, intrigued to find out who the mystery caller was.

Sarah found Kate sitting by the fire, reading a trashy magazine. She hadn't picked her out as someone who enjoyed celebrity gossip.

'Kate? What are you doing here?'

'Good to see you too,' laughed Kate, standing up and pulling a reluctant Sarah into a hug. 'I wanted to see how you're getting on, but thought I'd give you enough time to settle in before I pitched up.'

'Tea or coffee, Sarah?' Hattie called from behind the counter.

'Just a tap water, please.' Sarah didn't want to drag out the meeting with Kate longer than necessary. It felt weird seeing her out of context.

Kate sat down and stuffed the magazine into her bag. She caught Sarah looking and laughed. 'Don't tell Bob. Those gossip magazines are my guilty pleasure. He thinks I'm becoming more cultured now I'm in my thirties, but I love seeing what all those celebs are getting up to. I've almost finished it, so I can leave it with you if you fancy a read?'

'Go on then,' said Sarah with a smile.

'Right. So how's it going here? I expected to find you behind the counter.'

'Yeah, it turned out I was more suited to working in the kitchen,' said Sarah. She'd never admit to Hattie how much she enjoyed working with Fran. She still believed Hattie had hired her under false pretenses.

'So, are you helping with the cooking? Those cakes look delicious.'

'Have one on the house,' said Hattie, bringing over Sarah's water.

'Ooh, are you sure?'

'Of course, Sarah works so hard she deserves a few perks for her friends.'

'Thanks, that's very kind. I'll have a slice of coffee cake, please.'

'Coming right up.'

Hattie moved back to the counter, and Kate turned to Sarah. 'So are you the cake chef?'

'No, I do the washing up.'

'Not true,' said Hattie, reappearing with a chunk of coffee cake. 'Sarah's turning into quite the chef. She's a dab hand at scones and quiches, and I'm sure Fran will add to her repertoire in no time.' Hattie beamed at Sarah. Sarah gave a tight smile. She wished Hattie would leave them in peace. She hated people complimenting her when it was undeserved.

'Wow, this is good,' said Kate through a mouthful of crumbs.

'Fran is an amazing cook,' said Sarah, offering a genuine smile. 'She's a brilliant teacher, too. I've got a lot to learn, but if anyone can teach me, it's Fran.'

'I'm so pleased it's going well for you. How's the accommodation?'

'Interesting.'

'Sounds intriguing.'

'Let's just say it's taken a bit of getting used to.'

'Can I see it?'

'Oh, I don't think I have time.'

'You've got time,' called Hattie from behind the counter.

Sarah smiled and stood up. 'Come on then.'

Kate scoffed down the rest of her cake, standing up to brush crumbs from her dress. They were walking out through the garden gate when Kate said, 'I suppose you've heard Mark stayed with us last week?'

Sarah stopped in her tracks. Her throat dried out, her pulse raced. 'No, I didn't know.'

'Oh, sorry. I thought you said you two were friends?'

'We're on good terms. I wouldn't call it a friendship ,though.'

'Ah, sorry. I've put my foot in it, haven't I?'

'No, not at all. It wasn't like I would have had time to see him, even if I knew. I've not been into Bodmin since I stayed with you. There's not much public transport around here, and I'm working loads.'

'True. Right, where's this house of yours?'

Sarah smiled. 'I'm not sure house is quite the right word for it.'

They walked along an overgrown path, and the tipis came into view. 'Don't tell me this is where you're staying?'

'It sure is.'

'Well, I didn't have you down as a camper.'

'Me neither.' Sarah would never admit she was getting used to tipi life. If anything, she was almost on the verge of enjoying it. She opened up the doors and let Kate explore inside.

'Wow, this is cool! Is it warm enough at night?'

'Not too bad. The nights are warming up now. It was a bit of an icebox when I first arrived.'

'You know you can always call if you fancy a few extra creature comforts?'

'Thanks, but I'm managing OK.'

Kate walked out of the tipi just as Felix was arriving at his. 'Hi,' he said, waving and walking over to Kate. Sarah held her breath. Felix had been polite since their argument, but that politeness hadn't stretched beyond a few words, and they still weren't on proper speaking terms. 'I'm Felix.'

'Kate. Nice to meet you.'

'You too. Are you a friend of Sarah's?'

'Yes, I am.' Kate smiled at Sarah, who felt an unfamiliar warmth spread through her. 'We met a couple of years ago when Sarah came to stay in my Airbnb.'

'I see. Well, I'd better get on, but maybe see you again.'

'Bye.' Kate waited till Felix was out of earshot before turning to Sarah. 'I knew you had delightful views here, but he takes them to another level.' She wiggled an eyebrow at Sarah, who blushed.

'I'm not sure Bob would appreciate you eyeing up other men.'

Kate laughed. 'I'm only looking. Bob's the only man for me. Speaking of which...' she held out her left hand.

'What am I looking at?' asked Sarah.

'The ring! We got engaged last week.'

'Wow, congratulations.' Sarah wondered if Kate had any idea how lucky she was. Beautiful, smart, able to chat with anyone, and with a man who adored her. Some people had it all.

'Yes, I have to admit, whilst I came here to visit you, I also had an ulterior motive.'

'Oh?'

'I heard on the grapevine they've started doing weddings here. I thought I'd come and scope the place out.'

Sarah's stomach dropped. 'Right. Well, Hattie's the one to talk to about that. I'll take you back to her, I need to be getting back to work.'

Sarah kicked herself. All that pretense at friendship. As if someone like Kate would visit her. All Kate wanted was to look round a wedding venue, and visiting Sarah was a good excuse to do it. Of course, they'd never be friends in real life. Sarah rushed back to the café, said a curt goodbye to Kate, and left her chatting weddings with Hattie.

Back in the kitchen, Sarah pounded her pastry dough with renewed force, gaining a raised eyebrow from Fran. Next, she set upon an oil-caked pan, scrubbing it so hard the metal scourer cut through her skin, sending pink blood swirling through the dirty water.

'Everything all right, love?' asked Fran.

'Yes, fine.'

'You don't seem fine.'

'I am.'

'You sure you don't want to talk about it?'

'No!' Sarah turned back to her dirty dishes, but not before she'd registered the look of hurt on Fran's face. 'Sorry,' she mumbled into her soapy water.

The rest of the day held a veiled tension. Fran made her best attempt at cheeriness, but there was distrust in her voice, her eyes darting back and forth to Sarah as though she were a feral dog who could bite at any moment.

As the day drew to a close, Sarah rushed from the café, keen to escape the atmosphere she had created. In her bag were leftovers from the café; a sausage roll, cheese and pickle sandwiches and a slice of fruit cake. Hattie made sure all the staff ate a hot meal during their lunch break, then shared out leftovers between the staff at the end of the day.

There were still plenty of walkers and mountain bikers hanging about, so Sarah chose a path that rose from the valley, guarded on either side by rows of pine trees. She stopped halfway up to catch her breath, congratulating herself on the improvement. The first time she'd attempted the path, she hadn't been able to make it halfway before thinking she was dying and panting back the way she had come.

Sweat prickled her skin, but rather than the heat of embarrassment, it was from achievement. She had pushed her unfit body through the pain barrier, ignoring the voice in her head who said she couldn't do it. She was growing fitter with each day, and the thought made her smile.

The smile disappeared as she remembered the way she had snapped at Fran. Why did she have to do it? Fran was only trying to be a good friend. Without her, Sarah would be isolated from all the other staff. Hattie, who seemed incapable of hating anyone, seemed wary around Sarah, Felix was still ignoring her, and the Saturday girls didn't know she existed.

At the top of the hill, Sarah turned to admire the view. Somehow, the forest was seeping into her bones, pulling her into a world of peace and beauty that was difficult to ignore. She sat down on a clump of grass, looking out at the valley spread before her. So far she had stuck close to the café, too unsure of herself to venture beyond its gaze. Even within the narrow confines she'd set herself, the view was ever changing. Trees were bursting with new life, leaves appearing in neon-green, banks carpeted by delicate yellow and white flowers.

'Just wait for bluebell season,' Fran had said, when Sarah mentioned her walks. 'You've seen nothing like it.'

Sarah pulled out her food and looked around her. Would she still be here when the bluebells came? Would she be here when the leaves turned from green to burnt orange, or when they dropped to the floor, creating a crunching carpet under foot? She pushed the thoughts away. *Take one day at a time*, she told herself. *And don't forget to apologise again to Fran.*

Chapter 24

During her first few weeks living and working in the woods, Sarah dreaded Mondays. Too unfit to tackle anything but the easiest paths, she'd whiled away lonely hours in her tipi, watching the minutes tick by with painful lethargy. Four weeks in, and she looked forward to her day off. During the previous week, Sarah had forced herself to venture further into the woods, discovering new vistas, pretty clearings, and even spots she could swim should the weather ever be warm enough. By the time her fifth Monday morning rolled round, Sarah had highlighted paths to explore on her map, and had borrowed a *guide to forest plants* from the café ready to learn more about her surroundings.

Several times Hattie had offered to drive her into Bodmin for supplies, but each time Sarah turned her down. Soon, she would need to accept the offer of a lift. She'd need to replenish some of her toiletries and buy a few more T-shirts to prepare for the warmer weather.

Sarah wasn't looking forward to leaving the woods. As much as she'd hated them when she first arrived, the trees acted like a cocoon, an alternate reality where she could hide from the real world. In her tipi, or out on the forest trails, she could pretend her parents were still living together in her old house. She could pretend she was on holiday, or taking a short career break before returning to the real world.

The trees were becoming as familiar as friends. Although she'd never admit it to anyone, sometimes she spoke to them, telling them about her day, about her latest creation in the kitchen, or what she'd had for lunch. Surrounded by nature, the loneliness which haunted her waking hours subsided. As her heart rate increased with the gradient of a path, a fleeting feeling would pass through her. Was it happiness?

As the sun rose on her fifth Monday in the woods, Sarah pulled on her backpack and let herself out of the tipi. Telling herself the early start had everything to do with pastel skies, and nothing to do with avoiding Felix, Sarah made a quick detour to the compost toilet, before setting off through the undergrowth.

The morning air held a chill, but scrabbling up animal tracks made up for it. By the time Sarah reached a small clearing, her skin was sticky, and she removed her jumper and spread it across the ground to sit on. She pulled a savoury muffin from her cool bag, enjoying every bite all the more for having baked it herself. Any tension between her and Fran had dissipated, and as the weeks wore on, they were making a formidable team. Sarah worried that teaching her the tricks of the trade was giving Fran too much extra work, but she said she enjoyed it, and seemed offended when Sarah suggested they limit the lessons to every other day.

The days in the café were so busy with so little spare time, Fran had taken to staying behind an hour after each shift to teach Sarah a new recipe. Sarah was grateful, not just for the skills she was learning, but for the way her lessons shortened the long evenings alone.

With Felix showing no sign of thawing towards her, Sarah developed a routine which meant she spent as little time at the campsite as possible. It would be seven before she and Fran finished in the kitchen. After waving Fran off, Sarah took whatever she had made that evening out into the woods. It didn't matter if it was raining; the trees provided enough cover so long as she found the right spot. Once she finished her food, she'd either lie down and read, or sit staring at the view, watching the tree branches as they danced in the wind.

After four hours hiking, Sarah descended a steep track, longing to bathe her tired feet in the shallow river which hugged the valley floor. When she reached the bridge, she stopped short. Felix stood leaning against a wooden fence, gazing down at the river.

Before Sarah had the chance to turn back the way she came, Felix turned his head and their eyes met. He gave an awkward wave. There was no way she could turn around now. Sarah scrambled down the last few metres of hill.

'What are you doing here?' asked Sarah as she walked onto the bridge.

'I heard you go out this morning and thought I'd come and find you. It's about time we had a chat. I didn't expect to be waiting so long. How far did you get?'

Sarah looked behind her, secretly marvelling at how far she had walked. 'Oh, not far, just a stroll.'

'It must have been quite the stroll,' said Felix, following Sarah's gaze to the line of trees perched on a far-off hill. 'So you're enjoying the forest now, are you?'

'I never said I wasn't.'

Felix laughed. 'You know what you remind me of?'

'Enlighten me.'

'That,' said Felix, pointing to a bush beside them.

'I remind you of a plant?'

'Not just any plant. You remind me of Holly.'

'Holly?'

'Yes. Spiky, painful if you get too close.'

Sarah humphed. 'Thanks for the compliment,' she said, her voice laced with sarcasm.

'Hey, it's not all bad. Holly is beautiful when its berries appear.'

'Well, I'm sorry you think of me as spiky.'

Felix laughed. 'I'm not trying to be mean, just making an observation.'

'How kind of you.' Sarah stalked off across the bridge. Felix jogged up to her and blocked her path.

'You don't see it, do you?'

'See what?'

'How you treat people, how you speak to people. You can be rude when you want to be, not to mention distrustful.'

'I don't suffer fools. There's nothing wrong with that.'

'Maybe not, but the people you're dealing with here aren't fools, Sarah. They're good, kind people who are trying to be your friends.'

'Friends? Give me one example of someone here who's been a genuine friend to me.'

'Fran.'

'Apart from Fran.'

'What about your friend that came to visit you at the café, Kate, wasn't it?'

'Oh, her,' said Sarah, letting out a mirthless laugh. 'She didn't come to see me, she just wanted to look at wedding venues. She probably thought by cosying up to me she'd get a discount.'

'Or maybe she wanted to involve you in her plans?'

'I doubt it.'

'Fine then. What about Hattie?'

'You mean the same Hattie that demoted me to the kitchen and laughed at me in the pub?'

Felix scrubbed his hands through his hair. 'God, you are something. First off, working alongside Fran is no demotion. Do you have any idea how many aspiring chefs would give their right arm to be trained up by her? Second, from what I remember of that night in the pub, we were all joking around. Taking the piss out of each other like friends do. There was no malice behind it. You really have a low opinion of people, don't you?'

'Maybe I've just been let down one too many times.'

'Look,' said Felix, leaning against the wooden fence and staring at the river, 'I understand what it's like to want to protect yourself. But if you don't take a risk on people, how will you ever find the people who are good, who won't let you down?'

'And I suppose you're one of them?'

'Yes,' said Felix, turning to face Sarah, 'I am.'

Sarah leaned against the fence beside him, picking at a patch of mud with her boot.

'I'm sorry I've been ignoring you. What you did hurt me, accusing me and all that. It was a genuine mistake, but I get why you might not have believed me. The reason I wanted to talk to you was to see if we could start again?'

'How do you mean?'

'I mean, start again as friends. Hattie invited me to watch a band in town tonight. Why don't you come with me?'

'I'm not sure.'

'Why? Do you have other plans?'

Sarah frowned. He knew she had no plans other than hiding away in her tipi.

'Come on, it might be fun, you may enjoy yourself?'

'Fine.'

'Just fine? Well, I guess that's a start.' Felix's eyes twinkled. He was teasing her, but for once Sarah didn't look for malice behind the action.

Chapter 25

S arah walked up the high street in Bodmin feeling at home. Whilst her woodland hideaway proved a tonic, it was only when walking from shop to shop that Sarah realised how much she'd missed being in a town. Despite being much smaller than her hometown, Bodmin was full of life. Their arrival into the town had coincided with school kicking out time, and gaggles of teenagers milled around the streets, while harassed mothers gave in to small children demanding after-school treats.

'Did you get what you needed?' asked Felix as Sarah emerged from the pharmacy.

'Yes,' said Sarah, holding aloft a bag of toiletries.

'We've got half an hour before we meet the others. Is there anywhere else you need to go?'

'I'd just like to wander around for a bit if that's OK with you? I didn't get to see much of the town the last time I was here.'

'No problem. Tell you what, how do you feel about the prospect of another hill?'

Sarah groaned, remembering the miles she'd hiked only that morning. She was about to complain, then remembered being likened to a holly leaf and faked positivity, even if she wasn't feeling it. 'Nothing I'd like more,' she said, taking Felix by surprise.

'Town life seems to suit you,' said Felix. 'I've never seen you so cheerful.'

'Not so holly-like now, am I?' said Sarah, smiling.

'Come on, this way.'

Felix led Sarah past a grand square dominated by an even grander building. 'They're the old courtrooms,' said Felix. 'Tourist information's in there now.'

'You grew up in the town?'

'No, but I've lived here long enough to get a feel for the place. Come on, this way.' They climbed a flight of steps beside another grand old building. 'That's a cinema now. We should come and watch a film sometime.'

'Maybe,' said Sarah, blushing and turning her head away from him. *Don't be stupid*, she told herself. *Someone like him wouldn't be asking someone like you on a date.*

Sarah followed Felix through a car park until they found themselves in woodland. 'You've brought me to some woods? Don't you think we have enough of trees already?'

'It's a means to an end,' said Felix, climbing a steep path edged by crumbling stone walls and dense trees. They emerged from the woodland onto a narrow road, flanked by small terraced houses. 'Almost there,' he said.

'You weren't wrong when you said there'd be a hill,' said Sarah, catching her breath. 'How much further?'

'Five minutes at the most.'

'OK.'

They carried on until they came to a small car park. Dog walkers stood chatting beside cars, their furry companions sniffing each other and barking with impatience. Several people said hello as they passed, and Felix returned the sentiment.

'Wow, what is this place?' asked Sarah, as they emerged onto a large patch of grass surrounded by gorse and trees. A large stone monument dominated the top of the hill.

'It's the local nature reserve, local being the operative word. Most people who visit the town don't know about this place despite its proximity to the town centre.'

'Maybe they just don't like hills?'

'Could be. Come on, I want to show you something.' They skirted the edge of the grassy field until Felix stopped at a gate that separated the nature reserve from a field. 'Look at that,' he said, pointing in the distance.

'My God, you can see the whole town from up here.'

'You said you wanted to see more of the town, so I thought this would be the best spot.'

'It is, thank you,' said Sarah, throwing Felix a smile of genuine warmth.

'Want to see some more?'

'Yes, please.'

Despite her newfound love of the forest, the uninterrupted views spreading out for miles were welcome. They walked through fields, down paths, up grassy embankments, gazing on neat rows of houses and open expanses of fields. Conversation flowed, the tension and misunderstandings that had plagued them unmentioned if not forgotten.

'How are we doing for time?' Sarah asked as they made their way back to the beacon monument.

Felix glanced at his watch and frowned. 'We'd better get going.'

They walked back down the hill and into the town centre, reaching the restaurant with five minutes to spare.

'Looks like we're the first here,' said Felix. 'Where do you want to sit?'

'It says there's a courtyard. How about we sit outside? It's warm enough?'

'Good plan.'

They settled themselves at a table and ordered drinks. Hattie was the first to join them, followed by a beautiful willowy redhead.

'Hi guys. Sarah, this is Millie.'

Millie held out her hand, and Sarah shook it. It was impossible to feel anything but comfortable under Millie's warm gaze. 'Lovely to meet you. Hattie tells me you're a whizz in the kitchen.'

'That's kind of her.'

'She's giving me a run for my money,' said Fran, joining them at the table and pulling up a chair.

With Fran beside her, Sarah's shoulders relaxed. Felix had shown a different side to himself, but not enough for her to lay aside all her mistrust. As for Hattie, Sarah would try to keep an open mind.

'Joy!' Fran jumped out of her seat and rushed to a hunched old lady making her way through the courtyard with the help of a stick. The women embraced, Sarah experiencing a twinge of jealousy at the rapturous greeting. 'Sarah, this is my friend Joy. Joy, this is Sarah.'

'Pleased to meet you, dear,' said Joy, holding out a wizened hand.

Sarah threw a questioning glance to Felix, and he mouthed back 'Kate's friend.' *Great, so did that mean Kate would come too?* Sarah shivered in annoyance. Felix forgot to mention this would be a large gathering. If she'd known, there was no way she would have agreed to come.

'Good evening ladies and gents,' said Bob, ducking beneath the door to the courtyard, Kate holding on to his hand. 'Sorry we're late, I had a few things to finish up at the office.'

'Well, I'm sorry we're eating so early,' said Millie. 'I got out of prepping for tonight's dinner service, but they need me back by seven to oversee things.'

'Can't manage without you, can they?' said Hattie, giving Millie's hand a squeeze.

'More like I'm a control freak.' Millie laughed off the compliment and Sarah warmed to her even more.

Sarah turned her attention to Joy. 'How do you and Fran know each other?'

'Me and her mum go way back. She's a good girl, is Fran.'

Sarah smiled at Fran being called a girl. She must be pushing fifty. Her smile faded as Joy lit a cigarette and Sarah found herself smothered by a cloud of smoke. She should have picked a table inside.

'How are things going with your *situation?*' Hattie asked Felix under her breath, but not quietly enough.

'What situation is this, then?' Joy asked Felix.

Felix blushed. 'Oh nothing, nothing, just something to do with the café.'

The café? Sarah hadn't heard of any problems at the café.

'Sorry,' Hattie mouthed to Felix.

'It's all right,' Felix mouthed back.

What the hell was going on? Sarah hated secrets, especially if she were the only one not in on them.

'Shall we order?' asked Bob. 'I'm starving.'

'You're always starving,' laughed Kate. 'Speaking of which, Fran and Sarah, I could do with your opinion on a menu for the wedding.'

'Hey,' said Bob. 'No wedding talk tonight, you agreed.'

Ah, thought Sarah. *This is why you're here.* 'Yes, it's best if we discuss it at work. This is our day off, after all.'

'Sorry, sorry,' said Kate. 'I just get a bit carried away.'

'And so you should,' said Fran, frowning at Sarah. 'You're entitled to be excited about your wedding day. Sarah can enjoy her day off, me and you can have a chat about food in a bit.'

'Thanks,' said Kate.

Sarah wished she was back in her tipi by herself. Somehow, she'd upset Fran again. This friendship malarkey didn't suit her.

Chapter 26

S arah picked at the food in front of her, remembering why she didn't enjoy group situations. How was it possible to be in a group, yet feel so alone? The others chatted around her, over her, despite her. She couldn't keep up with their discussions about current affairs or politics. Even when the conversation turned to favourite TV shows, she couldn't join in, the only person at the table not to have a Netflix account.

'You're quiet there, dear,' said Joy.

Sarah recoiled at her bitter, tobacco-scented breath. 'There's not much opportunity for TV or watching the news when you live in a tent.'

'I don't suppose there is. How are you finding life under canvas? I used to love a bit of camping in my youth. These days my arthritic bones require a proper mattress.'

'I'm getting used to it,' said Sarah with a polite smile.

'So what are your plans once the season's over?' asked Joy. 'You can't stay in a tent over winter.'

Sarah winced. The old lady had an uncanny way of looking at you, like she could read your mind, or worse, your soul. 'I haven't thought that far ahead. A lot depends on my parents and their plans.'

'What have your parents got to do with anything? It's your life.'

'Joy,' said Kate, her voice holding a note of reproach. 'Leave poor Sarah alone. She's only just moved to Cornwall, let alone had time to think about what she does next.'

'It's fine,' said Sarah, staring at the table and avoiding catching Joy's beady eyes. Now would be a wonderful moment for Hattie to offer her a job through the winter, but she stayed quiet. Not for the first time, Sarah wished she'd signed a proper contract, so she'd know where she stood.

'I met your fella the other day,' said Joy.

'Pardon?'

'You know, the chap you were engaged to? What was his name, Kate?'

Kate had the good grace to blush. 'Mark. Sorry, Sarah, we haven't been gossiping about you. Joy came round while Mark and Gary were staying, and your name came up in conversation.'

'It's not a problem,' said Sarah, taking a large gulp of wine.

'Shame it didn't work out between the two of you,' said Joy. 'He seemed a lovely chap. Very brave. I wish my son had the guts to come out of the wardrobe.'

'I think you mean closet, Joy,' said Kate, suppressing a smile.

'Wardrobe, closet, chest of drawers, I don't give a fig what they call it. Each to their own, I say. If my son ever bothered to pick up the phone, he'd know I don't care a jot who he's sleeping with.'

Bob chuckled and leaned towards Sarah. 'You'll get used to her,' he whispered to Sarah, pointing a finger in Joy's direction.

Sarah didn't want to get used to Joy. The old lady's directness made her uncomfortable. The conversation moved on to safer topics, and Sarah ordered another glass of wine. As the alcohol reached her system, she relaxed.

'Sarah,' said Kate, pulling her chair closer. 'I know it's your day off, and I'll respect that by keeping wedding talk to a minimum, but there was something I'd like to ask you.'

'What is it? If you want to chat about wedding food, Fran's the best person. It's her kitchen, her menu.'

'Our kitchen,' said Fran, smiling at Sarah. 'And I'm sorry, love, you're right to protect your day off. We'll arrange a separate time to talk about wedding menus.'

'Of course,' said Kate. 'But it wasn't just the food I wanted to talk to you about. I wondered, given you know the place so well, whether you could help me come up with a few wedding plans?'

'Me? Hattie would be a better person for the job.'

'But as we're friends, I thought it would be something fun to do together?'

Friends? Did Kate count her as a friend? Sarah's feelings towards Kate thawed. 'I don't know...'

'I'll throw in a bottle of wine, how about that? Are you free on Wednesday evening? Bob's taking his mum to a pub quiz and I'm rubbish at those, so I'll have an evening to myself.'

'Please say yes, Sarah. I'm hopeless at all this wedding planning. You'd be taking the pressure off me.' Bob gave Sarah a winning smile. She may be suspicious of Kate, but as much as she hated to admit it, there was nothing Sarah could find to dislike about Bob.

'All right.'

'Brilliant,' said Kate. 'I'll pick you up about seven-thirty. How does that sound?'

Sarah wasn't sure how that sounded. 'Great, I'll look forward to it. Excuse me, but I must pop to the toilet.'

Sarah was washing her hands by the toilet window when she heard her name mentioned in the courtyard beyond.

'She's a strange one, that Sarah,' said Joy. 'Not the friendliest girl I've ever met. Nothing like Mark, who seemed such a lovely young man. No wonder they didn't work as a couple.'

Sarah held her breath, waiting for Kate, Hattie, or Felix to agree with Joy.

'Hmm,' said Kate, 'I know you're usually spot on in character assessments, Joy, but I'm afraid I think you've got Sarah wrong. Yes, she's prickly, but it's only because she has her guard up all the time. I think she's rather shy.'

'It's a defense mechanism,' said Hattie.

'I think she's rather splendid,' said Bob. 'She can be blunt, but I find it refreshing. So many people are trying to be something they're not these days.'

'We had a great time together this afternoon,' said Felix. 'I saw a totally different side of her.'

'I get the impression she's not used to having friends,' said Millie. 'I may be wrong, but if that is the case, it's no wonder she's awkward around people.'

'She's lovely to me, most of the time,' said Fran. 'And goodness me, that girl can cook.'

Sarah leaned against the toilet wall. It wasn't just the three glasses of wine causing her head to spin. Were these people genuine, or did they know she could hear them through the open window? Sarah waited until the conversation moved on, then emerged back into the courtyard.

'Sorry, everyone, I've got to run,' said Millie, hugging each member of the group. It took Sarah by surprise when she also received a warm embrace. 'It was lovely to meet you, Sarah. Hope to see you again soon.'

'Likewise,' said Sarah, meaning it.

The group spilled out onto the street, and Sarah walked beside Fran.

'Is everything OK, love? You've gone quiet.'

'I'm fine,' said Sarah, 'just tipsy after three glasses of wine.'

Fran laughed. 'I'm pleased you came. It's good to see you enjoying yourself for once.'

Sarah smiled. 'I didn't want to come. I'm not used to going out in a group, but I'm enjoying myself.'

Fran linked arms with Sarah. 'Welcome to the gang,' she said. 'We're a motley crew, but we know how to have fun. Just wait till you hear the band.'

'You've heard them before?'

'Oh yes, we get tickets every time they come to town. I hope you've brought your dancing shoes with you.' Sarah and Fran looked down at Sarah's scruffy trainers. Fran laughed. 'They'll do.'

The packed pub left standing room only. Hattie led them through the bar to a larger room at the back where the band was setting up. She rushed over to the long-haired musicians, hugging each of them.

'Some of the lads used to work at the café before they went off to university,' explained Fran, leaving Sarah to dish out hugs of her own.

Bob bought a round of drinks, and somehow Joy secured them a table. 'She's a dab hand at playing the frail old lady card,' explained Bob as they sat down.

The music started, and Bob wiggled his shoulders.

'Oh no,' said Kate, throwing her head in her hands in mock horror.

'Bob's a demon on the dance floor,' shouted Fran over the sixties rock classics blasting out from the band.

Bob grabbed Kate's hand and yanked her to her feet. 'See you in a few hours,' she called behind her as Bob spun her round onto the dance floor.

'May I have the pleasure of this dance?' Fran asked Joy.

Joy's eyes sparkled. 'Race you there,' she said, dropping her walking stick to the ground and shimmying her way across the floor.

Sarah assumed Felix would invite Hattie to the dance floor, but he slid along the seat until sitting beside her. 'Let me guess,' he said. 'You hate dancing?'

'I've got two left feet,' said Sarah.

'Prove it,' said Felix, taking Sarah's hand in his own and standing up.

'No, I can't. It wouldn't be fair to leave Hattie by herself.'

'I'd be pleased to have a rest,' said Hattie. 'Go on, get up there.'

Sarah wondered if the wine had affected her more than she thought. She couldn't remember ever dancing in public, having avoided school discos like the plague and not having friends to go out with when she left school.

Felix took both her hands in his and began jiggling her around to the music. Sarah couldn't help but laugh. 'I've discovered your weakness,' she shouted above the music.

'What do you mean?' asked Felix, wiggling his hips.

'You may be good at most things, Felix, but dancing isn't one of them.'

Felix responded by pulling Sarah close and attempting to tango across the dance floor. Laughing so much her stomach hurt, she felt a fizz of excitement at Felix's hand on her waist, the other hand wrapped around hers. Sarah shook her head to rid the foolishness.

'Felix, looks like you need some help from the master,' said Bob, sidling up to them and taking Felix in hand. Felix looked back at Sarah in mock horror as Bob took him in a ballroom hold. Sarah and Kate joined Fran and Joy, and Hattie appeared beside them.

Amidst the heat, noise and sweat-scented air of the dance floor, Sarah lifted her arms in the air, moving to the music, filled with freedom and happiness the likes of which she'd never experienced before.

Chapter 27

S arah's foot tapped against the platform, her legs jiggling as she perched on the edge of the bench, checking the train times.

'Relax,' said Felix.

'I just feel such a fraud. It's kind of you guys to invite me to the awards ceremony, but they nominated you before I even started at the café.'

'Yes,' said Hattie, 'but we're a team, and you're an important part of it.'

'Enjoy it,' said Millie. 'A free dinner, free hotel room, what's not to love?'

'I wish you'd let me contribute something. You've been saving those tips for two years. It doesn't feel right I should take such a large share.'

'I'm happy to come for the jolly and I haven't worked at the café for years. If it makes you feel better, you're much less of a scrounger than me.' Millie grinned at Sarah.

'I'm more worried about Fran,' said Hattie. 'Where is she? The train leaves in five minutes.'

'Have you tried calling her?' asked Felix.

'Only a hundred times. It keeps going to voice mail.' Hattie pulled her phone from her pocket. 'Shit. No.'

'What is it, hun?' asked Millie, draping an arm over Hattie's shoulder.

'A message from Fran. She says she's ill and won't make it.'

'No, but tonight's all about her!'

'I know. Have you noticed she's been cagey ever since we started talking about making a night of it? Like she doesn't want to be away from home that long? Or someone else doesn't want her to be...' Hattie frowned.

'It's only twenty-four hours,' said Felix. 'Besides, it's not like Fran to lie. She must be really ill.'

'Hmm,' said Hattie, an inscrutable look on her face. 'Oh well, we'll do our best to represent her. Come on, here's our train.'

They climbed aboard and settled themselves around a table. Millie grinned as she pulled a bottle of Bucks fizz and four paper cups from her bag.

'It's only ten in the morning,' said Hattie, frowning at her partner.

'I know, but this is a celebration. Even if you don't win, just being nominated for *Best Cake in the Southwest* is an honour. Here's to Fran,' she said, filling the cups.

'To Fran,' they chorused.

Excitement warmed Sarah as much as the booze as the train sped its way towards Exeter. Sarah couldn't remember ever going on a group shopping trip, never mind to an awards ceremony. She'd been warned not to expect much from the budget hotel, but Sarah didn't care where they slept. It still surprised her they had invited her at all.

Sarah pulled out her phone and texted Fran. *I hope you're OK. It won't be the same without you. xxx.*

Moments later, a reply came. *I'll live. Have fun xxx.*

An hour later, the train pulled into the station and Felix took charge of all the overnight bags. 'I still think it's sexist that you won't let me come shopping with you,' he said.

'You'd only be bored,' said Millie. 'We'll meet you back at the hotel in a couple of hours.'

Before Felix could protest further, both Millie and Hattie linked arms with Sarah and near enough dragged her out of the station. After complaining she had nothing smart to wear, Millie and Hattie had insisted on arriving early in order to fit in a spot of shopping. Sarah couldn't remember the last time she'd bought new clothes.

'What if I can't find anything I like?' she asked, as they headed to the main shopping area.

'Then you'll have to wear that,' said Hattie, looking down at Sarah's jeans, T-shirt and trainers.

After an hour of trailing round high street shops with no luck, Sarah was feeling despondent.

'Let's try in here,' said Hattie, striding into a large charity shop.

'But if I buy something from here, I won't be able to wash it first,' said Sarah.

'Don't worry, they wash everything before they put it out for sale,' said Millie, winking then grimacing at Hattie over the top of Sarah's head.

Sarah trawled through the rails, feeling a creeping sense of panic that she wouldn't find anything and would end up in jeans at the event.

'Come here,' called Hattie, pulling a black dress from a rail.

'Hmm,' said Sarah, 'I'm not sure it's me.'

'You won't know unless you try it on,' said Hattie, thrusting the dress into Sarah's arms and pushing her towards the changing room.

Five minutes later, Sarah emerged. Millie gripped onto Hattie's arm and let out a dramatic sigh. 'You look gorgeous,' she said.

'I'm not sure...'

'Not sure about what?' asked Hattie. 'Sarah, you look stunning. It's a perfect fit. Come on, give us a twirl.'

Sarah obliged, turning around in the black, 1950s-style halter neck Hattie had picked out for her. The hem skimmed her knees, the boned bodice making her feel curvy rather than lumpy.

'Come on,' said Millie. 'You can't deny you look good.'

Did she? Sarah studied herself in the full-length mirror. She didn't look *bad*, and perhaps that was good enough.

*

By the time they reached the hotel, Sarah had been forced to sit at a makeup counter while a teenage girl painted her face with products she'd never be able to afford, and hustled into a shoe shop to buy a pair of heels she'd never be able to walk in.

'Looking good,' said Felix as they walked towards him in the bar.

'Wait till you see her outfit,' said Hattie, flopping into a chair beside him.

Millie checked her watch. 'We've got two hours till we need to leave. How about a quick drink, then we'll go to our rooms to get ready?'

'Good plan,' said Felix.

One drink turned into two, and by the time they headed to their rooms, there was only an hour before they'd need to meet back in the hotel lobby. Sarah located her room, grateful to find a clean, bland space. She paused by the mirror, startled by her reflection. She'd never had so much makeup applied, and yet the young girl had done a good job of making it look natural. It accentuated her features without being garish. Sarah smiled and flicked on the kettle.

It was only as she climbed into her new dress that the nerves hit. What was she doing prancing round in a posh dress and high heels? She'd look ridiculous. With an undignified dance, Sarah did up the zip on the back of her dress. She slipped her feet into her high heels and practiced walking back and forth across the room. She only twisted her ankle once, and decided that as long as she took tiny steps, she'd just about manage.

A knock on the door made Sarah jump. She swore under her breath and gave her twisted ankle a quick rub before hobbling towards the door.

'Hi,' she said, feeling heat rushing to her cheeks as she took in the sight of Felix in a suit.

'Hi,' he said, his cheeks matching Sarah's as he stared at her, his mouth hanging open. 'You look...'

'We'd better get going,' said Sarah, throwing a handbag over her shoulder and stepping out of her room.

It was a quiet ride down to the lobby, both Sarah and Felix feeling tongue tied and out of place in their finery. Millie and Hattie were waiting on a sofa for them.

'Oh my God,' said Hattie when she spotted them. 'You two look like you're a Hollywood power couple on your way to the Oscars.'

Sarah gave a tight smile, desperate to be out in the fresh air, which she hoped would douse her flaming cheeks. 'You both look lovely,' she said, admiring their outfits. Hattie wore a flowing silk tie-dye dress, and Millie looked gorgeous in a figure-hugging green velvet trouser suit.

A horn beeped outside. 'That will be our taxi,' said Millie. 'Come on, we've got a free bar to make the most of.'

*

Sarah didn't notice how long and boring the award ceremony was. She didn't notice the sub-par food, the deafening noise around them, the smell of hot, over-excited bodies filling the air, the cheap sweetness of the champagne. She experienced a flutter of disappointment on Fran's behalf when they didn't win, and a pang of regret that her friend wasn't there to share the evening with them. But on the whole, all

Sarah felt was happiness. It was such an unfamiliar feeling, at first she wondered if she were drunk. But she'd sipped her two thimblefuls of cheap champagne with restraint. The atmosphere was more intoxicating than any amount of alcohol could ever be.

Hattie caught Sarah's eye and smiled. 'It's a shame Fran didn't win,' she said. 'But I'm loving being out with you all. How about we ditch this sweaty ballroom and find ourselves a friendly pub somewhere?'

'Good plan,' said Felix.

After his earlier awkwardness, he'd relaxed into the evening, leaving his friends in stitches with his impressions of café customers. Sarah had laughed as hard as Millie and Hattie when he recalled Sarah's terror at meeting Madge the Badger. Her face ached, and she vowed to make better use of her facial muscles from now on.

As they pulled on coats and began weaving their way through the packed ballroom, Felix took Sarah's hand. *It's an act of friendship*, she told herself, as her heart tried to jump out of her chest and she prayed her palms weren't clammy. When they stepped out into the cool night air and Felix let her hand drop, she savoured the warm imprint where it had been.

With every pub they visited packed to the rafters, they decided a decent night's sleep was preferable and headed back to the hotel. They said goodnight, and Millie and Hattie disappeared through the double doors to their ground floor room, while Sarah and Felix made their way to the lift.

Perhaps it was the alcohol wearing off, but as they waited for the lift to come, some of their old awkwardness slipped into the space between them. A bell tinged and the lift doors opened. Sarah stood beside Felix, the small space and proximity to the man beside her causing her breaths to come fast and light. Felix attempted some banal small talk, and both were relieved to exit the lift on their floor.

They reached Sarah's room first. 'Goodnight,' she said. 'I can't wait to get out of this dress and into that enormous bed.' Like a tidal wave, a flush spread up her face. She prayed Felix hadn't picked up on the innuendo. Sarah turned to unlock her door, hoping her long hair concealed the colour of her face.

'Hey,' said Felix, touching her arm. Sarah turned and looked up at him. 'I meant to tell you earlier, but didn't.'

'What?'

'I just wanted you to know how beautiful you look tonight. I'm not sure you always see what other people see.'

Sarah struggled for words, convinced her face had now turned from red to purple. 'Thanks,' she muttered.

Felix took a step closer, leaned over and kissed her cheek, then with a gruff 'Goodnight', turned and walked off down the corridor.

Sarah fumbled with her key card, dropping it twice before she made it into the room. As the door closed, she sank to the floor, leaning against it, fanning her steaming face with her hand. Had Felix just called her beautiful, or had she imagined it? Sarah pulled herself to her feet and stood in front of the mirror. For the first time, the reflection staring back at her wasn't grotesque. Beautiful was a step too far, Sarah decided, but the woman staring back at her looked like someone who fitted in, an ordinary woman with friends and a life.

Sarah pulled off the dress, kicked off her shoes, and climbed into bed. The smile on her lips remained long after she'd fallen asleep.

Chapter 28

Despite being the middle of May, the weather was terrible. It had rained for weeks, and showed no sign of letting up. Fran and Sarah took their break under a shelter designed to protect the bins.

'It stinks out here.'

'I know.' Fran chuckled and took another sip of her tea.

'What's on the menu today?'

'Chickpea stew, caramelised onion tart, carrot cake and triple chocolate brownies.'

'Yum. Can I make the brownies?'

'No, you could do that standing on your head. You can make the onion tart.'

'But I've never made one before.'

'I know. It will be a good learning curve. It's not as complicated as it sounds, and I'll be right there with you if you get stuck.'

'You're an excellent teacher, you know.'

Fran pretended to faint. 'Was... was... was that a compliment?' she asked, fanning herself.

'Hey, I give compliments.'

'You do? I'm not sure I remember receiving one.'

'You've seen me eat your food, you know I love it.'

'I know you finish it. You could just be doing that to be polite.'

Sarah laughed. 'You've known me long enough to know I do nothing for the sake of politeness.'

'How very self-aware of you,' said Fran, grinning. 'Come on, we've got work to do.'

Two hours later, Sarah pulled a delicious-smelling tart from the oven. 'Ta da!'

'That looks wonderful. You've come on so much these past few months. Let's add this to the menu for tomorrow.'

Sarah baulked. 'What if my first attempt is a fluke?'

'Pah,' said Fran. 'Have a bit of confidence, love.'

Sarah turned back to the washing up and took deep breaths to settle the nerves in her stomach. Tomorrow was going to be a big day. All the local dignitaries were coming for an official fund-raising event, and there were even rumours royalty may attend. Agency staff had been hired to help with waitressing, and a KP was being brought in so Sarah could work on the food with Fran. The pressure weighed down on Sarah's chest. There would be no room for error, no second chances. Everything had to be right first time. What if she messed up?

'Are you OK to stay behind today? I'd like to finalise the menu and get a bit of prep done before tomorrow.'

'Of course,' said Sarah.

'Mmm, something smells good,' said Felix, walking into the kitchen with a tray of dirty dishes.

'Sarah made it,' said Fran.

'You're wasted washing dishes,' said Felix, causing Sarah to flush with pride.

Over the past few weeks she'd been enjoying the novelty of friendship. After their night at the awards ceremony, Sarah embraced the ease of being in the company of her new friends. She'd been out for drinks a few times with Hattie, Millie, and Fran. And while she hated to admit it, helping Kate with wedding preparations was proving enjoyable. Their original Wednesday evening planning session had become a regular event, and Sarah looked forward to her evenings at Kate's house.

But it was the newfound friendship with Felix that brought Sarah the most pleasure. She hadn't realised how lonely she'd been until she started hanging out in his tipi each evening. Sometimes they talked, sometimes they read, sometimes she lounged on a beanbag while he strummed away on his guitar. Spending time with him felt easy, and over time, her guard was slipping. Whilst conversation flowed freely, they hadn't strayed onto any difficult topics, or revealed much to each other about their lives. *Baby steps*, thought Sarah, smiling into the soap suds in front of her.

'What's put that grin on your face?' asked Fran, adding a cake tin to the growing pile of dirty dishes.

'I guess I'm just enjoying being here with all of you.'

'All of us, or one person in particular?'

'Well, you're my favourite,' said Sarah, deflecting the teasing note in Fran's voice.

'Of course,' said Fran with a smirk. 'I'm pleased you're settling in. You seem so much happier than when you arrived. And a lot less spiky.'

'Hey!' said Sarah, flicking Fran with a tea-towel. She continued washing up, then dried her hands and turned to Fran. 'Sorry about how I was at first, spiky, as you call it. I'm not used to having friends, or having things go well for me. It's hard to trust people.'

'So, what's changed?'

Sarah felt a blush creeping up her neck. 'You remember when we went out for dinner in Bodmin?'

'The night we watched the band?'

'Yes, well, I overheard you talking about me when I was in the toilet.'

'You did, did you?'

'Yes. I wasn't eavesdropping, it was impossible not to hear through the open window. Anyway, the point is, you were all so nice about me. It made me wonder if I'd misjudged you all.'

'Misjudged us?'

'Yeah, I thought you all hated me.'

'Hate's a strong word,' said Fran. 'It would be true to say we were a little wary of you, I suppose. You weren't all that friendly. Anyway, enough chitchat, we've got work to do.'

*

By the time Sarah got back to her tipi that evening, her body was exhausted, her mind skittish with nervous energy. Finalising the menu should have been relaxing, but all it did was highlight how much there was to do the following day. Fran had been ambitious in her choices, meaning the canapés and lunch buffet contained many opportunities for messing something up.

'Hi,' said Felix, poking his head into Sarah's tipi. 'You're back late.'

'We were going through the menu for tomorrow.'

'How's it looking?'

'Delicious, providing nothing goes wrong.'

'You'll be fine. Between you and Fran, you're going to blow those VIP's socks off, or should that be taste buds?'

Sarah laughed. 'Are you off to bed?'

'Not yet, I wondered if you fancied a nightcap before we turn in?'

'Sounds good.'

Sarah followed Felix to his tipi. She'd added a few little touches to hers in the time she'd lived there, but it never felt as cosy as Felix's, and there was never a discussion as to whose place they'd hang out in.

Felix handed Sarah a beer and pulled out a pack of cards. They sat cross-legged on Felix's bed, sharing out playing cards and chatting through their day. They stopped talking as the serious business of Gin Rummy began, peering over their hands to outwit each other.

'Yes!' shouted Sarah once all their totals were counted.

'Yeah, all right, just remember, no one likes a bad winner.'

'No one likes a bad loser,' said Sarah, collecting up the cards and stacking them in a pile.

'Play again?' asked Felix.

'No, I need to be up early tomorrow. It's a good game, though. Where did you learn it?'

'From my nan when we were little. She thought it would help with our maths.'

'She wasn't wrong there.'

'I used to play it with my sisters,' said Felix, his voice becoming husky.

Sarah leaned over and took his hand in an action that surprised them both. 'Fran told me about what happened. I'm so sorry.'

'Yeah, well, it's water under the bridge. I'm OK, it's just random moments like this,' said Felix waving a hand towards the playing cards, 'remind me of all I've lost.'

Felix's eyes filled with tears. Sarah reached up with her free hand and brushed them away with her thumb. The atmosphere in the tipi changed. Still holding hands, they sat opposite each other on the bed, neither breaking away from the look which held them transfixed.

Before she knew what was happening, Felix leaned forwards and his lips met Sarah's. She snapped her head back.

'Sorry, sorry that was wrong of me.'

Sarah flushed. 'No, it wasn't, you just took me by surprise.' She leaned towards Felix and placed a tentative kiss on his lips. Felix pulled back. 'Sorry,' said Sarah, 'are you OK?'

'You took me by surprise,' he said, a grin spreading across his face. He pulled Sarah closer and their lips met once more.

Half an hour later, Sarah stumbled out of Felix's tipi. The skin on her face was sore from rubbing against his stubble, her lips dry, but her heart so full she felt it might burst. As soon as Sarah entered her tipi, she flung herself down on her bed and let out a long breath. Her body was screaming to return to Felix, but her mind knew it was better to have left things as they were.

Felix proved the perfect gentlemen. There had been no suggestion she stay with him. He had pulled away from her, telling her she had a big day in the morning and needed her sleep. Part of Sarah wished he hadn't been so gentlemanly about the situation, but with her body leaden with tiredness, she knew it had been the right decision. Besides, there was no rush. It wasn't like she was going anywhere.

Chapter 29

Sarah opened her eyes and listened. All was quiet. For the first time in ages, she wasn't waking to the sound of rain hammering on canvas. She climbed out of bed and poked her head out of the tipi door. The sun beamed down, warming the ground, drying off the mud-clogged earth. It was only seven, but the sun's strength warmed her face as she tilted it to the sky.

It would have been easy to stay like a cat in a patch of sunlight all day, but there was work to do. Sarah dressed quickly, heading over to the café as soon as she was ready. There was no time to lose. When Sarah walked into the kitchen, Fran was already there.

'What time did you get here?'

'Half six. I'd rather miss out on a bit of sleep than be in a rush.'

Sarah marvelled at the woman's dedication. 'Right. Where do you want me?'

Fran issued instructions and the two of them set to work, the sound of the morning radio soothing any nerves as to what the day would hold.

*

Sarah stared at the wall, lost in thought, her arm stirring the bowl in front of her on autopilot.

'Sarah? Sarah?'

'Hmm?' Sarah turned her head to see Fran standing behind her, hands on her hips.

'I'm not even going to ask what's put that soppy smile on your face, but you need to save thoughts of a certain person till later.'

'A certain person?'

'Oh, come on. It's been obvious to everyone there's something going on between you and a certain gentleman,' said Fran, cocking her head in the café's direction.

Sarah stopped stirring. 'Really? It wasn't obvious to me.'

Jan laughed. 'You are a one. That boy's been mooning over you for weeks and you're telling me you hadn't noticed?'

Sarah caught her reflection in the window. No one would moon over her, least of all Felix. 'I think you're wrong.'

Fran laughed again. 'So there's no evidence to suggest I'm right?'

Sarah flushed.

'I want to hear all the gory details, but not right now. We've got lunch to cook for a hundred people. I need you focused and on top of your game. You think you can do that?'

'Yes, boss,' said Sarah, dragging her thoughts away from the previous night and back to the present.

Five hours later, and with cakes and savoury pastries cooling on a rack, Fran instructed Sarah to find Hattie and check she was ready for the canapés to be sent out. Sarah walked out of the café and over to an enormous marquee set up the day before. The transformation was incredible. What had been a bare, grassy space was now filled with trestle tables groaning under the weight of spring flowers. Colourful rugs filled the floor, fairy lights criss-crossed the ceiling and hay-bale sofas lined the edge of the tent.

Hattie was standing at a wooden bar, clipboard in hand, Felix beside her. Sarah hadn't seen Felix since she left his tipi, and took a deep breath as she walked over to him. Hattie had her back to Sarah, but Felix saw her, his cheeks turning rosy before his lips curled in a smile. Sarah returned her own shy smile and tapped Hattie on the shoulder.

'Sarah, what can I do for you?'

'Fran was wondering whether you're ready for the canapés to come out?'

Hattie looked across to the grass outside the marquee, where men in suits and women in pretty dresses stood milling around, glasses of champagne in their hands. 'Can you wait another thirty minutes? We're still waiting for a few people to arrive.'

'Sure, no problem.'

'Great. How's it going in there? You look hot and bothered.'

Sarah flushed an even deeper red, aware her increased heart rate had nothing to do with the heat of a kitchen or the stress of the morning. 'Oh, yes, it's all go in the kitchen, but Fran's doing a wonderful job.'

'I don't doubt it. Once the canapés come out, you'll have a bit of time to relax before we begin the lunch service.'

'Thanks, I'll let Fran know.'

Sarah walked back through the giant tipi, feeling Felix's eyes on her with every step.

*

At three o'clock, Fran pulled off her apron and told Sarah to do the same. She walked over to Sarah and enveloped her in a tight hug. 'Thank you so much for today. I couldn't have done this without you.'

'I'm pleased I could help.' Sarah looked over to where two of the agency staff waded through the mountain of washing up left by the guests. Relief flooded her, for once soap suds and wrinkled skin were not her concern.

'How about you nip across to the bar and get us both a drink? I think we've earned one.'

'Good idea,' said Sarah, heading off towards the marquee.

If the kitchen seemed stuffy, it was nothing compared to the marquee. An unexpected shower had forced the lunch guests inside, and the mass of bodies sucked all fresh air from between its walls. Voices rose with each glass of wine consumed and the din made Sarah's head pound.

Sarah pushed through the crowds to the bar, where Hattie was replenishing the bottles of wine in the fridge. Her hair had escaped its bun, sticking to her face in places as it met with the sheen of sweat. She looked both tired and harassed.

'Are you OK?' Sarah asked. 'It's crazy in here.'

'I know,' said Hattie, wiping her forehead with her sleeve. 'This lot drink like fish. I'm worried we'll run out of wine before they head home.'

'Maybe now isn't the best time to ask if there's a drink going spare for me and Fran?'

Hattie laughed. 'You two deserve a bottle. The food was incredible. Loads of people have come up to me asking me to pass on compliments to the chef.'

'I'll see they reach her,' said Sarah.

'And accept a few compliments yourself,' said Hattie, stretching out her back and suppressing a yawn. 'From what Fran's told me, you're as much responsible for the success of today as she is. Here you go,' said Hattie, placing two glasses of wine on the counter.

'Thanks,' said Sarah. 'Is there anything I can do before I head back to the kitchen?'

'Could you grab more bottles of wine from the trailer out the back? I'd get them myself, only the barman we brought in disappeared off for a cigarette break an hour ago and hasn't reappeared. I've been manning the bar on my own ever since.'

'Isn't Felix around to help?'

'He disappeared too. If you see him, tell him he needs to get his arse back here ASAP.'

'Will do. I'll get the bottles for you, take a drink to Fran, then if Felix and your barman haven't returned, I'll give you a hand myself.'

'Thank you. You're a star.'

Sarah left the marquee, buoyed up by her usefulness, Hattie's praise, and the thought of an evening with Felix lying ahead. As she rounded the corner of the marquee, Sarah saw Felix leaning against the side of a trailer. He had his back to her, but just as she was about to run up and surprise him, Sarah realised he wasn't alone.

Stepping closer to the marquee so he wouldn't see her, Sarah watched in horror as Felix took the hand of a young woman. There was no way the woman was part of the event. She wore cut-off shorts, a baggy jumper, hiking boots and her tied-back hair was twisted into long dreadlocks.

Bile rose in her throat as Sarah watched Felix lift a hand to stroke the woman's cheek. The woman leaned against him, Felix wrapping his arms around her, holding her tight. After several minutes, they pulled apart. Felix looked at his watch, then back to the marquee. Sarah held her breath, praying he hadn't seen her. Felix turned back to the woman. Sarah watched him hold up his wrist and point at his watch. The woman nodded, gave him another quick hug, then disappeared towards the forest.

Sarah strode towards Felix. 'Hi, what are you doing here?'

'Oh,' he said, jumping and avoiding Sarah's eye, 'just taking a breather. It's crazy hot in there.'

'It is, and Hattie's on her own behind the bar. She asked me to find you, said she's been by herself for ages.' *Now's your time to explain,* thought Sarah. *Tell me there's an innocent explanation for what I just saw.*

'Oh right, yeah, sorry. I felt ill in there, to be honest. I must have been out here longer than I thought.'

Liar. 'I told Hattie I'd grab some wine from the trailer. Could you do that, then help her?'

'Will do. Hey, Sarah, is everything OK?'

'Yes. Why?'

'You just sound pissed off. I thought after last night...'

Sarah flushed, not through embarrassment, but shame. How could she have been so stupid? She'd put her trust in a man who didn't deserve it. Could she trust anyone? 'I'm fine. See you later.'

Sarah walked back to the bar, explained to Hattie she'd have help soon, and carried two drinks back to the kitchen.

'Goodness me, I needed this,' said Fran, taking a sip of her wine and closing her eyes. The rain showers had passed, and they sat outside the kitchen enjoying the warmth of the sun. 'You were such a help today. Thank you so much for everything you've done.'

'There were lots of compliments about the food,' said Sarah, trying to raise a smile.

'Good, that's what I like to hear. Now, I want to know all about you and Felix.'

'There is no me and Felix.'

'Oh? Trouble in paradise so soon?'

Sarah sighed. 'Something happened last night, but it shouldn't have. I got him wrong, so wrong.'

'In what way?'

'He's a liar and a cheat.'

'What makes you say that? Doesn't sound like the Felix I know.'

Sarah considered telling Fran what she'd seen, but it only made her seem more of a fool for trusting him in the first place.

Chapter 30

F elix's tipi lay in darkness. Sarah paused outside the door and listened, wondering if he'd opted for an early night. The only sound to reach her was the gentle rustle of leaves as a spring breeze teased them. Where could he be? It was unlikely he'd gone out with Hattie, as she seemed dead on her feet by the time the last guests left the event and all the clearing up was done. Checking no one was around, Sarah lifted a corner of the tipi door and peered inside. Empty.

Disheartened, Sarah trudged back to her own tipi and changed into pyjamas. She climbed into bed and picked up the book of poems Felix had loaned her. She remembered him slipping the bookmark from it. *I love you.* Why had he hidden it from her? Was it the mystery woman from earlier who gave it to him?

Sarah threw the book onto the ground and clenched her fists. He'd made a fool out of her. She banged her fists against her forehead. She knew she shouldn't have been so trusting. It never ended well. Sarah's phone rang, and she sighed as Cynthia's name flashed up.

'Hello?'

'Hello, only me.'

'Is everything OK?'

'Yes, why wouldn't it be?'

'Because you haven't called me the entire time you've been in Spain.'

'I've been busy.'

Busy lounging by a pool. 'Right. Were you just calling for a chat?'

'No, I was calling to let you know I'll be back in the country for a week.'

'Why? Is Spain not working out as you'd hoped?'

'God, no, I love it here. I need to come back to sign some paperwork for the house.'

'I see.'

'Yes, anyway, I'm bringing Marjorie with me. She heard you're living in Cornwall these days and fancied a holiday.'

'You can't stay with me,' said Sarah, looking around her canvas home.

Cynthia huffed down the phone. 'I wasn't asking to stay with you. Didn't you stay in some little bed-and-breakfast the first time you went down there? I thought perhaps we could stay there. Thought they may give us a discount, as you know the owners.'

The thought of Cynthia staying with Kate induced the familiar early signs of panic. Only now they weren't so familiar. Sarah realised she hadn't had a panic attack in weeks.

'When are you thinking of coming to visit? Last I heard, Kate's place is booked up for the next few months.'

'Damn it, we're coming next week. Do you think you could check just in case? I wouldn't be coming to Cornwall at all if it weren't for bloody Marjorie. Waste of money.'

A visit to your daughter is a waste of money? 'Right.'

'So, if we have to come, I'd rather it didn't cost the earth.'

'I'll message Kate,' said Sarah, with no intention of doing so, 'but I can't promise anything.'

'Good girl. I'll text you when we know the exact dates we'll be visiting. Don't worry about booking time off, Marjorie has a list of places she'd like to visit. We'll pop in and see you at some point, obviously.'

As an afterthought. 'It will be lovely to see you.'

'Good. Speak soon.' Cynthia hung up, and Sarah threw her phone on the floor to join the book. Why did nothing good last? Was she cursed?

'Knock knock.'

'Hello?'

'Only me,' said Felix, strolling into Sarah's tipi. He walked over to the bed and bent down to kiss Sarah. She turned her head and his kiss met her nose. 'Everything OK?' he asked.

'Yes, I'm just tired.'

'Me too.'

'Where have you been?'

'Been?'

'Yes. I came over to your tipi to find you, but you weren't there.'

'Oh. I was having a shower.'

That would be far more believable if your hair was wet. 'OK. Well, like I said, I'm tired.'

'Right, I guess I'll leave you to it then,' said Felix, his forehead drawn into a frown. 'You're sure everything's all right?'

'Yes, why wouldn't it be?' Sarah held his gaze, daring him to tell the truth.

Felix shook his head. 'Night then.'

'Good night.'

Sarah made sure the door was closed after he had left. He might have made a fool of her once, but she wouldn't fall for his charms a second time. Everyone else may lap up his good guy act, but more fool them. If anything, seeing him with that woman had been a blessing in disguise. If she hadn't, she'd be with him now, exposing more of her heart, leaving herself open to more hurt.

*

'Sarah,' said Hattie as she walked into the café. 'Thank God you're here. Fran's not coming in today. I need you to run the kitchen.'

'What's wrong with Fran?'

'She said she's tired after yesterday's event.' Hattie frowned. 'To be honest, I'm a little worried, it's not like her.'

'Yes, she's never struck me as flaky.'

'Flaky?'

'She may well be tired, but so are we. We all worked hard yesterday, but I don't see you or I calling in sick.'

'I thought Fran was your friend?'

'She is, I just don't see why she should have a day off when the rest of us have to keep working. Never mind, show me the menu and I'll see what I can do.'

'Thank you. I'll get it for you, then I'll give Fran a call and double check she's OK.'

'Sure,' said Sarah, grabbing an apron and making her way to the kitchen. Was this why Fran had been training her up? So she could take a day off whenever she felt like it?

Despite her annoyance, Sarah missed Fran. Hattie had drafted Dave the KP in to help, but he wasn't what Sarah would describe as a conversationalist. She thought working in silence would help concentration. Instead, she felt alone and abandoned. She wished Fran was on hand to ask for advice. When Sarah pulled a coffee cake from the oven, the middle had sunk; the scones were singed on top, and while cake and scones had distracted her, the soup had stuck to the bottom of the pan. So much for being Fran's protégé.

Sarah set about rectifying her mistakes and by the time the café filled up with hungry mouths wanting lunch, there was more than enough food to go round. Sarah took a break and carried a cup of tea outside. There seemed little point in having a break without Fran to chat to. Sarah tipped her half-drunk tea on the ground and went back inside.

A timer beeped, and Sarah bent down to retrieve a tray of flapjacks from the oven. When she stood, Felix was beside her.

'That smells amazing,' he said. 'You're doing Fran proud.'

'Did Hattie speak to her?'

'Yes, seems like she's fine, just coming down with something.'

'OK.'

'Do you have time for a quick chat?'

'About what?'

'Us.'

'You can see I'm rather busy,' said Sarah, waving to the tray of flapjacks and half-full mixing bowls lying on the counter.

'Just a quick chat. Dave?' said Felix, turning to the KP. 'Could you give us a minute?'

'Sure,' said Dave.

'I wanted to check you're OK,' said Felix once Dave was out of earshot.

'Why wouldn't I be?'

'I don't know, you seemed a bit off with me last night.'

Sarah let out a mirthless laugh. 'I bet you're not used to women resisting your charms.'

'That's unfair.'

'Is it?' asked Sarah. 'I think what happened the other night was a mistake. It's never a good idea to blur the boundaries.'

'Blur the boundaries? What are you talking about?'

'We're colleagues. Anything going on between us affects the entire team.'

'Sarah, we work in a café, not some Footsie One Hundred company.'

'I know, but team dynamics are important.'

Felix laughed. 'You're talking to me about team dynamics?'

'What's funny about that?'

'You're hardly a team player.'

How was it that despite Felix being in the wrong, he was making her out to be the bad guy? 'I think you've said enough. In case you hadn't noticed, I've got work to do.'

'Fine, if you want to be like that.' Felix marched out of the kitchen, letting the door slam behind him.

Sarah pounded her fists into a bowl of dough. The fragile happiness she'd built was at risk. She thought back to the call with her mother. There couldn't be a worse time for Cynthia to drop in on her new life.

Chapter 31

S arah stared at the tray of scones not long out of the oven. She frowned, counting them for the sixth time.

'Fran? Has anyone been in the kitchen while we were on our break?'

'How would I know? I was out there with you,' said Fran.

'I think someone's been stealing.'

Fran laughed. 'Sarah, it's a few scones. You must have miscounted.'

'I didn't. I was careful to make the exact amount, just like you asked. Someone's been in here and taken some.'

'Why don't you look on the counter? Someone's probably come in and plated a few up while we were on our break.'

Sarah walked through to the café. She studied the counter. Cakes and pastries filled every inch of surface space, but there were no scones to be seen.

'Who took the scones from the kitchen?' demanded Sarah. Hattie looked up from the till, Felix turned from the coffee machine, and the two Saturday girls sniggered.

'Sarah? What's this about?' Hattie asked.

'Someone has stolen five of my scones.'

One of the Saturday girls spluttered and covered her mouth with her hand.

'It was you, wasn't it?' said Sarah, pointing her finger at the young girl.

The Saturday girl flushed a deep red and shook her head. 'I've been nowhere near the kitchen,' she said to Hattie. 'I've been here with you all morning.'

'Sarah, if there's a problem with the food, it's best we discuss it in the kitchen,' said Hattie, glancing at the customers turning to look.

'It's a simple matter. We can sort it out now if someone will just own up.'

Hattie apologised to the customer she was dealing with, grabbed Sarah's arm, and guided her back to the kitchen.

'Whatever's going on?' asked Fran.

'That's what I'd like to know,' said Hattie, red-faced and nothing like the relaxed, friendly woman Sarah knew. 'Sarah has just come through to the café and accused the staff of stealing scones. Scones for goodness' sake! Of all the things to get your knickers in a twist about, she picks a few bloody cheese scones.'

'It's the principle of the matter,' said Sarah, standing her ground despite her confidence slipping. She'd been on edge ever since things with Felix went wrong. Was she overreacting? She took a deep breath. 'Stealing is stealing, whether it's a Rolex watch or a cheese scone.'

'I don't think they're comparable,' said Hattie, taking a deep breath.

'Hattie's right, love,' said Fran, walking to Sarah and putting an arm around her. 'What's this really about?'

'It's about what I said it's about. Can none of you see the problem here? Someone is stealing food and you don't give a damn about it.'

'Perhaps some of us have bigger fish to fry,' said Fran, moving away from Sarah and turning back to the cake she'd been icing.

'Fran,' said Hattie. Fran looked up and shook her head to stop further comment.

Great, thought Sarah, *so now they're keeping secrets from me too.*

'Sarah, regardless of the rights or wrongs of the situation, the way you behaved in the café is unacceptable. Consider this an official warning. I think it would be best if you take the rest of the day off to calm down.'

Calm down? Hattie was telling her to calm down? Sarah pulled off her apron and stomped out of the café. Why hadn't Fran stood up for her? She'd been behaving strangely all week. There had been none of the usual chatter. She'd been withdrawn, quiet, distracted. In all the weeks Sarah had worked at the café, she had never seen Fran make a mistake until this week. One day she put salt instead of sugar into a cake mix, another day she forgot to add the butter. Only yesterday morning, Sarah had walked in to find chicken soup left out of the fridge all night and needing to be thrown away.

Something was going on, but Sarah had no idea what. Weren't friends supposed to confide in one another? Hattie knew something. Perhaps she knew about Felix's mystery woman, too? Was there was a web of lies and secrets being shared between everyone but Sarah?

Sarah walked back to her tipi but found she couldn't settle. Instead, she packed a bag with her phone, purse and water bottle and pulled on her walking boots. Rather than comforting, the forest felt oppressive. She needed to get away for a few hours.

Sarah was two miles along the road to Bodmin when her phone rang. She climbed onto the grass verge and pulled the phone from her pocket.

'Hi, Mum.'

'I'm calling to say we're in Bodmin.'

'What? I thought you weren't arriving till Monday?'

'Change of plan. Marjorie saw a great deal on a coach holiday heading down this way, so we snapped up the offer. We've come for a long weekend rather than a week, and are staying at a hotel in Bodmin.'

'You're staying at the jail hotel?'

'Good Lord, no. Do you think we're made of money? No, we're staying at the one in town, I can't remember the name. It's not what you'd call five-star, but it's clean and comfortable, so will do for a few nights.'

Sarah should have known her mother would do her own thing. Determined not to impose Cynthia on Kate and Bob, Sarah had spent hours scouring the internet for suitable accommodation, sending an extensive selection of B&Bs, apartments, and cottages to her mother. The only place she hadn't sent was the one her mother and aunt had chosen. *What a waste of time*, thought Sarah, taking a deep breath as her mother chattered on.

'Are you free this evening? We're going to brave one of the local pubs for tea.'

'I'm coming into Bodmin this afternoon. I should be there by six.' *Better to get it over with.*

'Perfect,' said Cynthia. 'I'll text you the name of the place and we'll see you there.'

By the time Sarah made it to the town centre, her legs were leaden. Sweat glistened on her skin and looking down at her walking clothes, she realised how poorly dressed she was for an evening out. She checked her phone for the name of the pub and found it with ten minutes to spare.

As she walked in to the recently refurbished building, Sarah relaxed. A fire blazed in the hearth despite the warm evening outside. The walls were navy, the woodwork white, lush plants sat in corners and fresh flowers took centre stage on tables. She found herself a table by a window and waited for her mother to arrive.

The pub doors flung open and Cynthia and Marjorie arrived in a haze of lurid colours and overpowering perfume.

'Sarah!' yelled Marjorie, flinging herself at her niece and covering her cheek in fuchsia lipstick.

'Hi, Auntie. How are you?'

'Never mind her. Come here, pequeno,' said Cynthia, kissing Sarah on both cheeks to show her newfound European-ness. *Has she forgotten she voted for Brexit*, Sarah wondered?

'Nice to see you Mum, you look... um... very tanned.'

Cynthia did a twirl, purple silk flying around her. She didn't look tanned; she looked orange, and Sarah wondered how much of her tan was natural.

'The Spanish life suits me, doesn't it?' said Cynthia, posing like she was on a magazine shoot. To Sarah, it looked like her mother had gained at least two stones in the time she'd been away, but kept her thoughts to herself.

'Aren't you going to order some drinks?' Marjorie asked Sarah. 'I'm gasping over here.'

And I'm on minimum wage. 'Of course. What would you like?'

'Let's go wild and get a bottle of champagne. It's years since the three of us have been together, we should celebrate.'

Sarah slunk over to the bar. She ordered a bottle of prosecco and hoped neither Cynthia nor Marjorie would notice the difference.

'Here you go,' said Sarah, pouring out three glasses.

'To us,' cried Marjorie, clinking her glass so hard against Sarah's half the contents spilled out. *Thank goodness I didn't fork out for champagne*, thought Sarah.

Marjorie and Cynthia embarked on a lengthy monologue about their lives in Spain. They interrupted one another to correct details, or exaggerate them.

'Has your mother told you about Marco?'

'Um, no, I don't think so. Who's Marco, Mum?'

Cynthia grinned. 'Marco is your soon-to-be step-dad.'

'My what?' asked Sarah, her face falling as Cynthia held out a hand to show off a cheap, tacky ring.

'You're invited to the wedding, of course, but I've asked Marjorie to be my bridesmaid.'

'Hold on, you're getting married?'

'Yes, wonderful news isn't it,' piped up Marjorie. 'I must admit I'm jealous. I've lived over there ten years and never found the right man. Your mum's been there five minutes and has a ring on her finger.'

'Isn't there the slight problem you're already married?' asked Sarah, thinking the day couldn't get much worse.

'Oh, that will be sorted soon. Your father and I are going to speak to a solicitor while I'm over here. He wanted to do it all online, but I don't trust those internet forms.'

'So what's he like, this Marco?'

'Well... he's younger than me...'

'How much younger?'

'He's in his mid-thirties.'

'He's twenty-nine,' corrected Marjorie.

'Twenty nine? But that's only four years older than me! You're old enough to be his mother.'

Cynthia scowled. 'Age doesn't matter when you're in love.'

Sarah sighed. What could be more depressing than her irritating, overbearing, orange mother having a better love life than her? Sarah took a large gulp of fizz and prayed the day would soon be over.

Chapter 32

Each step closer to the café filled Sarah with a deeper sense of dread. What would she find when she arrived? Would she still have a job? After a long night thinking about it, Sarah could see that she might have overreacted to the scone-gate, but she stood by the principle of the matter. Stealing was stealing.

'Morning,' said Hattie as Sarah walked in.

'Morning.'

'Everything OK now?'

'Yes.' Sarah watched Hattie from the corner of her eye as she gathered up an apron from behind the counter.

'No Fran today, I'm afraid.'

'Again?'

'She's got an appointment this morning. I told her to take the rest of the day off.'

And lumber me with two people's workload? 'OK.'

'Here's today's menu,' said Hattie. 'Fran asked me to let you know she did all the prep last night.'

'Thanks.' At least that was something.

'I've asked Dave to come in too.'

Great, a whole day with silent Dave. Mind you, it was better than having to work alone, just. 'What time's he getting here?'

'Should be here any minute.'

'OK, I'll make a start in the kitchen.'

Sarah walked through to the kitchen, wondering why Hattie hadn't mentioned yesterday's incident. Had she concluded Sarah was right? She should have taken the accusation more seriously, after all.

By half past ten, there was still no sign of Dave, and by eleven it was clear he wasn't coming. Sarah juggled cooking with the dirty dishes, feeling overwhelmed by the workload and struggling to keep up. Hattie and Felix offered their help, but soon the café was so busy they were tied up with their own work.

The lunchtime rush was manic. As another long order came in, Sarah felt the beginnings of panic. 'I'm just getting something from the freezer,' she called through to Hattie. She let herself out the back door and leaned against the shed which housed the freezers. *In two, three, four, hold two, three, four, out two, three, four, hold two, three, four.* With her heart rate settling, Sarah walked back to the kitchen. *You can do this*, she told herself.

Sarah's heart sank as Felix appeared in the kitchen, carrying a mountain of dirty dishes on a tray. 'Sorry,' he said. 'If you need to, let the dishes pile up and I'll help you deal with them later.'

'You can't spare a minute now?'

'No, it's mad out there. Poor Hattie is dealing with two awful customers. Nothing's right for them. They've already complained five times and are now trying to haggle a refund.'

'Something was wrong with the food?' asked Sarah, her heart hammering in her chest.

'Hmm, well, they're not about to leave a glowing review. They said the cake was dry, the soup too salty and the butter on the turn.'

Sarah fought back tears. She'd let Fran down, she'd let everyone down. Why did she believe them when they told her she could do this?

'Hey,' said Felix, walking over to Sarah and putting a hand on her back. 'Don't take it to heart. All the other customers have commented on how delicious the food is. Even more so once they heard those two old hags complaining.'

'Thanks,' said Sarah, unable to say more for fear the tears would fall.

Hattie burst into the kitchen, biting on her arm to stifle a scream. 'I need a minute or I'm going to kill that pair out there.'

'Felix told me they're unhappy with the food. Hattie, I'm so sorry.'

'Don't you go apologising. You've done nothing wrong. I tasted some of their leftovers and the food was delicious. If it makes you feel any better, it's not just you who's been on the receiving end of their wrath.'

'What else did they complain about?'

'Everything. The café's too stuffy, the café's too noisy, the hot drinks weren't hot enough, the water not cold enough, the staff aren't friendly enough, the service isn't quick enough. God, I'm close to throttling them. Now they're asking for a refund. I know the customer's always right, but they've had two full meals, two coffees, and three slices of cake between them. If I refund all of that, we'll go bloody bankrupt.'

'As chef I should apologise.'

'No,' said Hattie. 'They're scroungers trying to get a free meal.'

'Sending Sarah out there might not be such a bad idea,' said Felix. 'Maybe your bluntness will come in handy for once?'

'Thanks,' muttered Sarah, disliking the amusement in Felix's tone.

'Felix could be right,' said Hattie. 'You can be very matter of fact when you need to be. Perhaps a bit of bluntness is called for on this occasion. To be honest, I'm not sure I can face them again.'

'Fine,' said Sarah.

'I'll come with you,' said Felix, following Sarah out of the kitchen. 'There they are,' said Felix, pointing to two women tapping their fingers against the counter.

Sarah froze. All her breathing work undone, heat raced through her body, turning her face tomato red. She sucked in air, but it came in quick shallow bursts, which left her feeling dizzy. One woman turned round.

'Sarah, thank goodness you're here. I don't know what kind of place this is, but the service has been terrible. And as for the food...'

After a lengthy pause, Sarah found her voice. 'Mum, what are you doing here?'

'You told us you worked here, so we thought we'd come and see the place for ourselves. Wish we'd gone with the group on their outing to Charlestown, though. This place is a rip-off. I'd like a word with your chef. He doesn't know his arse from his elbow.'

'Mum, I'm the chef today. It was me who made your food.'

Cynthia burst out laughing. 'You made the food? Good God, whatever were they thinking, letting you loose in the kitchen?'

'Sarah's a superb cook,' said Felix, stepping forward and standing by Sarah's side.

'A superb cook? A superb cook who can't boil an egg.' Cynthia and Marjorie giggled like schoolgirls. 'I thought you were waitressing?' she said, once the laughter had subsided.

'I was, but then I started working in the kitchen and found I was rather good at it.'

'I've heard it all now,' said Cynthia, rolling her eyes. 'Now, why don't you run along and find that manager? We need to speak to her about what sort of discount she's going to give us.'

'There won't be a discount, Mum. The food was fine, the service was fine, it was you who was the problem.' Sarah's legs felt like jelly.

All her life, she'd done her mother's bidding. Worse still, she'd admired her sharp tongue and forceful personality. Now, for the first time, she saw the woman standing in front of her not as strong, but as a bully.

Cynthia glared at Sarah from beneath her false eyelashes. She slapped a twenty pound note down on the counter. 'You're just like your father,' she said, turning on her heel and storming out of the café, Marjorie in tow.

'That woman's your mother?' said Felix once he was certain the coast was clear.

Sarah couldn't look at him. A toxic mix of shame, embarrassment, anger, and despair swirled in the pit of her stomach. She turned on her heel and ran.

By the time Sarah reached the top of the hill, her lungs were burning, her limbs losing feeling. She slumped against a tree, pulling her knees up and placing her head between them. Her breaths came in painful gasps, sweat prickled her forehead, the world around her spinning as her vision blurred. Sarah grasped at her chest, the pain so severe it could be a heart attack. Would she die here, alone in the woods?

When they arrived, the tears brought some relief. How could Cynthia embarrass her like that? Sarah thought back to when she'd been at school. She remembered her mortification when Cynthia came in to complain to her teachers about inconsequential matters. All her mother achieved by her complaints was ensuring Sarah was disliked not only by pupils, but by staff members, too.

Now here she was, wrecking the first job Sarah felt good at. Tears of despair turned to tears of anger. Without a tissue in her pocket, Sarah blew her nose on a leaf, wiping her tears with the sleeve of her shirt. She couldn't go back to the café again. How could she face everyone?

'You're a hard woman to find.' Felix appeared through the undergrowth, a bottle of water in his hand. 'Here,' he said, holding the water out to Sarah.

She drank greedily, then passed the bottle back. 'Thank you,' she said.

'Your Mum's a piece of work,' said Felix, sitting down on the forest floor beside her.

Sarah gave a joyless laugh. 'Can you believe for years I admired her? I thought she was strong and brave. I thought my dad was in the wrong for leaving her, now I'm not so sure.'

'It's hard when we realise our parents aren't the people we'd hoped them to be.'

'Yes, but I expect most people realise that before the age of twenty-five. Thanks for sticking up for me back there. I appreciate it.'

'No problem,' said Felix.

'Do you want to hang out this evening? As friends, I mean.'

Felix's demeanor changed. 'Ah, I'd love to, but could we do tomorrow instead? I'm afraid I have plans.'

'Sure. Going anywhere nice?'

'Um, no, just a drink with a friend.'

He was lying, Sarah was certain.

Chapter 33

S arah sat by the entrance to her tipi, listening. She checked the time on her phone. Almost an hour of waiting and her legs were losing feeling. She stretched and allowed herself a silent yawn. Ignoring the voice inside her head telling her she was becoming a stalker, she peeped out of her door.

As Felix emerged into the night, Sarah whipped her head back inside and waited. If she strained her ears, she could just make out the tread of his feet on the grass. As his footsteps faded, Sarah risked another look. He was wearing a head torch, its light bouncing up and down with each step.

Sarah climbed out onto the grass and ran to his tipi. She poked her head around and spotted the torch's beam disappearing towards the forest. So he had lied to her. There was no pub in the direction he was heading.

A torch of her own would be too risky. There was no way Felix could find out he was being followed. He'd never speak to her again. Sarah scuttled along as fast as she could in the direction Felix had taken. Several times she stumbled on the roots of trees, but she pressed on.

Beneath a waning moon, the forest lay black as pitch. Now accustomed to its cacophony of nocturnal creatures, it didn't scare Sarah as it once had. Instead, she worried about losing sight of Felix and becoming lost in the mass of trees around her. At least the night was warm, spring sliding in to summer with each passing day.

The torch light disappeared, and Sarah increased her pace. As she rounded a bend, the pool of orange light came into view and Sarah hung back, pressing in to a moss-covered bank for fear of being seen. Sarah watched as Felix paused and pulled out his phone. The light caught his face and exposed a smile playing on his lips as he tapped out a message.

With his phone back in his jacket pocket, Felix pressed on up the hill. Sarah's foot caught a stone, which went spinning across the path. Felix stopped in the middle of the path. Sarah crouched beside a bush, cursing her mistake. The head torch's beam spun around, illuminating all corners of the path. Sarah's heart hammered as the light drew near.

In one swift movement, the light retreated, Felix satisfied he was alone in the woods. As the path reached the summit of the hill, Felix turned and disappeared into what looked to Sarah like dense undergrowth. She sped up, hugging the bank beside the path, aware that on the far side was a sheer drop to the valley floor. The torch light had vanished beneath the mass of ferns, trunks and dense undergrowth.

Sarah proceeded with caution, climbing the steep bank by clinging on to tree roots and using protruding stones as steps. As she stepped further into the leafy darkness, thorns tore at her clothes, nettles stroked and stung her bare hands. After walking a few more metres, Sarah felt the beginnings of fear surfacing. It would be very easy to get lost in a place like this. What the hell was she doing? Perhaps Felix just fancied a night walk?

Amidst the sounds of the forest, human voices reached Sarah. They were too far away to make out the words, but close enough to tell one was male, the other female. So Felix had come out here to meet his mystery woman, after all. Sarah took a few tentative steps towards the voices. She heard laughter, and from nowhere, a burst of orange pierced through the black night.

The light grew in intensity, its flicker and multitude of oranges, reds and yellows confirming Felix had lit a fire. A thin swirl of smoke danced above the forest floor. Sarah was closer to them than she'd thought. Too close. She took a step back and a storm-felled bare branch spiked her back. She let out a cry, then clapped a hand across her mouth. The voices paused. The sound of a snapping branch told Sarah they were coming to find the source of the cry.

With as much speed as the undergrowth would allow, Sarah retraced her steps, finding the steep bank and sliding down it. Stones battered against her skin, thorns tore at her clothes. She landed in a heap at the bottom, the sound of voices not far behind her. Sarah turned and ran. Gravity propelled her forward, and she flew down the wide path.

As she neared the bottom of the path, Sarah's boot caught on a tree root. She flung forward, her palms skidding along the gravel floor, her forehead meeting with a jutting rock. Sarah looked behind her. In the distance, the light of a torch punctured the forest's darkness. Felix and the mystery woman were only a few minutes behind her.

Sarah heaved herself off the ground, rubbed her hands against her jeans and sprinted back towards the tipi. With minutes to spare, Sarah rushed inside, closing the doors behind her. There was no time to remove her clothes, so she kicked off her boots and climbed beneath the duvet, fully clothed. She pulled the duvet up around her chin and arranged her hair to cover the gash on her head.

Sarah lay as still as she could as footsteps approached her tipi. A thin line of blood trickled down her face, but Sarah didn't dare rub it away.

'Is she in there?' asked a woman's voice.

'I don't know. I'll check.'

Sarah swallowed down anger as she heard Felix open the door of her tipi. So much for privacy and personal space. She kept her breathing slow, adding in the occasional light snore.

'She's fast asleep,' said Felix, closing the door to her tipi. 'It couldn't have been her out there.'

'Then who was it? Felix, no one can know I'm here.'

'I know. Don't worry, it was just an animal.'

'An animal? You heard the noise, it was human.'

'It couldn't have been. There's no one around except us and Sarah, and she's fast asleep in there.'

'She could be faking.'

'I know what her snoring sounds like. Trust me, she's asleep.'

I don't snore, thought Sarah, keeping her body still as a corpse.

'Come on, I'll walk you back, then I'd better get some rest.'

'Thanks, you're the best,' said the woman. Sarah heard the unmistakable sound of a kiss being planted on Felix's cheek.

Sarah waited till the voices had faded into the night before she dared to move. She slipped on her boots, creeping out of the tipi towards the compost toilet. Once inside, she checked herself in the rusty mirror hanging on the door. The gash on her forehead would be hard to explain. She cleaned it the best she could, then scrubbed her grazed hands until certain all gravel and dirt had washed away.

Back in her tipi, Sarah removed her clothes and folded them in a pile. Her jumper, torn in so many places, would need to go in the bin. Her jeans were grass-stained, a brown layer of dirt clinging to the knees after her tumble. She'd deal with them tomorrow.

Exhausted by her midnight excursion, Sarah had no time to ponder over what Felix was up to, for as soon as her head hit the pillow, she fell into the deepest of sleeps.

*

Sarah washed and dressed early. Despite the sunny day, she wore a long-sleeved top to hide the bramble scratches on her arms. With her jeans covered in mud, Sarah pulled on a pair of leggings, hating how they exposed her too-large thighs and enormous bum. The concealer in her makeup bag had covered some of the bruising around her head wound, but a bright streak of red still lay dashed across her forehead.

Fran was already in the kitchen when she got to work. 'My God, what happened to you?'

'I fell on my way back from the toilet last night,' said Sarah, feeling the lie was justified.

'It looks nasty. Get it checked out by a doctor.'

'It's not as bad as it looks. How come you're in so early?'

'Oh, I just fancied the chance to get ahead of things.'

'Right, well, I'm here now, so let me help you.'

When Fran asked Sarah to chop lemons for the lemon drizzle cake, she kept quiet about her grazed hands. As the acidic juices bled into her skin, Sarah fought back tears. Despite her wounds, she remained convinced following Felix had been the right thing to do. It was better to know what she was dealing with.

As she was thinking of him, Felix walked into the kitchen. He stopped in his tracks when he saw Sarah. 'What the...'

'Silly girl fell on her way back from the toilet,' said Fran. 'You'd think she'd learned by now to take a torch with her.'

'Yes,' said Felix, eyeing Sarah through narrowed eyes, 'you'd think she would. What time did this happen? I heard nothing. I'd have helped if I'd known.'

'Oh, I'm not sure,' said Sarah. 'I woke in the small hours with a dicky tummy. I guess I was in a rush and not looking where I was going.'

'Hmm,' said Felix. 'Well, I wish you'd told me. That gash looks nasty.'

'It's just a scratch.'

'If you say so,' said Felix. He gave Sarah one last inscrutable look before turning on his heel and heading back into the café.

'What was all that about?' asked Fran.

'What?'

'You could cut the atmosphere with a knife. Have you two been falling out again?'

'No,' said Sarah. 'Nothing like that.'

There was no point speaking ill of Felix. She was the only person who recognised his true colours. She'd wait until she had enough evidence, then expose him for the liar he was.

Chapter 34

When Sarah arrived at Kate's house, she found her cheerful friend quiet and withdrawn. Kate sat under a blanket on her purple sofa, a glass of wine in hand, magazines spread across her lap.

'Hi, everything OK?'

'Urgh,' said Kate, throwing a magazine down onto a growing pile. 'I think my head's going to explode. Who knew organising a small wedding could be so stressful?'

Despite looking forward to their weekly meetings, the late night chasing Felix through the woods had caught up with Sarah. She wasn't in the mood to be picking someone else off the floor. She had enough of her own problems to deal with. 'I don't understand why you're getting so stressed.'

Kate stared at Sarah, a frown creasing her skin. 'Haven't you been listening to me these past few weeks? The seating plan is a nightmare, the dressmaker isn't sure she can get the alterations done in time, and I've got Bob's mum trying to invite the whole of Bodmin. I've got less than twenty people coming from my side. His list is pushing two hundred.'

'Just tell him they can't come.'

'Easier said than done. Apparently, it's rude not to invite second cousins, even if he's seen none of them for twenty years. He wants his mum to invite all her friends, and I get that, but it's our wedding, not hers.'

'Is it a money thing?'

'What? No. It's just not the simple wedding I want.'

'At least the menu's sorted.'

'Thank goodness for small mercies.'

'So who's coming from your side?'

'My friend Flo, Joy of course, some friends from uni and a few guests I've had to stay.'

'You've invited B&B guests?'

'It's not as though I've got any family to invite.' Kate looked downcast, but Sarah struggled to be sympathetic. Couldn't she see how lucky she was planning a wedding in the first place?

'Top up?'

'Why not?'

Sarah carried the bottle of wine through to the living room and topped up their glasses.

'Sorry for going all Bridezilla on you,' said Kate. 'How are things going with you?'

'They've been better.'

'What's happened?'

'First off, someone stole five scones from the kitchen. Everyone thought I was in the wrong trying to find out who the culprit was.'

Kate sniggered behind her hand. 'Scones?'

Sarah smirked. 'I know, not my finest hour. I was upset by something else and blew the scone debacle out of proportion. Mind you, I stand by the principle. Nobody should steal anything. But that was just the start. I pissed off Hattie by being rude to the Saturday girls, but you should have seen their faces, they looked guilty as hell.'

'OK...'

'Then my mother shows up in town and made a fool out of me in front of all my colleagues. You had a lucky escape, she wanted to stay here.'

'Oh, you should have said. It would have been nice to meet your mum.'

'Trust me, you're lucky you didn't have to. If you do ever have the misfortune of meeting her, you'll thank me for keeping her away.'

'She sounds intriguing. So is it your mum that's put you in a bad mood?'

'I'm not in a... fine, OK, so I'm feeling a little grumpy, though you're a fine one to talk, sitting here all glum. Anyway, it's not just Mum. There's also Felix...'

'What about Felix?'

Sarah blushed and took a sip of her wine. 'I thought we were becoming friends. We were getting close, you know?'

'Close like friends, or close like something more?'

'I thought it was something more, but I was wrong. He's a liar and a cheat.'

'What happened?'

'I saw him hugging some girl, then one night I followed him when he said he was going to the pub, but he wasn't. He was meeting *her*.'

'Have you asked him about it? There could be an innocent explanation.'

'Of course I haven't asked him about it. He's made a fool of me once already. I'll not humiliate myself by showing I'm bothered.'

'I'm sorry to hear things aren't going well with him. He seemed a lovely guy the couple of times I met him.'

'Appearances can be deceptive.'

'How about we look at table decorations this week?'

'Sure.'

For the next hour, Kate and Sarah rifled through magazines, cutting out pictures of floral displays and sticking them into Kate's scrap book. Not for the first time, Sarah wondered why she'd been drafted in to help. It wasn't like she had an artist's eye. Most of the table decorations looked the same to her.

'This is nice,' said Kate, pointing to one design. 'I reckon I could have a go at making that myself. We could collect some greenery from the forest.'

'Yes, that sounds good.'

Kate sighed and placed her wine down on the table. 'Look, Sarah. I can't hold off telling you any longer.'

'What?'

'We've invited Mark and Gary to the wedding.'

'You've what?'

'We got on well with them when they came to stay and the invite just kind of slipped out.'

'Oh.'

'I'm sorry, I know you said you were friends, but I understand it could be awkward.'

Sarah flushed. She should have known lies would get her nowhere. 'Weddings are hard enough for me without my ex being there.'

'Maybe you'll have patched things up with Felix by then? Anyway, as you're doing the catering, I doubt your paths will cross that much.'

Sarah frowned. 'I think I'd better get going.'

'Sarah, don't be like that.'

'I'm not being like anything.'

'At least wait till Bob's back so he can drive you home.'

'I told my dad I'd call him this evening. It's getting late and I know he likes to get to bed early. Tell Bob not to worry about a lift tonight. I'll get a taxi home.'

'You're sure you're not angry with me?'

Sarah swallowed down her hurt. 'I'm sure.'

'And you'll be there for my fitting next week?'

'Of course.'

'OK then.' Kate drew Sarah into an awkward hug. 'I'll text you the details of the fitting. You're sure you'll be OK getting home?'

'Yes.'

'OK.'

Sarah left the house and walked along the dark street. She liked Bodmin in daylight, but felt vulnerable walking the streets after dark. She told herself she was safer here than in the town she grew up, but that didn't stop her jumping at noises and being spooked by shadows.

A call to a taxi firm informed Sarah there would be a forty-five minute wait. She should have swallowed her pride and waited for Bob to give her a lift, but then she would've had to pretend she wasn't hurt that Kate and Bob had invited Mark to the wedding.

Sarah found a bench positioned below a street light and pulled out her phone. The lie of needing to call Colin held an element of truth. She'd had three messages from him that week asking when was a good time to call. He picked up on the third ring.

'Sarah?'

'Hi, Dad. Where are you?'

The noise on the other end of the phone was deafening, and Sarah struggled to hear her father's voice.

'I'm in the pub with a couple of mates. Hang on, it's pretty noisy in here, I'll just go outside.'

'That's better,' said Sarah, as the racket on the other end of the phone lessened. 'Sorry it's taken me a while to call, it's been a busy week.'

'No problem. Are you in your tipi? I loved the photos you sent, by the way. It looks just my kind of place.' Sarah struggled to imagine the father she'd known sleeping under canvas.

'No,' said Sarah, 'I'm...' *On a bench in the middle of town, in the dark, on my own.* 'I'm at a friend's house.'

'That sounds nice. You can call me another time if you're busy with your friends.'

'No, it's fine.'

'OK.'

Did she detect disappointment in her father's voice? Was it he who wanted to get back to his friends?

'Are you still sailing your way around the Norfolk broads?'

'Yes, I am. I could get used to the lifestyle. In fact, I'm thinking about buying myself a boat.'

'Right. How are things going with the house?'

'There have been a few delays with the buyer's chain, but it should all be done and dusted in a month.'

'Great,' said Sarah, struggling to keep the disappointment from her voice.

'Would it be OK if we had a longer chat another time? Only it's karaoke night at the pub and I've signed up to sing a Beatles number with my mates.'

Mates? Karaoke? Who was this man she was speaking to? 'No problem. I'll get back to my friends too. Speak soon.'

Sarah hung up the phone and looked around her. While her father was having the time of his life in a pub with friends, she was sitting alone in the dark, her only company the odd drunk stumbling by. So much for a new life, a fresh start. Sarah checked her watch, praying the taxi wouldn't be much longer.

Chapter 35

Sarah looked from the paper in her hand and back to the cupboard. 'Fran? Something's not right here.'

'What's wrong?'

'You know that delivery we had yesterday?'

'What about it?'

'I don't understand. I've been checking the inventory and lots of the items are missing.'

'They can't be. I checked everything in myself.'

'I know. But look at this.'

Fran looked over Sarah's shoulder. 'It looks like all the perishables are there, it's the tinned goods that are missing. This is strange. You know, it could be me. I've been distracted lately.'

You're telling me, thought Sarah. Fran hadn't been her usual self for weeks. Sarah had tried to broach the subject, but Fran wasn't having any of it. 'Distracted by anything in particular?' asked Sarah, deciding to try one last time to prise information from Fran.

'I think it's just old age,' said Fran. 'I'll call the suppliers later and check if it's a mistake at their end. I can't see anyone here pinching a few tins and a couple of packets of dried fruit.'

'Hmm,' said Sarah, unconvinced.

The day dragged. It was quiet in the café and Sarah spent more time standing around than working. Outside, the sun blazed, giving an early taste of the summer to come. The few walkers around sat under canopies of trees in the dappled sunlight, drinking from flasks and eating home-made sandwiches.

'It's so quiet today,' said Sarah, leaning against the worktop and taking a sip from her tenth cup of tea.

'It always happens around this time of year,' said Fran. 'The first hot day of the year, all the locals flock to the beaches. They try to get their beach fix before the tourists descend and take up every spare inch of sand. I'm grateful for the rest.'

'You're sure everything's OK?' asked Sarah, looking over at her friend. Fran's sudden change in appearance worried Sarah. The plump, jolly woman she'd met when she first arrived had become a grey shadow. The skirts and blouses Fran wore like a uniform hung off her and Sarah guessed she must have lost at least a couple of stone in as many months. As much as Sarah would love that kind of weight loss, it didn't suit Fran. Her skin hung from her face, aging her by several decades. Her rosy cheeks were a light shade of grey, purple crescents sitting beneath her eyes.

'How many times do I have to tell you,' said Fran, 'everything is fine. Apart from your nagging, that is. Sarah, you're driving me up the wall with your concerned looks and constant questions.'

'I'm only worried about you. You don't seem yourself at the moment.'

'And how would you know what I'm like when we've known each other five minutes?'

Fran's words landed like a slap. What had happened to the woman she counted as a friend, with her endless patience and ever present ability to make Sarah smile? 'Sorry to have troubled you,' said Sarah. 'I'll get on with cleaning the oven, seeing as there's nothing else to do.'

'Good idea,' said Fran. 'I'll phone the suppliers and check about that order.'

Sarah hunched beside the oven, fighting back tears. She took her confusion and frustration out on the oven, scraping and scrubbing at its metal until it gleamed as new.

'I've spoken to the suppliers,' said Fran. 'They said they sent over everything we'd ordered, so there must be a problem at our end. Also, Sarah, I'm sorry I snapped. I've got a few things going on at home, but I don't feel able to share them with you just yet.'

'I understand. But you know I'm here if you need me.'

'Thank you,' said Fran. 'That means a lot. Now as we're quiet, why don't I teach you how to make hommity pie?'

Sarah smiled. Fran may have changed, but her enthusiasm for food was as strong as ever.

Throughout the day, the café remained quiet. At four o'clock, Hattie announced she was going to close early. 'There's no point us all hanging around with no one about. Enjoy an evening off. The school holidays are only just around the corner, so rest while you can.'

Sarah went to the staff toilet to collect her bag and coat. Felix walked in behind her, the space small for two people.

'I'll only be a minute,' said Sarah, unhooking her bag from a peg.

'Don't worry, no rush, I just need to get my bag.'

'Where is it? I can get it for you?'

'Don't worry about it.'

'Felix,' said Sarah, 'I know things are awkward between us, but there's no need to be like that.' Sarah looked around and saw Felix's bag poking out from beneath a bench. 'Here it is,' said Sarah, pulling it out. She tried to lift it and almost dropped it back down. 'My God, what have you got in there?'

'Nothing,' said Felix, leaning forward and snatching the bag from Sarah's hands. 'It's just my camera. I thought I'd head into the forest and take a few photos after work.'

'Right,' said Sarah. As she handed over the bag, she felt something cylindrical pushing at the fabric.

Felix took his bag and rushed out of the room. Sarah watched him leave, her mind pulling together pieces of information. Felix was the thief. There was no doubt about it. But why would he feel the need to steal from them? Hattie fed them well. *Oh*, thought Sarah. *Maybe the food isn't for him.*

*

Sarah waited for Felix to leave. Tonight, rather than following him, she wanted him out of the way. As the sun slunk low in the sky, she heard him undo the door of his tipi. She grabbed a towel and wash bag and stepped outside.

'Hi,' Sarah called.

'Oh, hi,' said Felix, looking shifty.

'Off anywhere nice?'

'Just heading out to take some photos of the sunset.'

'Ah yes, you said. I didn't realise you were into photography.'

'It's a new hobby,' said Felix, his words clipped, his hands playing with the strap of his bag.

'You seem in a hurry.'

'Don't want to miss the sunset, that's all.'

'Right,' said Sarah. 'Well, I'll leave you to it. I'm just off to have a shower. Keep your fingers crossed there's some hot water.' She gave what she hoped was a carefree laugh.

Felix mimicked her laugh with one of his own. He held up a hand and crossed his fingers. 'Have a good evening.'

'You too. Oh, and I'd love to see the photos you take,' said Sarah, enjoying watching him squirm.

'I'd wait till I've had a practice if I were you. I haven't quite got the hang of focusing yet. Everything seems to come out in a blur.'

Oh, Felix, you're such a terrible liar. 'OK then, see you.'

'See you.'

Sarah headed toward the shower. As soon as she was out of sight of the tipis, she crouched behind a bush and set her phone timer to five minutes. She had to time this right. After what felt like an age, Sarah's phone vibrated in her palm and she crept out from her hiding spot. She approached the tipis with caution, wondering if five minutes had been long enough.

As light slipped from the sky, Sarah ran to Felix's tipi and darted inside. She pulled the door closed behind her and stood, hands on hips. There was no way Hattie would take her seriously without evidence, and it wasn't as if Felix had many places to hide it.

Over the past few weeks, Sarah had been totting up the value of all that went missing. She'd kept most of the missing items to herself, a few slices of flapjack here, a couple of pints of milk there. Now that the total had exceeded two hundred pounds, and with the latest order showing the stealing was ramping up, now was the time to act.

The last puzzle piece was collecting irrefutable evidence. If she shared her suspicions without it, Hattie would laugh her out of the café. Sarah could picture the scene... *Let me get this right. You felt Felix's bag, and it was heavy? You're accusing him of stealing because he has a heavy bag?* Oh, how they would laugh. She'd be back to spiky Sarah, the troublemaker, the staff member who couldn't work as part of a team. Well, she wouldn't have that happen again. This time, she'd be prepared.

Sarah looked through the chest of drawers beside Felix's bed. All she found were a few books and plenty of well-worn clothes. She tried the chest at the end of the bed, disappointed as her hands rifled through woollen blankets. Flat on her stomach, Sarah began pulling items out from under Felix's bed. She'd removed three suitcases before she found what she was looking for.

The large plastic tub took quite some effort to drag out. Sarah eased it from under the bed, but when she tried to lift it, found she didn't have the strength. She clicked open the lid and began removing the contents and laying it out beside her. Tins, jars, bags of pasta and rice. There was enough food hidden in the box to feed an army. Was he preparing for a nuclear fallout?

As vigilant as she'd been, Sarah discovered she had underestimated the extent of Felix's light-fingered behaviour. Mental maths had never been her strong point, but besides all the fresh food she'd witness go missing, this new find had to bring the total closer to five hundred pounds. Five hundred pounds worth of stock. What the hell was Felix thinking? Was he suffering from kleptomania? Whatever the cause, he needed to be called out on it.

Sarah took her phone from her pocket and photographed the contents of the box. Next, she replaced everything as she found it and slid the box back into its original position. With one last check everything was in its rightful place, Sarah left the tipi and returned to her own.

She'd need to pick her moment with care. There was no rush, it might be fun to watch Felix go about his business unaware for a few days. Soon enough, he'd learn that Sarah was not someone you messed around. Soon enough he'd be exposed as the lying, cheating, kleptomaniac he was.

Chapter 36

'This is all I need,' said Sarah, hands on her hips, surveying the damage.

'Somewhere you need to be?' asked Felix.

'Yes, Kate has her final dress fitting this morning. I'd booked a taxi for nine, which I've had to cancel.'

'Does Fran know about this?'

'Yes, Hattie's calling her now.'

'I'm sure she'd give you a lift back to Bodmin.'

Sarah grimaced. She'd hoped never to be in a car with Fran again.

'Fran's on her way,' said Hattie, walking into the kitchen with a mop and bucket. 'Felix, can you get on with mopping? Me and Sarah will empty the food. If we put it all on the counter, Fran can decide what to keep and what needs to be binned.'

The three of them set to work, Sarah cursing under her breath. Of all the days for a freezer to break, this was the worst. She hoped they could salvage enough food from the mess. Otherwise, it would mean even longer hours each day as they worked to replace it.

'Sorry for calling you in on your day off,' said Hattie as Fran arrived. 'I thought you'd want to be here before we chuck stuff.'

'Too right,' said Fran, rolling up her sleeves.

'Checking the clock every five seconds won't make us go any faster,' said Felix after they'd been cleaning and sorting for an hour.

'Don't worry,' said Fran, patting Sarah's arm. 'We're almost done. I know today's important to you.'

'Thank you,' said Sarah. She couldn't bear the fact she was letting Kate down on such an important occasion. It was an honour to be invited to the dress fitting. Despite having no mother or sisters, Sarah was sure there were other people Kate could have chosen for the task. But she'd picked her, and Sarah didn't take the responsibility lightly.

*

The clock on the car's dashboard taunted Sarah. She had promised Kate she'd be on time for the dress fitting and was already ten minutes late. Fran screeched around a bend, narrowly missing a collision with a motorbike.

'Don't worry, you'll only be a few minutes late.'

'I just wish I could call Kate and let her know I'm on my way. My stupid phone has no signal.'

'Use mine,' said Fran.

'Are you sure?'

'Of course I'm sure. It's in my bag. I'll get it for you.' Fran looked behind her and the car swerved.

'I'll get it,' said Sarah, grabbing Fran's bag from the back seat.

'The code's one, two, three, four,' said Fran.

Sarah bit her tongue, saving the lecture on online security for when Fran didn't need to concentrate on the road. Kate didn't answer the phone, so Sarah left an apologetic message explaining that she was on her way and would be in town any minute now. When Fran pulled the car to a stop on the high street, Sarah breathed a sigh of relief.

'Thanks for the lift,' she said, climbing out of the car, grateful to have all her limbs intact.

Sarah walked up the high street and knocked on Kate's door.

'Hi, Sarah,' said Bob. 'I'm afraid Kate had to go on ahead. I've borrowed Mum's car so I can give you a lift.'

'How far is it? I can walk if it's easier.'

'It's not far, but I know Kate wants you to be there for the big reveal, so I'll take you over there then make myself scarce.'

'Thanks.'

Compared to Fran, Bob drove like a grandad, his mother's car crawling up the hill, and coming to a near halt each time they encountered a speed bump. Sarah reached for her phone to check the time.

'Oh no.'

'What is it?'

'I borrowed Fran's phone to call Kate, but must have put it back in my bag.'

'Do you want me to drop it off to her?'

'No, I don't know where she lives. I'll go to the fitting, then call Hattie for Fran's address and drop it round to her once we're done.'

'OK, if you're sure.'

Bob pulled the car up outside what looked like an ordinary bungalow. The only sign of the business which operated from it was a discreet needle and thread design on the front gate. Sarah waved to Bob, then walked up to the front door.

'Just in time,' said a middle-aged woman with glasses perched on the end of her nose. 'She's in the dress and waiting for you before she comes out.'

Sarah followed the woman into the house. They walked through a kitchen and into a large conservatory. Where the rest of the house was tidy and bland, in the conservatory colourful fabrics hung from every surface. A large sewing machine sat centre stage in the room, surrounded by faceless mannequins. A silk curtain partitioned off a corner of the room.

'Hello, dear,' said Joy. Sarah hadn't noticed her sitting in an old rocking chair.

'Oh, hi, Joy, I didn't realise you'd be here too.'

'I couldn't resist the chance to get a sneak peek at Kate in her dress.'

'Thank God you're here,' came Kate's voice from behind the curtain.

'Yes, sorry I'm late. We had a disaster with a broken freezer and I couldn't leave till we had transferred all the food to another one. Fran drove like an F1 driver on the way to Bodmin.'

Joy tutted. 'As much as I love Fran, I'd never risk getting in a car with her. It's more than my life's worth.'

'I think you're onto something there, Joy,' said Sarah.

'Ready?' said Kate.

'Put us out of our misery,' said Joy.

'Ta da!' Kate emerged from behind the curtain, a vision in vintage lace. Sarah found herself lost for words. She looked over at Joy, whose cheeks were wet with tears.

'What do you think?' asked Kate, looking from Sarah to Joy.

Sarah fought the lump in her throat. 'You look incredible. I can't believe you got that dress so cheap.'

'I've always had an eye for a bargain,' laughed Kate, turning to see herself in the full-length mirror. 'How about you, Joy? Do you think my Nan would have approved?'

Joy dabbed her eyes with a hanky. 'She would have been crying more than I am. You're so beautiful, that Bob's a lucky man. Now, dear, there's something I'd like you to have. I won't be offended if you don't want it, but I thought it might finish the outfit.' Joy reached into her bag and pulled out a package wrapped in tissue paper. She handed it to Kate.

'Is this... is this...' Now it was Kate's turn to brush away tears.

'I know it's not the same as having an heirloom from your own grandmother, but it seemed silly keeping my veil all these years. It's not like my son's ever going to wear it.'

Kate rushed over to Joy and wrapped her arms around her. Sarah looked on with envy. Joy may not be related to Kate by blood, but Sarah couldn't imagine replicating this scene with her own family. When she'd been planning her own ill-fated wedding to Mark, all Cynthia had wanted to do was take over, imposing her own ideas as if it were her getting married. Sarah wondered if Kate knew how lucky she was.

The dress maker stepped forward and took the veil from Kate's hand. 'Here,' she said, pinning it to the back of Kate's head. 'It's perfect.'

'Thank you so much,' said Kate. 'You've done such a good job with these alterations. And thank you too, Joy. You don't know how much this means to me,' said Kate, running her fingers over the antique lace adorning her hair. 'Now, Sarah. I have a little surprise for you.'

'Really?'

'Yes.' Kate's eyes glinted. 'Have a look in that box.'

Sarah looked at the large box Kate was pointing to. Was Kate about to present her with a bridesmaid dress? Sarah had longed to be a bridesmaid ever since she was a little girl, but with no family members of marrying age, and no friends, she'd long given up on the dream.

'Go on,' said Kate, clapping her hands like an excitable child. 'Open it.'

Sarah reached down to the box with trembling fingers. She lifted the lid to reveal a layer of pink tissue paper. Her eyes filled with tears. This was the moment she had always dreamed of. Her whole body shook as she peeled back the top layer of paper.

Sarah's heart plummeted. She pulled the fabric from the box and held it to the light, lost for words.

'Try it on,' said Kate, grinning.

Sarah slipped the fabric over her head.

'Oh, my, that is marvellous,' said Joy, eyeing Sarah in admiration.

Sarah turned to look in the mirror. Never had she felt more foolish. An apron covered her body. An apron. Not the pastel taffeta dress she'd hoped for.

'Do you like it?' asked Kate. 'I had it made especially. I saw the fabric in a charity shop and fell in love with it. The flowers are the exact type we're having at the wedding.'

'It's great,' said Sarah, her voice monotone. Kate was right about the fabric, it was pretty. But as presents went, Sarah had never felt so undervalued. 'Sorry,' she said, pulling off the apron and putting it back in the box. 'I have to go. I picked up Fran's phone by mistake and need to drop it back to her.'

'Oh,' said Kate, her smile fading. 'That's a shame. I thought we were going for a drink after the fitting.'

'Yes, sorry about that. I'd love to go another time.'

'OK. Oh, and Sarah?'

'Yes?'

'Don't tell Fran about the apron. I've had one made up for her too and I want it to be a surprise.'

'OK.'

Sarah found her way out of the house, despite her vision being blurred by tears. All those hours she'd spent with Kate, thinking they were friends. All those hours listening to her moan about seating plans, grumble about her mother-in-law, pore over floral arrangements. All that time given in the hope of friendship, and all along, Kate only saw her as the hired help.

Chapter 37

'Hattie, hi, it's Sarah.'

'Sarah? Is everything OK? You sound upset.'

'I'm fine,' lied Sarah. 'It's just hay fever.'

'That's good. Not that you have hay fever I mean, but I'm pleased you're not upset. You sound like you've been crying.' Hattie laughed, and Sarah choked out a bitter laugh of her own. 'How did the dress fitting go?'

'Yeah, great. The reason I'm calling is that I picked up Fran's phone by mistake. Could you give me her address and I'll drop it back to her while I'm in town?'

There was a pause on the line.

'Hattie? Are you still there?'

'Yes, sorry. Um, how about you bring it back to the café? Fran will be in tomorrow and you can give it back to her then.'

'That's stupid, as I'm in Bodmin now. I may as well take it back to her while I'm here.'

'Yes, but I'm not supposed to give out staff details.'

Sarah laughed. 'Hattie, this is Fran we're talking about. I work with the woman every day. What do you think I'm going to do, burgle her house?'

'Fine, I'll give you the address, but could you post the phone through the letter box? Fran hasn't been too well and she might be sleeping.'

'She seemed fine this morning.'

Hattie sighed down the phone. 'Look, just put it through the letter box, please. I'll text you the address.'

'OK,' said Sarah, hanging up the phone.

After walking for ten minutes, Sarah stopped to check the map on her phone. She turned down a narrow street, ramshackle terraced houses packed together on either side of the road.

Number nine stood out from the other houses. A trimmed hedge lined the border between the property and the road. Herbs grew up between the gravel, trimmed into uniform sizes. A window box housed coloured bedding plants and a crazy paving path led to the front door, where two stone lions guarded the entrance.

The house was well cared for, but Sarah had been expecting something a little more homely, a little less regimented. As Sarah walked up the path, a net curtain twitched. Hattie had been specific about not knocking, but now, seen, Sarah felt she had little choice.

Before she knocked, the door opened a crack.

'What are you doing here?' Fran's voice held none of its usual warmth.

'I put your phone in my bag by mistake,' said Sarah, trying to peer around the crack to where Fran stood.

Fran slipped a hand beyond the door and held it out. 'Give it here then.'

Sarah fumbled in her bag.

'Please hurry.'

'Sorry,' said Sarah. 'I didn't realise you were busy. I was going to put it through the letter box, but I saw you at the window and thought it would be rude not to say hello.'

'Fine. You've said hello. Now, if you don't mind, I've got things to be getting on with.'

'OK,' said Sarah. She hadn't thought she could feel worse than when she left Kate, but it turned out she could. As Sarah turned to leave, the gate behind her creaked open. She turned to see a middle-aged man walking towards her. Dressed in chinos and a golfing sweater, he had a bag of clubs slung over his shoulder.

'Didn't you see the sign?' he snapped, pointing to the front door. 'No cold callers.'

'Oh, sorry, I'm not a cold caller. My name's Sarah, I work with Fran.'

'I see,' said the man, his demeanor changing. Gone was the snappy voice and squinting eyes. His face broadened in to a smile. 'I hope my wife's invited you in for a cup of tea?'

'Um...'

The front door opened, and Fran filled the doorway. 'I wasn't sure when you'd be home,' she said.

'What's that got to do with anything?' The man laughed, walking past Sarah and kissing Fran on the cheek. 'You put the kettle on.' He turned to Sarah. 'Michael,' he said, 'pleased to meet you, Sarah.'

'Pleased to meet you too,' said Sarah, shaking his outstretched hand.

'In we go then,' he said, leading Sarah into a narrow hallway. 'Shoes off, please.'

Sarah bent down to untie her laces, wishing she'd put a newer pair of socks on. She scrunched the end of her sock to hide the hole and tucked the folds of fabric between her toes. Michael exchanged his golfing shoes for a pair of slippers and propped his golf clubs against the wall.

'The sitting room is through here,' he said. 'Take a seat.'

Sarah followed him into the room, perching on the edge of a high-backed sofa. The room was formal, a three-piece suite more suited to an old folks' home filling most of the space. Beside the sofa sat a mahogany coffee table, polished to within an inch of its life. A fringed lamp stood in a corner, the television hidden in an old-fashioned cabinet.

'It's wonderful to meet one of Francesca's friends. I can't remember her ever inviting someone round. You know what she's like, a timid little mouse.'

Sarah wondered if they were talking about the same woman. Fran wasn't one to make a fuss, but she ruled the kitchen with quiet authority and wasn't timid about ensuring high standards.

'This is a lucky coincidence then,' said Sarah. 'It was silly of me putting her phone in my bag. I guess it's force of habit.'

Fran walked through carrying a tray. She placed it on the coffee table and began pouring tea from a teapot into bone china cups. Sarah hadn't had Fran down as a cup and saucer type of woman. At work, she enjoyed her tea in an over-sized mug with *World's Best Mum* painted on the side.

'I hope I'm not putting you to any trouble,' said Sarah.

'Not at all,' said Fran. She kept her eyes on the ground, her voice monotone. Sarah knew she'd made a big mistake, but wasn't sure what that mistake was. Don't friends call in on each other if they're nearby?

'Francesca tells me you're her dishwasher,' said Michael, accepting the tea Fran handed to him.

Dishwasher? What happened to protégé? 'Yes, that's about right.'

'And this is just a summer job, is it?'

'Yes,' said Sarah.

'Good for you. I've told Francesca to get out of that place till I'm blue in the face, but does she listen? Does she heck?' Michael laughed, but Sarah noticed Fran didn't join in.

'And why's that then?'

Michael laughed again. 'Baking cakes all day is hardly the job for a woman of Francesca's age. She'd be better off at home with me. Even when the boys were young, she insisted on going out to work. I told her there was no need. It's a man's job to provide for his family, and a woman's job to care for them.'

Sarah couldn't believe what she was hearing. She opened her mouth to reply, but Fran got there first.

'Michael, did I tell you I had a call from Elliot yesterday?'

'No, you didn't. Elliot is our eldest,' said Michael, pointing to a photograph on the mantlepiece of a young man in a cap and gown. 'And how was he? Still lounging about on a beach somewhere?'

'Elliot is a geologist,' said Fran, looking at Sarah for the first time. 'He's over in Thailand working for a conservation charity.'

'Wow, that sounds amazing.'

'Amazing? Goodness me, what is the world coming to?' Michael shook his head and took another sip of his tea.

'And what does your youngest son do?'

'Don't ask,' said Michael, scrunching up his nose like he'd just smelled something rotten.

'David is at art college,' said Fran.

'In Edinburgh of all places,' said Michael. 'Francesca wanted to visit him, but as I told her, he's got another thing coming if he thinks we're going to fork out to travel all that way. Silly boy should have gone to a proper university to study a serious subject somewhere we could get to. Do you know how long it takes to get from Cornwall to Edinburgh? An entire day! Can you believe that?'

'It sounds a long way,' said Sarah, burning her tongue as she tried to drink her tea with haste. She looked at her watch. 'I'm sorry, but I'd better make a move. Bob is giving me a lift home and he'll be expecting me. Would it be possible to use your toilet before I head off?'

'Down the corridor, first door on the left,' said Michael.

Sarah followed his directions and headed down a dark corridor. She found the toilet, but couldn't resist a quick peek behind the other two doors leading off the hallway. Checking behind her to make sure they didn't catch her, she poked her head round the first door.

An enormous mahogany dining table filled the room. Around it sat six uncomfortable-looking dining chairs. Ugly embossed wallpaper enclosed the room, a tall cabinet filled with dated crockery leaning against the far wall. There was nothing inviting about the room, and Sarah felt relieved at the certainty no dinner invite would be forthcoming.

Without making a sound, she closed the dining-room door and opened a second. Sarah stared at Fran's kitchen. Pine cupboards clustered around the small space, a narrow window looking out onto the garden. There was none of the organised chaos Sarah knew from work. Every worktop was bare, the polished sink empty. Where were all the appliances? Sarah knew Fran was particular about her workspace, but didn't have her pegged as a neat freak.

The murmur of voices filtered down the hallway and Sarah slipped into the downstairs cloakroom. A sickly shade of mint green paint covered the walls, the toilet and sink coloured peach. Sarah sat on the toilet and looked beside her. A doll in a ruffled skirt perched beside the toilet, hiding a toilet roll. Sarah had seen nothing like it. Nothing about the house fitted with the woman she knew. Had she got Fran so wrong?

'Thank you so much for the tea,' said Sarah, walking back into the sitting room. 'I'm sorry it's been such a brief visit.'

'You'll have to come for longer next time,' said Michael, standing and shaking Sarah's hand once more.

'I will.'

Sarah saw Fran flinch at her words. Why didn't she want Sarah to visit her at home? Sarah thanked her hosts once again and let herself out of the house. Her head was spinning. First Kate, now Fran. How had she got everything so wrong? These people didn't want to be her friend. Sarah fought back tears. How foolish to think she could begin again. How foolish to think she could form genuine friendships. Sarah plodded back towards town, vowing to keep herself to herself from now on. After all, why break the habit of a lifetime?

Chapter 38

What a day. Fran had barely spoken a word since she arrived, answering Sarah's questions with one word, refusing to meet her eye. *God*, thought Sarah, *who knew calling on a friend was the crime of the century?* Sarah glanced at Fran from the corner of her eye. Something wasn't right, and Sarah was sure it couldn't all be her fault.

Fran turned the radio up. *Fine, if she doesn't want to talk, I won't talk*, thought Sarah, keeping her back to her one-time friend as she scrubbed out her anger on an oil-encrusted baking tray.

A scream caused Sarah to turn. Fran stood clutching her side, a tray of muffins scattered across the floor beside the oven.

'What happened?' asked Sarah. Fran remained silent, her palm rubbing against her waist. 'Fran?'

'It's nothing. I must have twisted the wrong way.'

Fran tried to bend down to pick up the muffins, but fell back against the work top, clutching her side.

'Let me see.' Sarah fought off Fran's protests and lifted Fran's top. 'What the hell?' The whole of Fran's torso was covered in varying shades of green, blue, brown, and yellow. 'This is awful. What did you do to yourself?'

'It was a stupid mistake,' said Fran, eyes on the ground. 'I'd spilled some oil on the floor at home. I was rushing, not paying attention. I fell and caught my side on the corner of a cupboard door.'

'You've seen a doctor?'

Fran shook her head. 'There's no need to bother a doctor about it. It's only a bruise.'

'Fran, it looks to me like you might have broken a few ribs. When did this happen?'

'A few days ago.'

'And you've been working through the pain ever since?'

Fran nodded her head. 'It's nothing a few ibuprofen can't fix.'

'I think you should go to minor injuries.'

'There's nothing they can do, even if I've broken my ribs. They'll just tell me to rest and there's too much to do here.'

'I can cover for you. You need to take a few days off.'

'Please, just mind your own business. I don't need you mothering me, or poking your nose in. I just want to be left in peace to get on with my work.' Fran's voice rose with each word. Sarah took a step back, trying not to take Fran's words to heart. The woman was in pain. It was pride making her push Sarah away.

'Ladies,' said Hattie, strolling into the kitchen. 'I wonder if I could borrow you for an hour after work?'

Sarah looked at Fran. 'I think Fran could do with an early finish.'

'Is everything OK?' asked Hattie.

'She's injured.'

'I'm fine.'

'Fran, can you come with me for a minute, please?'

Unlike her response to Sarah's offer of help, Fran responded to Hattie with meek acceptance, removing her apron and following Hattie out of the kitchen. Sarah bent down and began clearing the muffins from the floor.

An hour later, Fran still hadn't reappeared. Sarah took the fresh batch of muffins out of the oven, admiring her handiwork as she laid them out on a cooling rack. She was washing the mixing bowl when Fran and Hattie reappeared.

Sarah studied Fran. Her face was puffy and blotchy, her eyes red-rimmed. What was going on?

'Sarah, can you hold the fort for the rest of the afternoon? Fran's going to head to my place and rest for a couple of hours.' Turning to Fran, Hattie handed her a set of keys. 'Are you sure you're up for coming later?'

Fran nodded. 'I want to be there.'

'If you're sure.' Turning back to Sarah, Hattie plastered a smile on her face. 'We've got a staff meeting after work.'

'Oh,' said Sarah, wondering what had prompted the sudden bout of staff management.

'We'll meet in the pub at six.'

'The pub?'

'Yes. I'll drive you all over there once we've closed up.'

'But why the pub? Wouldn't it would be easier just to meet here?'

'I thought I'd treat you all to a drink while we talk. We'll have had enough of coffee by then.'

'All right.'

At closing time, Sarah, Fran, Felix and Hattie climbed into her car and set off on the short drive to the local pub. No one spoke. If Fran and Felix knew the cause of the latest staff meeting, they weren't letting on.

As they made their way into the beer garden, it surprised Sarah to see Millie nursing a glass of wine at the furthest table. What was she doing there?

Just as she'd promised, Hattie bought the first round of drinks, setting them in front of everyone and taking a deep breath.

'I know this is unorthodox,' she said, taking a sip of her pint. 'But I wanted to talk to you all together. We have some news.' Hattie took Millie's hand in hers and smiled. 'Do you want to tell them, or should I?'

Please, not another wedding, thought Sarah.

'You do it,' said Millie.

'Right, well, my amazing, talented, incredible partner here...'

Millie groaned.

'Sorry,' laughed Hattie. 'My lovely partner Millie has been head-hunted.'

'Oh, that's wonderful, love,' said Fran, smiling for the first time that day.

'Yes, it is...' Hattie looked round the table. 'The only slight issue is that the restaurant is in Sydney.'

'Sydney?' asked Fran.

'Australia.'

'Congratulations,' said Felix, grinning from ear to ear and leaning over to give Millie a hug.

'They'll be lucky to have you,' said Fran, patting Millie's hand.

'What about the café?' asked Sarah.

'That's what I wanted to talk to you about,' said Hattie. 'There will be some changes. Millie's got another think coming if she thinks I'm going to let her go to Australia without me.'

'I wouldn't dare,' said Millie. Everyone laughed except for Sarah.

'What does that mean for our jobs?'

'Nothing in the short term. We won't be leaving until the end of summer, so for the next few months, everything will stay the same. When we leave, I want the café left in safe hands. That's why...' said Hattie, creating a drum roll on the table. 'I've asked Felix to take over managing the café. To my immense relief he said yes.'

'Well, isn't that wonderful,' said Fran. 'Not that you're leaving, of course, but that Felix will run it. You'll do a great job,' she said, patting Felix on the arm.

'I will with you by my side,' he replied.

Sarah felt sick. How could Hattie conceive of leaving the café in the care of Felix? He wasn't trustworthy. He was a thief. Sarah weighed up her options. If she exposed his stealing now, in front of the group, he'd worm his way out of it. Everyone would buy into his lies. He'd still get the manager's job and wouldn't hesitate to throw Sarah out on her ear.

'This calls for a drink,' said Sarah. 'Same again, everyone? Hattie, could you come and help me at the bar?'

'Sure,' said Hattie, following Sarah inside.

Before they reached the bar, Sarah grabbed Hattie's arm and pulled her into a corner.

'I need to speak to you in confidence.'

'Look, Sarah. I know you and Felix haven't always seen eye to eye, but you don't need to worry about your job. He's promised to keep you on, and even if he tried to get rid of you, he'd have to get past Fran first.' Hattie laughed, but Sarah remained grim-faced.

'That's not what I'm worried about. There's something you need to know about Felix. He's a thief.'

Hattie threw back her head and laughed. 'A thief? My God, Sarah, you've got a vivid imagination.'

'I knew you'd react like this,' muttered Sarah, pulling out her phone. 'Look at this. I've got evidence this time.' She scrolled through her phone and found the photos she'd taken in Felix's tipi.

'Sarah, I know what you're going to tell me, and it's not what you think.'

'You knew?'

'Felix hasn't stolen anything.'

'Hattie, I've seen the inventory myself. I know there were items missing, not to mention the scones you all teased me about. This is indisputable proof of what he's been up to.'

'Sarah, I promise you there is an excellent explanation for all of this. It's not my place to tell you what that explanation is, but you need to trust me.'

Sarah saw red. 'Trust you? TRUST YOU? You let staff members steal from under your nose, hold secret meetings with individuals to create rifts in the team and think it's an acceptable working practice to hold a staff meeting in a pub. A pub, for God's sake!'

'Sarah...'

'No, don't *Sarah* me. You can stick your job. All I've got from all of you since I've been here is a web of lies. There's no one here I can trust. If I never see you all again, it will be too soon. I QUIT!' Sarah stormed through the pub. Locals stared, pints halfway to their mouths, distracted by the drama unfolding in their sleepy establishment.

'Sarah. Sarah!'

Sarah ignored Hattie's calls, setting off at a sprint along the road. She'd cut through the forest and gather her belongings before the others got back. No way was she giving them the satisfaction of laughing at her again. She was done with this place. Done with her so-called friends. Done with this fresh start. She was going home.

Chapter 39

S arah escaped unseen. She'd packed her belongings in record time. Half an hour after arriving at her tipi she was leaving it for the last time, having had the foresight to book a taxi on her way back from the pub.

As her train carried her further and further from Cornwall, Sarah let her body relax. It had been the right decision to leave. If she were honest with herself, she'd never fitted in. Any suggestion of friendship had been on a surface level. Everyone had let her down, even reliable Fran. Sarah felt a pang of loss. Despite her recent behaviour, Fran would be the one person she'd miss.

What about Felix? Sarah pushed away the thought. He may have conned her with his good looks and fake niceties, but she'd never let a man do that to her again. Sarah pictured Felix arriving at her tipi to find her gone. Would he be pleased? Would he be disappointed? Perhaps he enjoyed stringing more than one woman along at a time?

The one thing Sarah was sure of was that none of her so-called friends would take any responsibility for what had happened. No, she'd be to blame. She'd become a legendary story shared each time a new staff member joined the team. *Remember that girl Sarah we had working here? What happened to her? Oooh, that's quite the tale, that is.*

Sarah's phone pinged with a message from Felix.

Where are you?

Sarah ignored it. Five minutes later, another message came through, this time from Hattie.

Sarah, we need to talk. You've got the wrong end of the stick. Please come back so I can explain.

Wrong end of the stick? Hattie was having a laugh. Even if Sarah went back, she'd only receive another pack of lies. They must think she was stupid. Sarah's phone rang. Fran. So Fran wouldn't talk to her at work, but was happy to call her now? Sarah turned the phone onto silent and placed it face down on the table.

It was close to midnight when Sarah arrived back in her hometown. She shivered, despite the warm evening. The relief of being home never arrived. She felt as though she were a stranger visiting a place for the first time. After spending more of her savings than she would have liked on yet another taxi, Sarah sped through the empty streets. As the car pulled up outside her old house, Sarah felt the beginnings of panic surface. She paid the taxi driver, took a deep breath and walked towards the front door.

Sarah looked for the plant pot used to hide the spare key. She shone her phone torch around the front step, but there was no sign of the pot. With her attention turned to the rest of the front garden, Sarah turned over every loose paving slab, felt beneath every bush and plant. No key.

Think, Sarah told herself, scrubbing her hands through her hair. She couldn't fall at the first hurdle. At the side of the house, Sarah reached behind the gate and lifted the catch. She looked behind her to check no nosy neighbours were watching and slipped into the back garden.

In the last few months of their marriage, Cynthia had nagged Colin daily about the broken kitchen window. Sarah prayed he hadn't got around to fixing it. As she reached the kitchen, Sarah tugged at the window. It rattled in its frame but didn't open. Torch on, Sarah scoured the garden for useful implements, breathing a sigh of relief as she stumbled upon a metal spike Colin used to mark out his vegetable patch.

Sarah squeezed the metal stick in between the window frame. With much effort and plenty of swearing under her breath, she caught hold of the catch and lifted it away from its fastenings. The window swung open. Sarah let out a silent cheer.

It took a few attempts to reach the opening, but with the help of an upturned crate, Sarah squeezed herself through the window, falling in a heap on the kitchen floor.

The first thing Sarah noticed was the silence. The house was still, as though holding its breath. Pulling herself up from the floor, she felt her way along the wall. Sarah's fingertips met the light switch. She flicked the switch up, but nothing happened. A surge of panic coursed through her. Without power, she was screwed. It wasn't as if there was anywhere else she could go.

Sarah found the cupboard which housed the fuse box. She flicked the switches, and the hallway flooded with light. Sarah leaned against the wall, sliding down it in relief. A full day's work, combined with emotional stress and a last-minute escape across the country, caught up with her. Sarah closed her eyes, tempted to give in to sleep there and then.

You can't sleep here, Sarah told herself. She pulled herself off the floor, clutched the banister and took deep, long breaths. This wasn't her home. As she looked around the hallway, she saw none of the familiar objects she'd grown up with. The coat stand had gone, a discoloured path of carpet the only sign that a shoe rack had once been there. Sarah walked back through to the kitchen. They had removed every appliance other than the oven. She opened cupboard after cupboard, finding all bare.

The sitting room looked enormous, devoid of all furniture. The conservatory was cold, the unmistakable smell of damp and dust filling the air. With trepidation, Sarah climbed the stairs to her bedroom. Tears filled her eyes as she opened the door. The only sign it ever held furniture was indents on the carpet. The room was empty.

Sarah cast her mind back over the few conversations she'd had with her parents over the past few months. Where had they put all her belongings? She hadn't cared, but now, seeing Blu Tack marks where posters and photographs had lined the walls, Sarah longed for the comfort of her stuff. God, she even missed the cuddly toys she'd long since grown out of.

Sarah walked from room to room, trying to locate anything that would aid in a comfortable night's sleep. With each room as empty as the last, Sarah carried her bag upstairs and made a make-shift bed from clothes and towels. The irony of her situation didn't escape her. The tipi she'd once considered primitive now seemed like a luxury hotel. At least the compost loo had toilet roll. At least she had a bed, with cosy bedding and blankets.

With her thin travel towel pulled up beneath her chin, Sarah tried to get comfortable on the floor. It was going to be a long night.

*

As the sun rose, Sarah reached over to pick up the glass of water she always kept beside her bed. Her fingers came away empty. And why was her mattress so hard? Memories of the previous night came flooding back, and Sarah forced her eyes open. She couldn't shake the feeling that she had made a huge mistake. Before she had time to process all that had happened, a knock came on her door.

Sarah heaved herself off the floor, smoothed down her hair, and headed downstairs. Who on earth would call at an empty house? Sarah's stomach somersaulted as she considered the possibility of the new owners dropping by. What would they think if they found her camping out in their soon-to-be home?

With a deep breath, Sarah opened the door. Her hand flew to her mouth as she took in the two uniformed police officers on her doorstep.

'What's happened? Oh God, is it my parents?'

The officers looked at each other before the older of the two cleared his throat. 'Good morning, madam. Could you please explain what you're doing in this property?'

'Huh? I don't understand?'

'We've had a call from a neighbour reporting a break in. They understood the house to be empty and when they saw someone creeping around, they called us.'

Sarah looked at her watch and laughed. 'So someone saw me breaking in, called you, and you're only turning up now? Thank God I'm not a real burglar or the house would be cleared out by now. What's that? A ten-hour response time? God, I'd heard about cuts to the police force, but this is just ridiculous.'

'Madam, you still haven't explained what you're doing in the property.'

'It's my parents' house,' said Sarah, wondering if that were true. Had they signed the final papers yet?

'And your name is?'

'Sarah Lint.'

'OK, we'll need to check you are who you say you are and will need to inform the owner.'

'My mum's in Spain and unlikely to be up yet. You're best off calling my dad. I'll get my driving licence for you.'

By the time Sarah arrived back at the door, driving licence in hand, the female officer was on the phone. The male officer checked Sarah's ID, nodding his approval and handing it back.

'Your father would like to speak to you,' said the female officer, handing over the phone.

'Hi, Dad.'

'Sarah, what on earth are you doing in the house? I thought you were in Cornwall?'

'I... um...' A wave of sadness washed over Sarah and to her horror, she found her eyes filling with tears. There was no point lying now, Colin would hear it in her voice. 'I had to leave my job. Everyone let me down, my so-called friends turned on me, I had no choice but to leave.'

'Oh my goodness, that sounds awful!'

'It was,' said Sarah, a tear slipping down her cheek. 'Can I stay here for a while?'

'Mmm,' said Colin, 'that could be tricky. It looks like we'll be completing on the house any day now.'

'Then what am I supposed to do?' The tears of sadness turned hot and angry. How could her parents have put her in such a difficult situation?

'Why don't I come and see you? I need to come back to town anyway to sort out a few things. Are you free tomorrow?'

Sarah laughed. What did he think she'd be doing? She was unemployed and about to be made homeless.

'I'll take it you're free. I'd rather not come to the house, too many memories. Can we meet by the duck pond at the park in town? Would eleven-ish be OK?'

'Fine, I'll see you then.' Sarah hung up and handed the phone back to the police officer. 'Satisfied?' she asked, hands on her hips, trying not to sniff.

'Yes, madam. We're sorry to have troubled you, but hope you understand we have to investigate reported burglaries.'

'I understand,' said Sarah. 'But maybe deal with it quicker in the future? I don't think you're going to catch many criminals if they have a ten-hour head-start, do you?' She slammed the door before the police officers could answer. Unable to face the day, Sarah trudged up the stairs and climbed back in to her makeshift bed.

Chapter 40

The day was too bright, in Sarah's opinion. A cold, drizzly day would have been better suited to her mood. Instead, a jovial sun beat down, sending locals into summer frenzy. Sarah resented the bright outfits of those she passed, with too much flesh on display for her liking. She'd opted for a grey T-shirt and black jeans.

Sarah ignored the cheery smiles on strangers' faces and kept her head down. That was the trouble with summer, it sent people mad. You weren't supposed to smile at strangers in this country. Bring back the good old days of winter, thought Sarah, when everyone hurried along the streets, eyes down, heads bent against the weather. All this summer love only heightened her own feelings of despair.

Sarah arrived at the park half an hour early and found a bench to wait for her father. Despite the sunshine, the park looked jaded. The children's play area had several rides cordoned off, waiting for repair. Bins spilled over, creating a feast for greedy gulls, and the duck pond emitted a stomach churning odour from its sludge-green water.

Sarah cast her mind back to the forest. The air had been fresh, the smell of pine and cut grass something she'd grown used to. Even the musty smell of leaves rotting in the rain held its own appeal. And the space, oh how she craved the space. Despite the visitors who flocked to the forest, Sarah could always find somewhere to be alone. Back in her hometown, there were people everywhere. She couldn't think with the noise of chatter and heavy traffic all around.

'Sarah?'

Sarah turned to see her father walking towards her. For the first time since he'd left, she realised how much she'd missed him. He looked different from the picture in her mind. He'd lost weight, grown a beard, and his skin spoke of long days in the sun. In his hands were two cups of coffee. Sarah accepted the one he held out and took a sip. It wasn't a patch on the coffee Felix made. Her stomach plummeted at the thought of Felix, followed by bubbling anger as she remembered how he had treated her.

'It's wonderful to see you,' said Colin, leaning in for an awkward hug.

'You look well.'

'I feel well. I feel like a new man.' Colin laughed, Sarah stayed silent. 'I'd like to say you look well too, but...'

Sarah humphed. 'I didn't sleep well last night.'

'Oh, I'm not talking about your physical appearance. You look sad. I can see it in your eyes.'

'Yeah, well, things aren't going great at the moment.'

'What happened?'

'Where do I start?'

'I thought things were going well. What changed?'

'It was OK down there for a while. Believe it or not, I rather enjoyed living in a tipi. Who'd have thought it, hey?' Sarah allowed herself a small smile. 'I enjoyed working in the kitchen, too. I was good at it.'

'And your colleagues? What were they like?'

'Nice at first. But one by one, they betrayed me. Once I realised they were faking friendship, I had to get out of there.'

'Betrayed is a strong word. What did they do?'

'Did I tell you about Fran, who I worked with in the kitchen?' Colin nodded. 'She was kind at first, taught me loads of different recipes, chatted to me on our breaks. Then she started withdrawing, acting weird. I went to her house one day, and it was obvious she didn't want me there.'

'And you did nothing to trigger a change in her?'

'No! What do you take me for?'

'Fine,' said Colin, holding up his hands. 'Then perhaps she had other things going on in her life?'

'Like what?'

Colin laughed, 'I don't know, I've never met the woman.'

'Anyway, I then caught one of my co-workers stealing. I took the evidence I'd collected to the manager, and she dismissed it, saying I didn't know the complete story.'

'Maybe you didn't?'

'Come on, Dad. I'd got photos and everything. It was so cliquey, everyone with their own little secrets, sharing them with each other, just not with me. I was an outsider from the start and it just went from bad to worse.'

Colin sighed. 'Take a few days to reflect on things. It's possible, like your boss said, that you don't know the full story. Not everything's always about you.'

Sarah spun her head round. 'How dare you suggest I'm trying to make things about me?'

'Listen, I've had time to think over things these past few months. I'm not sure your mother and I did you any favours. It's such a shame we couldn't have a second child.'

'Dad, what are you talking about?'

'We spoiled you.'

'Spoiled me? You're having a laugh.'

'I don't mean materially spoiled, I mean emotionally. You were our entire focus. We tried to make life easy for you, but in the end I'm not sure that helped anything.'

'I don't know what you're talking about.'

'You always found making friends difficult, so we let you retreat into your own safe world. We should have pushed you to join clubs, invite friends round, learn how to socialise.'

'God, Dad, it wasn't a lack of social skills that left me friendless. I was bullied.'

'And I'm not diminishing that. It was an awful time for you, I know. But that one experience has shaped the whole of your life. You've had your guard up ever since, pushing people away before they can hurt you.'

'You're supposed to be on my side.'

'I am, I am. But we could've helped you more than we did. I think your mother enjoyed having you to herself all the time. She never lost you to friends the way so many mothers do as their children grow up.'

'I enjoyed spending time with you and Mum.'

'I know you did, and that's to be commended, but spending time with parents shouldn't come at the expense of your own life. You've been living like a middle-aged woman since you were eleven.'

'I don't need to hear this,' said Sarah, standing to leave. 'You've got some nerve laying all the blame at my door. It was you who wrecked our family life. We'd all still be jogging along if it weren't for you.'

Colin took Sarah's wrist and pulled her back onto the bench. 'Sarah, you're not listening to me. That life we had, the one you look back on with rose-tinted glasses, was not a happy one. It was small, devoid of fun or adventure. The three of us sat there day after day, bringing out the worst in each other. You were becoming more and more like your mother and I couldn't let that continue.'

'There's nothing wrong with Mum,' said Sarah, squirming inside as she thought of Cynthia's behaviour in the café.

Colin took a sip of his coffee and stared out at the duck pond. 'I don't want to sit here and slag off your mum, Sarah. I'm just trying to be honest with you and tell you how I see things. Life was pretty awful for me, you know. I let you and your mother rule the roost. I let you boss me around, treat me like a second-class citizen. Perhaps if I'd stood up for myself earlier, you would have learned how to form a healthy relationship. I saw you treating Mark the way your mother treated me, and it broke my heart. When you split up, I hoped you'd take it as a fresh start, move away, get a bit more independence. Instead, you retreated further and further into yourself. It had to stop. We couldn't carry on as we were. That said, I'm sorry for the hurt I've put you through.'

Sarah sat stunned, struggling to process Colin's words. Did he think so little of her? 'If you hated me and mum so much, you should have left sooner.'

'Sarah,' said Colin, taking his daughter's hands. 'I don't hate you. That's why I'm saying all this. Look at me.'

Sarah turned her head away from her father. He cupped a hand beneath her chin and turned her face around so he could look into her eyes. 'In front of me, I see a beautiful, capable, interesting woman who deserves a life filled with friendship, love and fun. You were withering away at home, becoming the worst version of yourself. I couldn't bear to see what our marriage was doing to you. You're my precious, precious girl and I love you.'

'I can't do this,' said Sarah, pulling her hands from Colin's and standing once more. 'You've made your feelings clear. I'm leaving now.'

'Wait,' said Colin, pulling an envelope from his pocket. 'You can't stay in the house, there's nothing there. I'd invite you to come and stay with me, but I'm still renovating the boat and anyway, I don't think it will do you any harm to stand on your own two feet. Use this to tide you over until you have a plan in place.'

Sarah took the envelope from him. Inside was a wedge of twenty-pound notes. She wanted to throw the envelope back at him, but knew it would be a foolish gesture which would punish only herself. Sarah turned on her heel and strode off through the park.

'Can we meet up again?' Colin called, but Sarah ignored him, heading off to a future that seemed decidedly bleak.

Chapter 41

Sarah counted out the notes in her envelope. She was racing through them faster than she'd like and would soon be back to dipping into her savings. On the hotel's website, they had described the room she was staying as *bijou*. In reality, a better description would be cell-like.

The single bed was as narrow as a coffin, a wardrobe, and a sink filled up the remaining space. Sarah wished she'd opted for en-suite, but she had to watch her pennies. Besides, it was only a temporary arrangement.

Sarah sat cross-legged on the bed and spread a map of the UK out on it. Over the past week, it had become clear there was nothing to keep her in the town of her birth. Sarah knew from previous experience that the local housing market wasn't worth exploring, and as for the job market, unless she wanted to clean public toilets, there was nothing doing. Then there was the problem of ghosts. Not ghosts in the literal sense, but people from her past she had no intention of bumping into. Sarah could imagine Cathy and Miriam's faces if they witnessed her back in town after yet another downfall.

Sarah had spent most of the past week hiding out in her cramped hotel room, eating sandwiches and drinking cans of Coke. It was a far cry from the delicious home-cooked food made by Fran. Sarah felt the pang of loss as she bit into a tuna sandwich.

Colin's words had been whirring through her mind for the past week, and she'd thought of nothing else. The map was the first step on the road to proving her father wrong. She'd show him she could stand on her own two feet, that she wasn't the needy, scared, antisocial woman he thought her to be.

Sarah closed her eyes and waved her hand above the map of the UK. Her hand came down, and she opened her eyes. The middle of the north sea didn't scream *possibilities*. She tried again, this time her finger found itself in the highlands of Scotland. *Perhaps*, thought Sarah, *my new life needs more consideration that closing my eyes and pointing to a map?*

Frustrated by her own indecision and claustrophobia in the room, Sarah risked venturing outside. It was the middle of the afternoon, so everyone she hoped to avoid would be at work. She picked up her phone and pocketed it. Multiple calls from Felix, Hattie, and Kate lay unanswered. Fran was the only person not to call. Sarah tried not to let it bother her.

Sarah gave a curt greeting to the girl on the reception desk and let herself out onto the street, head down, not wanting to catch anyone's eye.

'Sorry,' she mumbled as she stepped into a man.

'Sarah.'

Sarah lifted her head and stared into Felix's eyes. 'What the hell are you doing here?'

'We need to talk.'

'But... but... how did you find me?'

'We dug out your emergency contact form and called your dad. He told us where to find you.'

Sarah regretted sharing her location with Colin. How dare he pass the information on after all she'd told him? 'I've got nothing to say to you.'

'Please, Sarah, it's important.'

'I said no. Go away.'

Sarah strode off down the street, Felix jogging to keep up. 'Sarah,' he said, panting for breath.

'Go away.'

'Sarah,' Felix grabbed hold of her arm.

'Let go of me,' said Sarah through gritted teeth.

'I will, but there's something you need to know. It's Fran. She's in hospital.'

Sarah stopped squirming beneath Felix's grip and looked at him in horror. 'What? Why? What's happened?'

'Not here,' he said. 'Is there somewhere we can talk?'

Sarah thought of her poky hotel room. 'How about we find a pub?'

They walked in silence, Sarah desperate for answers but knowing she'd receive none until Felix had a drink in front of him. They found a scruffy-looking pub.

'This will do,' said Felix, holding the door open for Sarah. He ordered two pints at the bar while Sarah found them a table in the corner of the room.

'Tell me what's happened,' she said as soon as Felix sat down.

'The first thing to say is that Fran's going to be OK.'

Sarah let out a sigh of relief.

'How much do you know about her home life?'

'Not much. I went round to her house once, but she didn't want me there. She seemed proud of her sons, but her husband struck me as pompous.'

'Yeah, well, that's a very generous description of Michael. He's the one who put her in hospital.' Felix's face scrunched like he'd caught the whiff of a foul smell.

'What do you mean?' asked Sarah. She'd assumed Fran had been in some sort of accident.

'He beat her up so badly the paramedics thought she was dead when they first got there. Thank God the next-door neighbour was home when it happened. They heard shouting through the wall and called the police and ambulance. If they'd been out, we'd be having a very different conversation today.' His jaw clenched, his fists balled.

'My God. I didn't know. How long has it been going on?'

'Years, I think. I don't think it was physical violence at first. Things escalated when he lost his job a couple of months ago.'

'But when I met him, he was just back from the golf course. I assumed he was some sort of businessman.'

'No, he worked in a factory, but liked to put on airs and graces. He gave a good impression of being an upstanding member of the community.'

'And how is she now?'

'On the road to recovery, but she'll be in hospital for a few weeks yet.'

'Why did he do it?'

'He found out she'd confided in Hattie about the abuse.'

Sarah felt sick. So that's what their secret meetings had been about. 'I've been such a terrible friend to her,' she said. 'If anyone, it should have been me who saw the signs first.'

'You weren't to know. It's not your fault.'

'Can I see her?'

'I'm sure she'd like that. You can get a lift with me, if you like? I borrowed Hattie's car to come up here.'

'No, thanks, I'll get on the train.'

'Sarah...'

'I appreciate you coming all the way up here to tell me, but it changes nothing between us.'

'You've got me wrong. I need to explain.'

'Felix, I've had enough of your lies. I want to see Fran, but nothing else has changed.'

Felix played with the glass in front of him. 'Look, Sarah. I need to come clean. We've been trying to call you all week to let you know about Fran, but that's not the only reason I came. I need to ask you a massive favour.'

'What?' asked Sarah, looking at Felix through narrowed eyes.

'Kate's wedding is next week.'

Sarah shook her head. In all the drama she'd forgotten. 'What's that got to do with me?'

'Fran is going to be in hospital for ages, so that leaves us with no one to do the catering.'

'Hire in a catering company.'

'We'd rather you did it.'

'I quit, in case you'd forgotten?'

'Sarah,' said Felix, sighing. 'You have issues with me and Hattie, and I know you've quit the café. I'm not asking you to come back to your old job, I'm asking you to do this one favour for Fran. She wants you to do it for her. It was her idea for me to come up here.'

Sarah knew she was beaten. How could she refuse Fran's request for help? 'Fine, I'll come down for one week. I'll visit Fran, cook for the stupid wedding, then I'm done. Understand?'

'Deal,' said Felix, holding his hand out for Sarah to shake. She ignored it, taking a sip of her pint instead. 'And listen, don't get a train. It will be quicker to come with me and the train is so expensive.'

'I don't think so.'

'What if I promise not to talk? You can tune the radio to whatever station you like, and I'll keep my mouth shut the entire way back to Cornwall.'

This time, it was Sarah's turn to hold out her hand. Felix shook it, Sarah ignoring the fizz of excitement passing through her as their skin met. An hour later, Sarah was piling her bag into the boot of Hattie's car, Felix waiting behind the wheel. She had to see Fran, but hoped she wasn't making a big mistake going back to the café. With a sigh of resignation, Sarah climbed into the car.

Chapter 42

Despite her reluctance to be near Felix, Sarah had to admit he'd kept his promised silence. The radio filled any space left by absent conversation, Sarah hoping the current discussion on the menopause was leaving Felix uncomfortable.

Twice he'd broken his silence, but each time it was for a mundane question- 'Fancy a coffee break?' 'There's a service station coming up if you need a wee?' Sarah replied 'no' to each question and they carried on, making good progress along the motorway.

After two hours, Felix pulled into a motorway service station to use the toilet. Sarah walked into the building with him, then they parted ways. Determined not to offer any sign of friendship, Sarah bought herself a coffee and a personal supply of snacks.

Once back on the road, they continued as before. It wasn't until they turned onto a smaller A road that Felix leaned over and switched off the radio.

'What are you doing?' asked Sarah.

'I'm going to tell you a story.'

'I don't want to hear a story.'

'Please,' said Felix. 'I'll keep it brief.'

Sarah considered fighting against him. She disliked the power imbalance of Felix behind the wheel and felt captive. In the end, she decided a fight wasn't worth the effort, so instead stared out of the window in disinterest as he talked.

'I want to tell you a story about a boy. This boy was lost in life. He struggled with school, drank too much on the weekend, and even dabbled in drugs from time to time. The one thing that stopped him from throwing his life down the pan were his little sisters. The boy adored his sisters. They were his world, his reason for waking up in the morning. His one goal in life was to protect them.'

Sarah risked a glance towards Felix. His tone was relaxed, but a pulsing vein in his neck suggested he wasn't as calm as he was trying to appear.

'One day, without warning, one sister changed. Before that day, she'd been fun-loving, full of life, excited for her future. Then, for no apparent reason, she became quiet, withdrawn, depressed. Instead of talking to her brother like she used to, the girl spent more and more time alone in her bedroom. The boy would hear sad songs blasting from her stereo, hear the muffled sound of crying as he went to sleep each night.'

'The boy should have been paying more attention, but the change in the girl coincided with exams starting. He knew he wouldn't do well, but as a bare minimum, he wanted to pass. The thought of retaking a year of school was unbearable. So, just like the girl, the boy spent more and more time alone in his room. The difference was, while the girl was falling into a pit of despair, the boy was trying to cram information from revision texts into his flighty mind. The boy and the girl drifted apart, each caught up in their own lives, their own problems.'

'One day, the boy woke up with a strange feeling, let's call it intuition. Every morning he'd call through the door of the girl's bedroom, telling her to wake up. On this morning, he did just that, only instead of the usual shouts and swearing, there was no reply. The boy opened the door to the girl's bedroom and found it empty. The bed was made, the floor clear of clothes, pens tidied away in their pots.'

'Propped against a pillow was an envelope addressed to the boy. He tore the envelope open and read... and read...'

Sarah turned her body to look at Felix. He cleared his throat, sniffing and shaking his head.

'You don't have to say any more,' she said.

'Oh, but I do.' Felix coughed. 'Right, where was I? The boy read the note, which read like a suicide note. In it, the girl spoke of an assault at a party, of not being able to tell anyone, of feeling alone and like she couldn't go on.' Felix took his hand off the steering wheel and brushed it against his eyes.

'What did the boy do?'

'He called the police. His parents were in a drunken stupor. He didn't know what else to do. He didn't expect the police to take him seriously, but after reading the note, they set up a search party to find the girl.'

'And did they find her?'

'Yes, no, not exactly. They traced her movements to one of the north coast beaches. There was CCTV footage of her getting on the bus in town, and getting off at the beach. That was the last known sighting of her. The police found her clothes and shoes left in a neat pile at the water's edge. In the shoe was a piece of paper with the word *sorry* written across it. It was another three weeks before her body washed up on a beach further down the coast.'

'Felix, I'm so sorry.' At that moment, Sarah could forget all her negative feelings towards him. So what if he was light-fingered? Trauma like that was bound to affect someone in many ways.

'Aha,' said Felix, 'but that's not where the story ends.'

'It's not?'

'No. The family went through the motions of a funeral, memorial service, they even had a plaque put up on a bench overlooking the beach where it happened. A stream of tearful teenagers came to lay flowers at the house. The girl's mum gave away clothes and jewellery, insisting the girl's friends take them despite the offer making them uncomfortable.'

'Anyway, the world moved on. The parents drank even more, the boy failed his exams and began heading down the same road as his parents, blocking out his sadness through drink and drugs.'

'Then one day, when desperate for money, the boy got himself a job. It was a crappy minimum wage job, waiting tables in a café. The café manager took a shine to the boy and began training him up. He found that although useless at most things in life, making coffee wasn't one of them.'

'Life got better. The boy moved away from his parents, his memories, and the dangerous crowd he'd fallen in with. He rebuilt his life brick by brick with the help of good people around him and a determination to make his sister proud.'

'Everything was fine until the day he saw a ghost. She was lurking behind a tree in the forest, watching him. The boy was terrified and tried to run away, but the ghost kept calling his name. The voice didn't sound spooky, or ghostly. It sounded just as he'd remembered. He walked to the girl and took her in his arms. At first he thought he was hallucinating, but she felt real, her body warm, her breath tickling his neck. He held her at arm's length, tears flowing down both their cheeks.'

'Your sister?' asked Sarah, open-mouthed.

'Yes, and no.' Felix pulled the car into a lay-by and turned off the engine. 'OK, enough of the stories. I've never been a great storyteller.

And I'm sorry, I know I promised not to talk, but I had to get all this off my chest.'

'Hang on, at the start of your story, you mentioned *sisters*, not *sister*.'

'Well spotted,' said Felix, managing a sad smile. 'There were two sisters, Lily and Mia. Mia was the eldest of the two. When things started going wrong for the family, Lily retreated into her own little world. It was almost like she had disappeared. After Mia's death, she became even more withdrawn. I'm ashamed to admit I didn't give her a second thought when I upped and left. Anyway, Lily came back into my life six months ago, not long before you started work at the café. She was fifteen, the spitting image of Mia, and had run away from home. Her resemblance to Mia brought everything flooding back, and for a while I was worried I couldn't pull myself together again, never mind look after a scared teenager.'

'Why was she scared?'

'After I left, Mum and Dad's drinking got worse. They became aggressive and very unpleasant to be around. It reached the point Lily couldn't take it anymore.'

'Hattie helped me process everything, just like she'd done when I first arrived at the café. She brought me and Lily together to talk things through, and I began getting to know my sister again.'

'Where did your parents think she'd gone?'

'She told them she was moving in with a friend. They never reported her missing, and when her school called to find out where she was, they said they were homeschooling. God, they didn't even come to ask me if I'd seen her! Lily had been missing for over a year before she came to find me. She hitchhiked up to north Devon, then fell in with some hippy types and travelled round the country with them, doing hair braiding in the summer, working cash in hand jobs in the winter.'

'Why didn't you tell me all this sooner?'

'Lily made me promise not to tell anyone. Hattie knew, but she agreed to keep Lily a secret until we'd figured out a plan. There are some pretty big consequences if you leave home at fourteen. There's no missing persons case open for her, but as soon as I tell the police where she is, she'll either be taken back to Mum and Dad, or put into care. We agreed to hide her for a while until we can find a way through that's in her best interests. Lily's been camping out in the forest. That's who I was with the night you followed me.'

'You knew about that?'

Felix laughed. 'Of course I knew it was you. I pretended I didn't as I didn't want Lily freaking out. So now we get to the food...'

'I think I can guess.'

'Hattie agreed I could take food from the café. I paid for it out of my wages, so there were no freebies, but being stuck in the forest without a car, it seemed the easiest thing to do. I couldn't get a supermarket delivery to the forest without raising a few eyebrows. Anyway, I'd just persuaded Lily to go to the police station and explain everything when we got the news about Fran. The plan is for me to convince social services to let me look after her. It should be easier now I've got the café manager's job and we can live in Hattie's old flat.'

'Felix, I'm so, so, sorry.'

'No, I'm the one who should be sorry. I should have told you all this ages ago. You were right to call me out when you thought I was stealing. I would've done the same had the tables been turned.'

'Does Lily have dreadlocks?'

'Yes. I don't think they suit her, but she likes them.'

Sarah slapped her hand against her forehead. 'So she's your mystery woman.'

'My what?'

'I saw you outside the marquee when we had that function. It was the day after we... never mind. Anyway, I thought you had another woman on the go. I should have asked you about it at the time rather than giving you the cold shoulder.'

'Yeah, but I can see how it must have looked.'

'Felix, I'm so sorry for the way I've behaved. Turns out my dad was right about me...'

'Huh?'

'Never mind. Can we start over again? As friends, I mean?'

'That sounds like an excellent idea,' said Felix, taking Sarah's hand in his. 'First, we've got another friend who needs us.' He started the engine and pulled out onto the road, Cornwall bound.

Chapter 43

'What's the matter?'

'I hate hospitals.'

Felix took Sarah's hand, pulling her towards the building. 'It will be fine. We're here for Fran, remember.'

Sarah nodded and let Felix guide her towards the entrance. It wasn't just a dislike of hospitals causing Sarah to hesitate. The thought of seeing Fran made her stomach churn. Shame and guilt mingled as Sarah considered all the ways she'd let her friend down. How had she not seen the signs when in Fran's home? *Because you were focusing on yourself, as usual. It's always all about you, isn't it?*

'You OK?'

'Yeah,' said Sarah. 'I'm nervous about seeing Fran, that's all. I've been a crappy friend to her.'

'We all missed the signs,' said Felix.

'I know, but I was so focused on myself, thinking the changes in her were to do with me. If I'd taken my head out of my arse for five minutes, I may have realised what was going on.'

'Stop being so hard on yourself. Do you mind if we pop into the shop on our way? It feels wrong turning up at Fran's bedside empty handed.'

Ten minutes later, armed with magazines, flowers and chocolate, Felix and Sarah walked into Fran's ward. As she approached her friend,

Sarah's heart fluttered, the familiar fizz of panic trying to make an unwanted return.

'It's OK,' said Felix, squeezing Sarah's hand and giving her a reassuring smile.

Fran's head was down, her eyes fixed on an iPad in front of her. When she looked up and saw Felix and Sarah, her face lit up. Sarah took a sharp intake of breath. Other than the wide smile, Fran was unrecognisable. Her face was black and blue, one eye disappearing beneath puffed folds of skin.

'I'm glad to see you two are friends again,' she said.

'Fran,' said Sarah, perching on the edge of the hospital bed and staring down at her battered and bruised friend. 'I'm so sorry for everything. I've behaved like a spoiled brat. The way I treated you, the way I treated all of you, is unforgivable.'

'Don't be daft,' said Fran. 'I did a good job of hiding my problems. You weren't to know.'

'And how are you now?'

'Alive,' said Fran, taking Sarah's hand. 'But I'm afraid I won't be up to much in the kitchen for a while yet.'

'You,' said Felix, pointing a finger at Fran, 'should not be thinking of work right now. Take all the time you need to get yourself well again. Sarah can hold the fort.'

'And your job will be ready and waiting as soon as you're better.'

'I'm sorry you got dragged back here,' said Fran. 'I know you were hoping for a fresh start.'

Sarah laughed. 'What I was doing was running away from my fresh start, throwing it away. Now I'm back where I belong.'

'I'm pleased to hear it.' Fran tried to heave herself up against her pillows, but didn't have the strength.

'Here,' said Felix, tucking his arms beneath Fran's. 'So how are you?'

'Sore. I don't want to talk about what happened if that's OK? Kate's given me the name of a counsellor to talk to when I'm ready.'

Kate. Sarah groaned. 'There's another person I need to apologise to.'

'Really? Why?'

'I took offence when she gave me an apron. I know,' said Sarah, seeing smirks form on Fran and Felix's faces. 'It was a stupid thing to do. If I'm going to be in charge of catering for her wedding, I need to apologise first.'

'You do tend to think the worst of people,' said Fran, shaking her head. 'Now, what have you got there? It looks like you've got a few goodies for me.'

Felix and Sarah handed over their last-minute gifts.

'No grapes? I can't believe you didn't get me grapes.'

'Sorry, they didn't sell them in the shop.'

'I'm teasing,' said Fran. 'I don't understand why people always take grapes into hospital. Chocolate is a much better choice.'

Fran shared out the chocolate and the three friends sat chatting until a doctor appeared on his ward round. 'That's our cue to go,' said Felix. 'Take care of yourself, Fran.' He bent down and planted a kiss on Fran's cheek. Sarah smiled as Fran's cheeks flushed pink.

'We'll come again later in the week,' said Sarah. 'Don't get up to any mischief while we're gone.'

'I'll try not to,' said Fran.

Sarah and Felix were silent until they left the hospital. 'I don't know about you, but I could do with a drink.'

'That sounds like an excellent idea,' said Sarah.

*

'Do you think she'll go back to him?' asked Sarah, as Felix set down their drinks.

'I doubt it,' said Felix. 'Hattie told me she's pressing charges. I don't think that evil husband of hers will be allowed within a mile of her when she's ready to be discharged.'

'It's so upsetting seeing her like that. I wish I'd done more to help.'

'Me too. All we can do is to be there for her now. Getting over her physical injuries is only the start. Aside from the emotional damage, she's going to have big decisions to make about what her life looks like from now on.'

'I just can't believe anyone could do something so awful to such an amazing woman.'

'Me neither. Hattie's spoken to her two sons. They were devastated but not surprised.'

'They knew what was going on? Why didn't they stay to help her? Why move so far from home?'

'It appears Fran insisted. She wanted to protect them at the expense of her own safety. Both her sons have come back to visit her. They'll help her get back on her feet.'

'I can't believe how much has been going on right under my nose, not just Fran, but all the stuff you've been dealing with too.'

'We've spoken about that. It's water under the bridge. There's no need to go over it all again.'

'No, but your situation is ongoing and I want to be there to support you. Can I meet her?'

'Lily?'

Sarah nodded.

'Yes, I don't see why not. Let me speak to her first, though. She can be wary of strangers.'

A waiter came and hovered by their table. 'Yes?' said Sarah.

'This table is reserved from six. If you don't mind hurrying your drinks, we need to set up for dinner.'

'Actually,' said Sarah, 'we do. You were quite happy taking our money and said nothing about there being a time limit on how long we had to finish our drinks. Now, if you don't mind, my friend and I are in the middle of a conversation.' Sarah turned back to Felix, and the waiter slunk away. Felix laughed. 'What?'

'Nothing.'

'No, what is it?'

'It's just good to see you haven't completely changed.'

'What do you mean?'

'It's just this new, improved, cuddly Sarah is strange. I like your feisty side, just not when it's directed at me.'

'Hey,' said Sarah. 'There's nothing wrong with standing up for yourself. Think of me as the same old Sarah, but a bit more self-aware.'

'Sounds good to me.'

Chapter 44

'Are you OK?'

Sarah turned to Felix and nodded. They'd been sitting in the car so long the windows had steamed up.

'You've got nothing to worry about.'

'I have. The way I spoke to Hattie was awful.'

'Then apologise. She's not someone to hold a grudge.'

Sarah took a deep breath and opened the car door. Hattie stood outside the café, bringing in the chalk boards for the night. When she saw Sarah, her face lit up with a smile.

'Hi,' she said, waving. 'The wanderer returns.'

'Do you need a hand with those?'

'That would be great, thanks.'

Sarah gathered up a heavy board and heaved it into the café. Hattie walked over to the sofa and slumped down.

'Come on then,' she said, patting the seat beside her. 'Let's have a chat.'

Sarah took her place on the sofa, eyes on the ground. 'I've been such an idiot. I'm so sorry for the way I spoke to you.'

'To be honest, it was upsetting, but I get where you were coming from. You came to a rational conclusion based on the information you had. Have you chatted to Felix?'

'Yes. I know about Lily.'

'Good. So you understand why I was so keen to protect him?'

'Yes. Look, Hattie, all that stuff I said...'

'Forget about it. Just make sure you learn from it. You see things as very black and white, but there's often more to a situation, or person, than surface level. Try not to judge too fast in the future.'

'I won't. God, I'm so embarrassed. I'm a twenty-five-year-old woman who's been behaving like a child. There's no excuse, but I'm trying to change.'

'Well, don't change too much. We like you as you are. Maybe just smooth off a few of those sharp edges.'

Sarah smiled. 'Thank you for being so kind.'

'I have an ulterior motive. I need you to come back to work. We're screwed without Fran. How was she when you saw her?'

'Putting on a brave face.'

'Typical Fran. She'll need us all these next few months. Anyway, back to business. I hope you don't mind, but I invited Kate over this evening.'

'Why?'

'We need to go through arrangements, check we're all on the same page now Fran's out of action. I suggested we meet at mine at seven. Does that sound OK?'

'Do you think we could meet at mine?'

'The tipi?'

'Yes, it's such a lovely evening, and I'd like a chance to settle back in if that's OK?'

'Fine by me. I'll head home and get changed, then meet you back here with a bottle of wine.'

'Thanks.'

'Come here,' said Hattie, pulling Sarah into a hug. For once, Sarah didn't stiffen. She let herself sink into Hattie's warmth, marvelling at the generosity of the woman she'd treated like crap.

Hattie set off home, and Sarah found Felix sitting on a bench outside. 'I thought I'd give you two some space,' he said. 'How did it go?'

'Better than I deserved.'

'Hattie's a good egg.'

Sarah laughed. 'She's invited Kate over this evening to go through wedding plans. I'd better get to the tipi and de-spider a bit before she arrives.'

'Sure,' said Felix, picking up Sarah's bag.

As she crossed the field towards the tipi, Sarah felt a swell of happiness. She was coming home.

'What is it?' asked Felix, as Sarah laughed.

'I was just thinking that if someone had told me six months ago, I would have missed living in a tent I would have thought they were mad.'

'These tipis have their charms.'

Sarah was expecting the tipi to be dusty and full of cobwebs. Instead, she found a fresh glass of wild flowers beside a newly made bed. Books were stacked on the bedside table. 'Did you do this?' she asked Felix.

'No. When we stopped at that service station, I gave Hattie a call and told her you were coming home.'

Home. Sarah smiled. 'Thank you.'

By the time Kate and Hattie arrived at the tipi, Sarah had unpacked and felt as though she'd never been away.

'Hi,' said Kate. 'How are you?'

'Good thanks,' said Sarah, noticing there was none of the usual hugging. 'I'm sorry I took off like I did.'

'You're back now, that's all that matters. Listen, I think I might have upset you the last time I saw you. The apron was supposed to be a thoughtful gift, but I see how it might have looked.'

'No, I was overreacting as usual. It is a thoughtful gift, and I'll be honoured to wear it while cooking for your wedding.'

'Right,' said Hattie. 'Let's get this open.' She unscrewed a bottle of wine and shared it out into their glasses.

'Mind if I join?' asked Felix. 'Or is this girls only?'

'You can be an honorary girl for the night,' said Hattie, handing Felix a glass.

Before he sat down, Felix dragged over the fire pit from outside his tipi and set about lighting it. Soon, warm flames danced in front of them, adding to Sarah's feeling of calm.

'I know I've already said it, but I am sorry,' said Sarah. 'I can't promise a personality transplant, but I can promise to try harder.'

'Sarah, we appreciate your apology, but you've said sorry enough. And please don't change, you're very good at dealing with difficult customers...'

'Like my mother?'

An awkward silence developed until Sarah let out a giggle. 'I can't believe her, I can't believe I was *becoming* her!' Sarah pulled off a very accurate impression of her mother and Marjorie, much to the delight of her assembled friends.

Talk turned to the wedding, stomachs rumbling as Sarah described the food she had planned. A bottle turned into two as conversation flowed as easily as the wine. Darkness settled around them and a distant car horn signalled Bob had arrived to drive Kate home.

'Kate?'

'Yes?' said Kate, pulling on her coat.

'I know this is cheeky, but would you be able to squeeze an extra guest in next week? Not at the meal, I just mean for the evening do...'

Kate raised an eyebrow. 'Have you got a hot date?'

'No,' laughed Sarah, 'nothing like that. But I would like to invite my dad down for a visit. He'd love it here. He'd love you,' said Sarah, waving her arm to include everyone around the fire.

'Of course he can come,' said Kate, 'to the whole thing if he wants.'

'Thank you, I'll ask him.' Sarah surprised Kate by pulling her into a hug.

Kate put her arms around Sarah. 'I'm glad you're back,' she said.

Sarah felt tears prick her eyes. For once, she believed Kate. For once, she trusted that someone would want to spend time in her company.

'I'm off too,' said Hattie. 'Are you OK to start back at work tomorrow, Sarah?'

'I can't wait.'

With Kate and Hattie gone, Sarah felt awkward, aware of Felix's proximity and the unresolved feelings they hadn't yet tackled.

'Right, um, I guess I'll head to bed.'

'Sarah.' Felix stood up and pulled Sarah into him. His touch was gentle, but she felt as though all her breath had squeezed out, her brain turning to mush as she slid her arms beneath his coat. They stayed like that for what felt like hours, but was probably only a few minutes. When Felix pulled away, he looked into her eyes, then leaned over and placed the lightest of kisses on her forehead. 'Sleep well,' he said, his voice muffled by all they hadn't said.

'Night,' whispered Sarah, releasing her arms and heading into her tipi. She glanced back to see Felix putting out the fire, then climbed into bed, her heart full of possibilities and what ifs. They had given her a second chance, and she didn't intend to waste it.

Chapter 45

S unlight streamed in through the tall glass windows of the hotel bedroom. Tiny silver horseshoes clustered around an open champagne bottle and the room smelled of flowers and hairspray.

'Here's to friendship,' said Kate, clinking her glass against her friend's.

'Here's to romance,' said Joy, before taking her glass to the balcony for a smoke.

'This is all rather wonderful,' said Fran, propped up against cushions on an armchair.

'Are you sure you're comfortable enough?' asked Kate.

'Goodness me, love, don't be worrying about me, it's your big day.'

Kate smiled. Sarah pulled out a small cardboard box and handed it to Kate. 'Your something blue,' she said with a shy smile, praying Kate liked the contents.

'Oh wow, I love them,' said Kate, examining two delicate earrings. Tiny blue flowers hung suspended in clear domes from silver hooks. Kate held one up to her ear. 'What do you think?'

'They look great,' said Sarah. 'You don't have to wear them today if you don't want to. They're to remind you of your wedding day. The flowers are from the forest.'

'You made these?'

'No,' laughed Sarah, 'I'm afraid my talents don't stretch to jewellery making. All I did was pick the flowers and take them to someone who knew what they were doing.'

'This is such a thoughtful gift,' said Kate. 'And of course I'm going to wear them today.'

'I'm afraid I only managed a card, and it's hardly appropriate,' said Fran, reaching into her bag.

Kate opened the card and burst out laughing. 'It may well be appropriate by tomorrow morning if I drink too much champagne today.' Kate showed Sarah the *Get Well Soon* card that Fran had brought along.

'I'm afraid there wasn't a great selection in the hospital shop,' she said, her eyes twinkling.

'It's a miracle you got me anything at all,' said Kate. 'It's also a miracle you're here. I can't believe they let you out so soon.'

'I channelled Sarah's brusqueness. It worked a charm on the doctor.'

'Hey,' said Sarah, joining in the laughter.

'I've got something for you too,' said Joy, closing the balcony door and popping a mint in her mouth. She pulled a black velvet bag from her pocket and passed it to Kate. 'I know you wish your mum and dad were here today. They may not be with you in person, but at least this is something.'

Kate pulled a silver locket from the bag and opened it. 'I... I...' her voice caught in her throat.

'Thank goodness you've not had your makeup done yet,' said Joy as Kate flung her arms around the old lady, her tears soaking into Joy's silver hair.

'Look,' said Kate, showing Sarah the locket. On one side was a picture of a young man, on the other was a photograph of a young woman. 'My parents.'

'They'd be so proud of you,' said Joy. 'As would your grandmother.'

'To family,' said Fran, lifting a glass of lemonade aloft.

'And surrogate family,' said Kate, smiling at her friends.

*

Sarah stood at the back of the enormous tipi, admiring the floral display Hattie and Millie had put together. The place looked magical, and Bob had even coordinated with the theme, sporting a bright floral waistcoat only he could get away with. Sarah waited with bated breath for Kate to arrive. She'd seen her in her finery, but as the gate opened and Kate walked across the lawn, arm in arm with Joy, the scene blurred with Sarah's tears. As Kate drew level, she gave Sarah's hand a quick squeeze.

'Good luck,' mouthed Sarah.

'I think I'm going to need it,' whispered Kate. 'I've just caught sight of Bob's waistcoat.'

Sarah hid her laughter behind her hand as Felix began playing a melody on his guitar and Kate set off up the aisle. As Sarah's heart swelled, she wondered if she'd ever felt so happy. She didn't think so.

As soon as the ceremony was over, Sarah rushed out of the tipi towards the kitchen, grabbing her new apron from its hook and tying it over her dress.

'How was it?' asked Colin, as Sarah ran into the kitchen.

'Wonderful, beautiful, amazing, pick any adjective and it won't be enough. Now, down to business. Have you whipped that bowl of cream I gave you?'

'Yes, chef.' Colin smiled at Sarah and she smiled back. It had been his idea to help her out in the kitchen after he admitted to the cooking classes he'd been attending for the past few months.

'This is nice,' said Sarah, as she plated up the canapés. 'Working with you, I mean. Who knew we'd both turn out to be half-decent cooks?'

'Life's full of surprises,' said Colin. 'I know now's not the time to bring it up, but now things are good between us, I don't want you going too hard on your mother.'

Sarah almost dropped the smoked salmon tart in her hand. 'What's brought on the change of heart?'

'I've just been thinking. I know she can be a right old battle-axe, but deep down she means well. There's a decent heart beneath her puff, bluster and unacceptable behaviour.'

'Dad, you know you've missed your chance? She's with a man-child called Marco now.'

Colin laughed. 'Don't worry, I'd never want to be married to the woman again, I'm just saying she's not as bad as she can seem. I don't want you ever to feel you have to take sides.'

'I don't. Now pick up that tray, will you? We've got over a hundred hungry guests out there who'll storm the kitchen if we don't feed them soon.'

*

The food was a roaring success. As Sarah mingled with guests at the evening do, her face lit up like a beacon each time someone complimented her on her cooking. She'd enjoyed some pleasant small talk with Mark and Gary, surprised at the ease with which the conversation flowed.

Sarah's eyes scanned the room, looking for Felix, but she could see no sign of him. She was about to give up her search when he appeared at the door of the tent. He signalled to her to meet him and Sarah weaved her way through the hordes of merry guests.

'Is everything OK? I've been looking for you.'

'Yes, everything's fine. There's someone I'd like you to meet.' Felix took Sarah's hand and led her outside into the field. Her eyes struggled to adjust to the dark, punctuated only by strings of fairy lights. From the shadows, a woman stepped forward. Her head down, she lifted her eyes to meet Sarah's.

'Hello, Lily,' said Sarah, smiling at the young girl.

'Hi.'

A moment of awkward silence filled the space between them. 'Do you fancy joining the party?' Sarah asked. 'We could get a drink in there and find a quiet-ish corner for a chat. There's still some food left at the buffet.'

'I dunno...' said Lily, looking up at Felix.

'I've told you already, Kate said it's fine.'

Lily shuffled her feet and Sarah took charge. 'Come on,' she said, offering a hand to Lily. 'Everyone's getting plastered in there, so no one's going to notice an extra body. I don't know many people, so you'd be doing me a favour coming in.'

'OK,' said Lily, taking Sarah's outstretched hand and allowing herself to be pulled into the festivities.

Sarah helped Lily load a plate with food, then found them a space on a straw bale away from the dance floor. At first, the conversation was stilted, but as each of them relaxed, Sarah found a natural affinity with the teenager beside her.

'You're nice,' said Lily after they'd been talking a while.

'You sound surprised,' said Sarah, laughing.

'Sorry, I didn't mean to sound surprised, it's just Felix warned me you could be a bit...'

'Of a cow sometimes? Don't worry, it's true, but I'm trying to be less of one these days.'

'Did I feel my ears burning?' asked Felix, walking up to them with a glass of wine for Sarah and a Coke for Lily. 'Do either of you lovely ladies fancy a dance?'

'No,' said Sarah and Lily in unison.

'Oh, come on, it's a wedding. Someone needs to join Bob on the dance floor.'

They looked over to where Bob was sliding down into the splits.

'Isn't he old to be doing that?' asked Lily.

'Don't let him hear you saying that,' said Sarah.

'Lily, come and meet some of my other friends.' Felix took Lily's hand and led her to where Joy and Fran sat giggling like schoolgirls. Sarah watched their faces light up as Felix introduced them to his sister. Returning to Sarah, Felix sat down on the hay bale beside her. 'Now Lily's taken care of, will you dance with me?'

'I'm not sure...'

'Come on.' Felix pulled Sarah to her feet, and they joined Bob, who was surrounded by a group of older ladies who'd taken pity on him.

'I remember your dancing from when we went to watch that band,' said Sarah. 'Are you sure I won't sustain an injury?'

'Not if we dance like this,' said Felix, pulling Sarah close to him and enveloping her in his arms. She sank into his warmth, feeling his heart beating against her own.

'Ow!' said Sarah, pulling away and hopping on one foot. 'I can't believe you trod on my toe when we're just shuffling from side to side.'

'Sorry,' said Felix, blushing.

'Let's try again,' said Sarah. They moved closer, only this time Sarah kept her head up, looking into Felix's eyes. He leaned forward. 'Wait,' she said, putting a finger against his lips.

'What is it? Have I trodden on your toes again?'

'No...' Sarah looked at the ground and took a deep breath. 'I want to know... well... I suppose what I'm trying to say is...' Sarah stopped moving. 'What I want to know is, what do you see in me? I've done nothing to earn your affection. I'm overweight, mean, damn right unpleasant at times. I have neither looks nor personality going for me, whereas you have everything going for you. You could take your pick from any woman in this room, even the married ones.'

Felix moved his arms away from Sarah's waist and held her face in his hands. 'I don't ever, ever want to hear you talk about yourself like that. You are a beautiful woman. Don't you ever look in the mirror? And you've apologised for your mistakes. I see the woman behind the barriers you've put up and I like what I see.'

Sarah's eyes filled with tears. 'But I...'

Felix silenced her as his lips met hers. Everything around them melted away as Sarah sank deeper and deeper into the rush of feelings sweeping through her. Here, in a tent, in a field in the woods, she was free to be herself. She'd finally come home.

Five years later...

'Quick, everyone, they're about to arrive.'

Bob tried to squeeze his body down, but couldn't stop his head from poking out over the top of the sofa.

'Get behind that armchair instead,' hissed Kate. Bob grinned at her and shuffled on his hands and knees to his new hiding place.

'Lily, are the streamers ready?' asked Sarah.

'Yes, boss.'

Sarah grabbed a balloon and threw it at Lily with a smile. 'Everyone shush...'

Felix peered around the counter and blew Sarah a kiss. She flapped her hand to move him away. The front door creaked open and Sarah heard boots rubbing against the mat.

'Where is everyone?' asked Fran.

'This is weird,' said Hattie, 'the door's unlocked but no lights on and nobody home. Millie, you told them when we'd be arriving?'

'Yes, I texted Sarah last week with all the arrangements.'

Hattie sighed and flung her bag on the counter.

'Goodness me, I'm exhausted,' said Fran, flopping down onto the sofa. 'The trip was worth it, but I'm afraid it might be a while before I come and visit you girls again. That flight was almost as bad as giving birth. I'm getting too old for twenty-four hours sat in a confined space.'

From her hiding place, Sarah motioned with her fingers, one, two, three... 'Surprise!'

Fran flew out of her seat, Hattie jumped a foot in the air, and Millie screamed.

'What the...' said Fran, clutching her chest. Sarah rushed over and enveloped her in a bear hug.

'Sorry for startling you, but we wanted to make your return home special.'

Fran laughed and flopped back in her seat. 'Well, you've woken me up.'

After much hugging and pulling of party poppers, everyone settled around the fire. 'You must be exhausted,' said Sarah.

'Yes,' said Millie, leaning her head on Hattie's shoulder.

'We could do with a coffee, if there's one going?' Hattie looked at Felix, who pushed his shoulders back with a smile and turned to Lily.

'Lily, perhaps you could make the coffee?'

'Sure,' said Lily, moving behind the counter.

'Just wait till you taste it,' said Felix to Hattie, his voice filled with pride. 'I hate to say it, but I think she may be a better barista than me.'

'You've been training her up?'

'Yes, I needed help with the coffees, what with everything else there is to do.'

'It seems like you're on top of things,' said Hattie, looking around the café and nodding her approval.

'We make a good team,' said Felix, pulling Sarah down to sit beside him.

'Can someone help me up?' came a voice from beneath a table.

'Oh my God, Joy, I'm so sorry I forgot you were under there.' Kate bent down and offered a hand to Joy, lifting the old lady to her feet.

'I'm too old for hide and seek,' said Joy, smoothing down her skirt. 'I got down there all right, but then my knees seized up and I was stuck.' Kate took Joy's arm and helped her into a seat.

'I can't believe you've all gone to so much trouble,' said Fran, looking around at the *Welcome Home* banner and balloons.

'We've missed you,' said Sarah. 'It hasn't been the same without you. As the weeks wore on, I worried you'd emigrated for good.'

'It was tempting,' said Fran, 'but they'd never let me settle in Australia at my age.'

'I'm sorry for you, but pleased for us,' said Felix. 'We've got a big event coming up next month and need your help.'

'What kind of event?' asked Fran. 'I could try out some of the fancy recipes I've been sampling at Millie's restaurant.'

Felix looked at Sarah and grinned. 'Fancy food sounds good. Go on,' he said to Sarah, 'show them.'

Sarah held out her hand, showing off a simple wooden band on her left ring finger.

Fran's eyes filled with tears as she took Sarah's hand and stroked the ring. 'About bloody time,' she said. 'I could have predicted this moment the second a frosty young Sarah arrived and started bickering with the handsome barista.'

Felix shuddered. 'I'm not sure I could have predicted falling for Sarah back then. She bit my head off at every opportunity.'

'Hey,' said Sarah, 'that's your future wife you're talking about.'

'Sorry,' said Felix, looking sheepish.

'Thank you,' said Sarah, as one by one her friends offered their congratulations.

'I get to be a bridesmaid,' said Lily, carrying a tray of coffees to the table.

'Mmm,' said Millie, taking a sip from her cup. 'This is good. If you ever fancy a change of scene, there'll be a job for you at my restaurant.'

'Hey,' said Felix, 'it's bad enough we only get her in the holidays, without you tempting her off to Australia.'

'How's uni going?' asked Hattie.

'Great,' said Lily, 'but I miss the woods. I'm hoping I can get a job with the forestry commission once I've finished my studies.'

'That sounds great,' said Hattie. 'And Sarah, how are things with you?'

'Good, thanks. Mum's still living in Spain, which is best for everyone. Dad's travelling the UK in a motorhome with his new wife.'

'Evil stepmother?'

Sarah laughed. 'No, she's sweet. They often come and visit. Did Felix tell you we rent out the tipis for holidays now we're living in the flat? Life under canvas is Dad's idea of heaven, he's our best customer.'

'Yes, Felix told me about renting them out. That's a great idea. I'm very pleased this old place is in safe hands.'

'It's been a team effort. Kate's been so helpful advising us on the holiday lets.' Kate grinned, and Bob cleared his throat. 'Sorry,' said Sarah, patting Bob's arm. 'Bob's been helping too, of course.'

'There's something else I thought I could help with,' said Bob, pulling a bag from beneath a chair and rummaging inside. He pulled out a bottle of champagne to cheers from the assembled friends.

Once Bob had filled all their glasses, he turned to Felix and Sarah. 'To Felix and Sarah, and their forthcoming nuptials,' he said.

'To Felix and Sarah,' they all chorused, clinking glasses.

'To friends,' shouted Felix, to another round of clinking.

'I'd like to add one last toast please,' said Sarah.

'Hurry up, love,' said Joy. 'I'm getting parched here.'

'Joy, let the girl speak,' said Bob.

'I'd like to make a toast to forgiveness, and family,' said Sarah. 'Anyone walking in here would look at us and think what a strange bunch we are. And it would be true. But aren't the best families the ones who all have their quirks but love each other anyway? You've all forgiven me, accepted me, loved me, and made this place home for me. So, let's raise our glasses to family.'

Echoes of cheers floated beyond the café and into the forest. Trees swayed, cocooning the makeshift family at the heart of them.

Afterword

If you'd like to keep in touch, find out about new releases, or receive the LK Wilde 'Bonus Bundle' you can sign up to my mailing list at lkwilde.com. You *won't* be bombarded with emails, but *will* receive a monthly dose of news, offers and general musings on Cornish life. Alternatively you can find me on your favourite social media platform at @lkwildeauthor. I love hearing from readers so feel free to get in touch!

If you enjoyed Sarah's story and would like to leave a review I'd be very grateful, reviews are the best way to help other readers find the book! As an independent author with no big publishing company behind me, reviews and reader recommendations are vital when it comes to competing with the 'big boys' of the book world and I'm incredibly grateful for each review that comes in!

Acknowledgements

Residents of Bodmin are fortunate to have several beautiful woodlands within easy reach of the town. Two of my favourites, Respryn and Cardinham, inspired this novel. Cardinham woods is home to a wonderful cafe, and while the location of the cafe was very much a starting point for this book, all characters and events are products of my imagination.

When I wrote The House of Many Lives, I was intrigued by Kate's first house-guest Sarah, and keen to explore her character in greater depth. This book has given me the chance to do just that, and it was a lot of fun dragging Sarah from her suburban comfort zone and landing her in the middle of a Cornish woodland!

As with all my books, there are a team of people behind them, cheering me on and giving sage, sometimes uncomfortable advice and feedback when needed.

Thank you Jen Beacham and Jo Egleton for your editing work. It's hard to believe just how awful Sarah was before you got your hands on her! Together you helped me pull my rough ideas into shape, fix plot holes, and create a more complete version of Sarah's story. Thank you!

Thank you to Audrey Davis for proof reading the final manuscript and adding much needed polish before it was sent out into the world. As well as being a top-notch proof reader, Audrey is also a wonderful writer, so do keep an eye out for her books!

Thank you to Leanne Davis, for not only your encouragement with the final draft but also for our cups of tea and slices of cake at the woodland cafe. Another coffee is long overdue!

Thank you to Pete, Joe and Tom for your encouragement and the interest you take in my writing. I couldn't do it without you. Special thanks to Pete, for reading messy, early drafts of my books and guiding me forward with patience and thoughtful critique.

Finally, thank you reader, for picking up this book. Writing books would be pointless without readers to read them, and the encouragement I've received from readers of my books is never taken for granted. Thank you all.

Also By LK Wilde

Kate is stuck in a rut, She works a dead end job, lives in a grotty bedsit
and still pines for the man who broke her heart.

When Kate inherits a house in a small Cornish town, she jumps at
the chance of a fresh start. A surprise letter from her grandmother
persuades Kate to open her home and her heart to strangers.

But with friends harbouring secrets, demanding house guests, and her
past catching up with her- can Kate really move on? And will her
broken heart finally find a home?

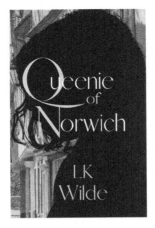

People say you get one life, but I've lived three.

I was born Ellen Hardy in 1900, dragged up in Queen Caroline's Yard, Norwich. There was nothing royal about our yard, and Mum was no queen.

At six years old Mum sold me. I became Nellie Westrop, roaming the country in a showman's wagon, learning the art of the fair.

And I've been the infamous Queenie of Norwich, moving up in the world by any means, legal or not.

I've been heart broken, abandoned, bought and sold, but I've never, ever given up. After all, it's not where you start that's important, but where you end up.

Based on a true story, *Queenie of Norwich* is the compelling tale of one remarkable girl's journey to womanhood. Spanning the first half of the 20th century, Queenie's story is one of heartbreak and triumph, love and loss and the power of family. It is a story of redemption, and how, with grit and determination, anything is possible.

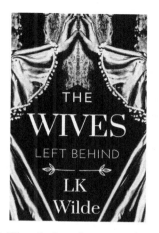

1840, Cornwall. The victim, the accused, and the wives left behind. Welcome to the trial of the century...

Based on a true story.

When merchant Nevell Norway is murdered, suspicion soon falls on the Lightfoot brothers. The trial of the century begins, and two women's lives change forever.

Sarah Norway must fight for the future of her children. Battling against her inner demons, can Sarah unlock the strength she needs to move on without Nevell?

Maria Lightfoot's future looks bleak, but she's a fighter. Determined to rebuild her life, an unexpected friendship offers a glimmer of hope...

With their lives in turmoil, can Maria and Sarah overcome the fate of their husbands? Or will they forever remain the wives left behind?

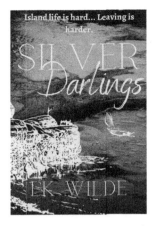

Island life is hard... leaving is harder.

In 1895, a Northumberland island welcomes two new residents. Clara and Jimmy are born on the same night to families poles apart. Clara is an islander through and through; Jimmy longs to escape. When tragedy forces them from their island and each other, they join the herring season in a bid to survive. As they follow shoals of silver darlings to Lowestoft, their paths are dogged by war, injury and misunderstandings.

Will they be reunited? And will they ever find their way home...?

Printed in Great Britain
by Amazon